San Barnabas
Mountains

Lake
Negro

Rendezvous

The Ridge

Massacre

NEGRO JUNGLE

East one

GROS MICHEL
PORT

GULF

WAR IS HEAVEN!

WAR
IS HEAVEN!

D. Keith Mano

DOUBLEDAY & COMPANY, INC.
Garden City, New York, 1970

For my Mother:

The source, the strength, the faith . . . who knew all these things, while I, a child, merely dreamed them.

WAR IS HEAVEN!

And as Jesus passed by, he saw a man which was blind from his birth.

And his disciples asked him, saying, Master, who did sin, this man or his parents, that he was born blind?

Jesus answered, Neither hath this man sinned, nor his parents, but that the works of God should be made manifest in him.

(John 9:1–3)

Dear David,

The ripeness is all. Things are coming to an end now. I only wish you were here, David, adding your skepticism to my dreadful excitement. The phenomena would fascinate you: I promise that. Perhaps, after all, if I come back (and I feel less and less certain that I will) I shall give myself up to your soft, black patent-leather couch and to the aweful wisdom of worldly men. To test myself. To vindicate myself before you. To burn away the prideful dross.

I have had seven visions in the past ten days (the last a coat upon a coat hanger?). On the 18th, 20th, 22nd, 25th, 26th (twice) and last night, the 27th. No pattern there that I can discern, and yet I sense an increasing urgency. I'm afraid now that I will never understand—or, worse, that I will misuse what has been given me.

It is still the same. A tall woman, naked to the waist, with breasts so perfect they stir my desire in retrospect (but never at the moment of seeing, never then). Her dark hair glistens. Her deep navel rests in a mound of soft flesh. Her face, white by contrast, broad with a crescent, unformed smile—an Old World face, the eyes almond-shaped and fierce, intent on me, unmoving. I hear you, David. A mother fixation, normal enough in one who never knew his mother. The product of 28 years' sexual repression. I hear you, David. Oh, yes—I hear you.

She comes toward me. I am lying on a bier (is it?) shrouded in yellow cloth. My body is somehow foreshortened, as though I had no legs. Mind you, it's not the dead me who is seeing but some other, some objective me. My upper chest is bared with the cross (the one I wear) upon it. She is close. She

1

touches her nipples. Then, with her forefinger, she anoints my head, my mouth, my chest, my groin, my legs. In that order: it is always the same. And she speaks. I seem to understand but afterward I cannot, for the life of me, remember what it is she has told me. For all my uncertainty, there is an immense goodness in it, a peace. There has been, since the first time 20 years ago. Oh, how frightened I was as a child. And the man, a stranger it seemed, had a beard even then. Did my vision foretell this, or did I grow the beard to satisfy my vision? Grow my beard. Cause my own skin to erupt. Am I insane or am I being fulfilled?

Don't answer yet. I must tell you first of other things—of outward and visible signs—things that I have never told you before.

Listen to me. In all my time here, I have never once been bitten by a mosquito. Don't laugh: sometimes we pass through dense clouds of them. They blind you, choke your breath. I use nothing on my skin; the others do and they're literally eaten alive. My men have noticed this. It embarrasses me: I hear them talking about it. Sand-flies, snakes, scorpions—I slept with a scorpion in Camaguay City. In the morning it was crushed dead beneath my body. But there was nothing. No puncture. Nothing.

Last week in San Pedro I saw a cuckoo land on the ledge of a public fountain. I know birds, David, these are the most skittish in the hemisphere. Yet the idea, the whim, came into my head that I would catch it. Sheer folly. I was perhaps twenty feet away, and the bird clearly saw me coming (I made no attempts at stealth). It twittered. It jumped—as though trying to rise, yet oddly thwarted. I picked it up in my hand as you might a salt cellar or a pack of cigarettes. When I opened my palm it wouldn't fly away. Yet it wasn't injured. It flew easily enough when I let it, when I willed it to. This isn't the first. I've caught snakes like that, David, parrots, bats, a howler monkey. Make your little jokes about St. Francis. There's worse yet to come.

2

It's made me a better soldier. A deadlier soldier. Four days ago there was an RFN raid on Las Casas airfield. The Riffs burned all our helicopters, 50,000 gallons of fuel, whatever else they could set a match to. The usual snafu. We got the word a quarter of an hour too late, and when I approached the airfield, the place was an inferno. We circled the perimeter, looking for stragglers. One other man and I were alone on the far edge when we saw two figures plunge through a gap in the fence. I shouted halt, but I was seventy yards to the right and they felt pretty safe. They were safe, that's the point. I had only a .45—virtually useless at that distance. And I had time for only one shot.

I killed them both. Both, with a single shot. Both dead through the neck. I counted the remaining rounds. The man with me didn't fire at all. Was there another man who fired simultaneously and with a .45? If so, where was he? A .45 simply cannot go through two bodies at that distance—ballistics forbids it. One hit would have been extraordinary enough. The man who was with me, a Camaguayan, spread the story around. I can safely say I am the most well-obeyed American in Camaguay. My men say I have an evil eye. I'm not so sure they're wrong.

My vision is incredible. It was always good, but now I see things as though with an instinctive intelligence. I can see the forest for the trees; the trees for the forest. I can separate things from their background at a glance. My nose, too: smells seem to have an odd significance they never had before. I run all day and I'm not even winded. I sleep two hours in forty-eight and I feel no fatigue. Things seem heightened. The way they say it is with pot or LSD. You would know, David, you who have tried everything.

I hate this war. I hate the suffering that brutalizes finally both the actors and the endurers. Yet I still feel we must fight, David, and I feel, with greater and greater certainty, that I have been chosen to fight. To die fighting. Chosen? What divinity, you ask, can sanction such a dreadful war? The same that sanctioned Joshua and St. Joan. The same that sanctions

3

martyrdom. The God who gave His only Son to torment. My God.

I pray a great deal now, but I have given up fasting since you warned me about self-induced visions. I don't know what you will think of all this—though I can imagine. I am terrified now of righteous pride. Yet, at this moment, I feel totally an instrument. And I want desperately, if I can, to make myself a still better instrument of His will. Whatever that will is. Whether or not I ever know.

Write me. Say I'm insane. Tell me all the long names for my insanity. It will do me good. Bless you for your patience.

Love,

Clarence.

4

I

RED DUST. Corpsman Andrew Jones, a Negro, scuffed the earth
with his heavy boot. It was a surly act, a typical act. He regretted it at once: sweat formed along his spine where the
unfamiliar black and green uniform shirt adhered to his back.
The red dust rose a few inches, struggled upward against the
oppressive air, then settled back. Jones scratched the letter F
in the dust with his boot tip. He spat at the letter, but his
saliva was viscous and unmanageable; it wet chiefly his own
chin. Jones took out a cigarette. It was bent; the tobacco fibers
were extruded at odd angles. Again he turned and peered
into the low mud-and-thatch hut.

There were four other Americans in the hut. Each wore the
Irregular Command insignia: a silver, double-pronged arrow
that probed into the hook of a question mark. "Into the unknown, bravely." Three white men and, happily (Jones
thought), a Negro. Their heavy gear was beside them, aligned
with the right thigh of each. Jones frowned. It irritated him:
their capacity to bear the close, unrelieved heat of the hut.
He sensed, and it irritated him yet further, that this was part
of their training, a limp, tactical giving way before the unal-
terable. It was a training that Jones did not have, that he was
constitutionally unfit for. It made him different. A large fly
cleaned its legs on the wall. Jones meant to slap at it, for he
considered all tropical insect life to be pernicious, but at that
moment, with obscene fastidiousness, the fly exuded a gluey,
opaque liquid dotted with black flecks of dirt. Jones turned
away.

The Camaguayans sprawled on the other side of the hut. A

5

foot-wide alley of unoccupied ground separated them from the Americans. There were twenty Camaguayans (Jones did not count them, he would have thought there were more), and it was difficult to judge where one ended and the other began. They, too, had given way before the heat, but this was an abject, not a tactical, surrender. They lay on each other's laps and chests; arms and legs extended from the mass, indefinitely attached. Now and then one would rise up and plump the thigh or the shoulder of the man beneath, as though arranging a bolster. Their equipment was disordered, seeming communal. Objects from one pack had, by contiguity, become part of another's pack. Jones was leery of these dark, small men. They reminded him of the hamsters (meant to teach him responsibility) that he had kept for a week when he was ten—kept, uncared for, until their droppings had covered the cage floor and his mother had given them away.

Jones winked at the other Negro, but there was no evident response. The other's eyes stared, as before, ahead and without blinking. Jones, sensing a rebuff, was surprised into sound: an awkward, unplanned clearing of the throat. He began to pat busily at his pockets. The matches were in his haversack, which leaned against the hut's outer wall, near the menacing ten-pound medical pack with its faded and alien initials: W.T.G. Jones bent down, and, as he did so, he saw something wriggle in the shadowed crevice between the haversack and the wall. Jones straightened, squinted, rubbed his fingers together nervously. He leaned forward again, then jerked the haversack quickly away from the wall.

The scorpion huddled in a shallow niche, dazed by this sudden access of light. Its jointed tail wavered in a torpid threatening above the unformed nub of its head. Jones pressed his palm to his chest; he had swallowed the full weight of air in his mouth and his breathing was suddenly distressed. The scorpion's lobster claws pinched tentatively, blindly at the light. To Jones the insect, the first he had ever seen, seemed oddly familiar. He remembered the names his mother had called him in anger, drawing on her foolish astrology, for he, her only child, had been born in early November. Jones was fascinated and near, he knew, to a sort of hysteria. He patted his chest spasmodically. Its size, its ugly efficiency seemed suited to the country—to all the strange, small, violent things he had been warned of. The thorn at the tail's end, now dipping and rising (he followed it with a fierce intentness) could cripple him—an animal, in volume, several hundred times the larger. Then a foot moved swiftly past his thigh and crushed the scorpion. The sharp crackling of its armored body sickened him. Jones whimpered.

"Scorpion. No good." As a child might in seeking approval, the small, plump Camaguayan (Armando, by name), peered around Jones' legs until he had engaged the corpsman's averted face with his eyes. He grinned upward. Jones laughed shrilly, nodded, and then belched as the captive air found release— so suddenly that his nostrils burned. The Camaguayan began shaking his boot over the mangled scorpion, a clumsy dance. The insect's stinger was imbedded, with its two nether tail joints, in his boot's sole. Armando carefully scraped it off. Then he stepped back, unbuttoned his fly, and began to urinate. He hummed, spraying in a circular pattern over the parched soil, his pot belly cradled in his arms. The stream spattered just inches from Jones' heels.

Jones had found his matches, but the cigarette was not now satisfactory. His body became, in imagination, a precious, sterile world; each aperture required a thoughtful defense. He was loathe especially to allow foreign objects to pass his lips. And so he tried to smoke without touching the cigarette's end, making a vacuum of the surrounding air, at last merely sniffing the fumes. He ignored the sounds of the jolly trickle that was puddling just behind him.

The sun shone so forcefully from Jones' sweaty dark cheeks that his own dark skin appeared in the foreground of everything he saw. The military compound on the outskirts of San Pedro seemed now anxiously quieted. The square in front of him was deserted but for a single spotted dog that lay on its back, front paws propped in the air, bent at the wrists and limp. They were prepared to move out; they had been prepared for three hours. Across the way, in what had previously been a shabby general store ("IC—GHQ—Sect. #2. Drink Coca-Cola," the signs said) their officers had been deliberating since dawn: the Americans eager and impatient; the Camaguayans fractious, uncertain, and quickly offended.

"Sig-rette. Yes. Please." The Camaguayan named Armando made the V sign with his fingers and then put the fingers against his lips. Expressively, he billowed out his cheeks, seeming some pudgy, cheerful god of the winds. A fly landed on the light brown forehead, camouflaging itself among a constellation of dark moles. Jones handed over the half-smoked butt. The little man pushed it greedily against his mouth, as though meaning to eat it, until only the hot ash protruded. Then he patted Jones amiably over the left kidney and waddled back to the hut. Jones now had a headache. He considered the five hundred-odd aspirins in the unfamiliar medical pack. He knelt, propping his chin on one knee. When he closed his eyes, yellow-red lights disintegrated, synthesized on the insides of his eyelids. He should have put his helmet on. Jones peered at his watch and the sun glanced viciously from the metal case, dazzling him. He cursed.

Corpsman Andrew Jones knew that he didn't belong where he was—near the city of San Pedro on the Gulf coast of Camaguay. Two nights before, the regular corpsman, W.T.G. (the name was William Tyndall Graham) had been drowned while swimming. An IC type, he imagined, gung-ho, trained to kill; Jones saw him challenging the Gulf tides . . . well, he had lost that one, hadn't he? Jones had been given a .45, a heavy, ugly gun, and he didn't at all appreciate this omen of violence pressing the soft skin of his hip. As a child he had possessed a cap gun with the same blunt, square shape: bah, bah, bah from between parked cars. Bah. Bah. To distract himself, Jones fingered the two Red Cross brassards—one on each bicep—that he had brought from the *Sting*. His safe conducts. Then he stared at the dead man's medical pack. There was a stain on one of the straps. It might have been blood; Jones assumed, pessimistically, that it was blood. He was depressed and intimidated. An indifferent medic in fair physical condition. A stranger here. A Negro. And anyhow, he thought, the Camaguayan war stank.

The engine of a heavy truck roared in the motor pool at the south end of the compound, waking the dog. The driver gunned the engine. Jones stood and staggered; he was dizzy, slightly nauseated. In twenty-four hours he had had little sleep; none at all since 3 A.M., when they had flown him in from the aircraft carrier *Sting*. They had been playing poker when the order came through. The other three corpsmen, eager, crew-cut professionals, had volunteered at once. Jones had seconded their enthusiasm cautiously and as a matter of form. The chief medical officer, not caring, Jones supposed, to bear the responsibility, had said, "Low card goes." Jones pulled a three of clubs (the other men had actually cursed his luck). The card, torn in half, was still in his haversack. "Of all the miserable tricks," he sobbed. His eyes began to water in the sharp sunlight. "Of all the rotten, dirty tricks. Stuck in this hell hole with a pack of honky career killers. Of all—" The door to GHQ opened.

Jones watched. The dog turned on its side to watch. Three men began to cross the dusty square. After a few paces they paused, and the tall man pointed first to the sky, then at the road that led north toward the Rio Negro bridge. Jones leaned against the hut wall. Hastily, worriedly, he examined the three officers through half-closed lids.

The Camaguayan lieutenant, Ulysses Sanchez, was on the left. He wore ivory handled Colt revolvers at either hip. Mornings, just before dawn, in a gorge behind the GHQ, he outdrew and murdered a six-foot-tall wooden mannikin with a paint can, now riddled and torn, for a head. There was a knife in his belt, sheathed behind, near his spine; three grenades dangled like hard, unripe fruits from his chest. Sanchez had a thin nose, broken once so that it angled to the right. His two front teeth protruded and were bent in on themselves to form an ugly wedge. The lieutenant was hated by all his men and

9

by the Americans in proportion to how frequently they were subjected to his arrogant, sadistic commands. His prized possession was a deep scar that ran from his left nipple, across his navel (obliterating it), over the left hip, and down to the crease of his buttocks. On special occasions he was not averse to stripping nearly naked to display it. Sanchez walked easily now, cowboy style. He combated a tic under his left eye by flicking the sunglasses up and down beneath his St. Louis Cardinals baseball cap. Jones grunted. Lieutenant Sanchez was four feet ten inches tall.

Lieutenant Storch, Sanchez's American counterpart, was between the other two, seemingly dependent on their support. Though the ground was level, he stumbled at each shuffling lurch of his large feet. Storch wore no head covering and his scalp, entirely bald, reflected the sun from a sheen of sweat. His eyes were small. His lower lip was a capacious flat platform, chewed raw. As he walked, he stared up and to the east, his eyes apparently uninjured, in their deep crevices, by the teeming sunlight. Storch stopped once—the others stopping patiently beside him—to grunt and blow snot onto his own left shoe.

On the right was Sergeant Hook. Jones had recognized him as soon as he saw the bushy, black beard. Even on the *Sting* there had been talk of Sergeant Hook.

Behind, in the hut, the four American IC's were already on their feet. The Camaguayans had begun to unpile, squealing and hissing like a full burrow of disgruntled rodents. They achieved a poor semblance of alertness, their packs gaping, disgorging items of equipment, their rifles pointed at their comrades' more vital parts, long before Lieutenant Sanchez had crossed the square. An open military transport scuffed up billows of red dust as it made its way toward the hut. Coughing and shuddering, it stopped. The driver peered out: Jones saw that he was watching their movements with an apparent sadness, mopping his brow as he did so, and this anonymous sympathy frightened Jones. The red dust floated over them. It embedded itself freely in the sweat that had formed already on their cheeks and temples.

"Up and in," shouted Sergeant Hook. He reiterated the command in Spanish, elaborated it. Jones shouldered his haversack, but was confused at first by the strange trappings of the medical pack. The Americans were silent; they moved at a semitrot. The Camaguayans, however, had been confounded by their own eagerness. It was evident they had not thought beyond the immediate, beyond the exciting ride in the big Yanqui truck. They shoved at each other, became ridiculously bottlenecked in the narrow hut door. Hook watched them, heard their happy shrieks, but his eyes were noncommittal between the helmet rim and the black beard fringes on his upper cheek. Yet when Jones passed him, his medical pack slung awkwardly under one arm, Hook said, "Corpsman," in a low, resonant voice.

"Yes sir, Sergeant," said Jones. He stopped, grinned.

"Corporal Purdy fit you out?"

"Oh yes, sir," said Jones. "He did that. He sure fit me out good."

Jones lifted the medical pack between both hands and, with exaggerated motions, shook it once or twice, suggesting heaviness, fullness. Then, as the sergeant seemed inclined to further conversation, he dropped the pack and put his right foot on it. Hook blinked. The thumb and forefinger of his right hand sought the pit just below his collarbone; there they pinched at something hidden under the black material.

"Jones," he said slowly. "A good man used that." Jones looked down, discovered his offending foot as though with surprise, and removed it from the pack. They stared at each other: one challenging, the other judging. To Jones, Hook's pupils seemed unnaturally dark, small, glossy black olives. They disconcerted him. "I know you're on loan from the Navy," said Hook, "and I know you haven't had much field experience—but you'll have to keep up. There are no short cuts out here now. We've got one helicopter on the Gulf since the Las Casas raid. You think you can manage?"

"Well, sir . . ." said Jones. He hesitated, intrigued by something. Hook turned his head. Lieutenant Storch was sitting on the running board, arranging his genitals in his pants crotch. Near him, Sanchez had drawn one of his revolvers and was aiming carelessly at the spotted dog. Sanchez saw that the sergeant was watching him. For a brief moment he pointed the muzzle at Hook, then he shrugged sullenly and reholstered the gun.

"You were saying, Jones?"

"Well, Sergeant. About keeping up—like, how should I know? This ain't my bag exactly. But I don't get much choice, do I?"

"You don't seem eager."

"Eager?" Jones smiled innocence. "Eager about war, Sergeant?" Jones shut his mouth, opened it, perceived the black pupils, shut it again. There was laughter: Armando tumbled out of the truck. Laughing, he made a fist, hoisted himself up, and was shoved out once more. "Anyway, them little wogs're having fun."

"Yes. Six may be alive by summer. Let's go, Jones." Hook turned and trotted away. Unseen, the corpsman's face became alive with contempt and loathing. He slung the pack over his shoulder and began to walk in aloof, determined slowness toward the truck. But the truck started at once when Sergeant Hook leaped on the running board of the cab, and Jones, gasping through clouds of red dust, had to run thirty yards to catch it.

The San Pedro plateau is an anomaly. Forty miles long and thirteen deep, it rises unexpectedly from the Negro jungle between the mouths of the San Gabriel and the much smaller Negro Rivers. The city of San Pedro, population fifty-three thousand (slightly higher since the war began), reposes like the tiered side of a stadium on the plateau's Gulf edge. It is the only considerable port, indeed, the only considerable city of any description on this jungled coast of Camaguay. Coffee, bananas, chicle, tin, and mahogany are exported, but since the war on the Pacific side of Camaguay began to move half-heartedly eastward, this activity has become sporadic and uncertain. The area around San Pedro is farmland. The soil, having endured two thousand years of cultivation, is much eroded, and after the first Revolutionary Front raids eighteen months before, the farmers, poor already, then terrorized as well, began to stream into the crowded slums on the northeast side of the city. The transport now followed the coast edge of the nearly desolate plateau, then it turned inland and started gradually descending toward the Rio Negro and the jungle.

Jones, seated on the rearmost left bench of the transport, remained winded for a long while: longer than he might have, for out of the perversity of pride, he had strained to conceal his panting from the IC's. Sweat dribbled down, over his belly, puddling at his groin and between his buttocks. The heat was excruciating; though there was considerable wind, it was warm and gritty and provided him no relief. He stared to the rear. Beyond twenty feet the road, the countryside were shrouded in billows of the ubiquitous red dust—it seemed to follow them, rushing forward, indefatigable. Jones felt apprehensive; he knew only very vaguely where they were going.

The Camaguayans had gone to sleep again. Fifteen or so lay heaped between the benches, cavalierly using their comrades as hassocks, head rests. Opposite Jones, the Negro IC stared disconsolately at his left arm. Jones had made up his mind to like this man. The IC was small, five-foot-five, and eight inches shorter than Jones. From the evidence of his forearm and wrist he was extremely thin. His lips inscribed a perfect circle, a small, brown doughnut; even in repose, he seemed to be expressing a mild astonishment. Jones required companionship. He stood, stretched. Then, when the transport struck a rut, he stumbled purposefully and sat, as though by chance, on the opposite bench.

"God-damned, fuckin' red dust," he said sociably. "It's all over everything." The smaller man looked up.

"Better than the God-damned, fuckin' red mud."

"That so?" said Jones. But the IC had once again given attention to his left arm. He flexed the elbow, and then studied the responses of his various sinews. Jones watched politely for a few moments. "That so?" he said again. "I guess mud must be pretty bad. Ah . . . my name is Jones. Andy Jones. Yours?" He invited a handshake. The IC did not grasp his hand, did not seem to notice it. Jones placed the back of his wrist near the other's forearm—to demonstrate the similar darkness. Grounds enough for intimacy.

"Horace Baxter." The little man touched Jones' hand lightly.

"What's the word, brother?" Baxter blinked. He seemed to study the brassards on Jones' arms, the red cross on his helmet. Another blink, this longer, as though to indicate disbelief. Baxter wetted the circle of his lips with his tongue. "I mean," said Jones, "where exactly are we goin' to? I didn't get my tour folders. Are we goin' to see the Riffs?"

"Maybe," said Baxter. "Maybe. Maybe they just gonna see us."

"I sure hope nobody gets hurt. I don't like the sight of blood."

"You got enough red crosses on."

"That's right, brother—I don't want nobody, nohow, mistakin' me for a soldier." Baxter stared at him. The face was perfectly impassive. He blinked—evidently it was a characteristic facial act—three times now in slow succession. Then he touched his collarbone, tentatively, with his right forefinger.

"I'm a soldier," he said.

"Yeah. Sure. Well . . ." Jones wasn't happy with Baxter's tone. He moved his head back and looked hastily, from the corners of his eyes, at the man's fists. Jones had always been big; always, too, he had distrusted small, wiry men. They fought, he imagined, with a tough desperation that was demoralizing. "See," he said. "No personal offense. I'm a college guy. I got me a good education. Someday I'll be a lawyer. I got big things t'do, brother, and this war don't fit in. If these guys got problems"—he indicated the Camaguayans—"I figure it's none of my business. I sure don't care t'get killed." Baxter blinked. Then he sniffed.

14

"You smell something?" Jones sniffed, shook his head.

"Funny," said Baxter, his face still impassive behind the fleshy O. "I smell something. What I'm gonna do, see. I'm gonna sit over there. Only don't you move. I don't want that smell coming with me." Baxter got up, stepped over the Camaguayans, and sat opposite. Jones laughed. He shook his head sardonically. But he was disconcerted.

The transport rumbled ahead and toward the northwest. It was now nearly ten o'clock. Jones didn't know it, but because of the indecision that morning, they would have to march during the day's hottest hours. Occasionally he could see the Gulf over Baxter's shoulder, a glaciated dazzle of reflected light. Behind, over his own shoulder, the ranks of the first foothills were visible fifty miles away, on the far edge of the Rio Negro and the jungle. A flock of pelicans soared toward the Gulf lowlands, projectile shapes in excellent formation. Broken, dried stalks of maize tottered at all angles in the red fields, like bits of some child's construction game not put away. It would be sowing time in three weeks, but the farmers' huts were empty, often roofless. By chance Jones touched the hot metal of his .45. He gripped it. He could not decide whether its shape reassured or distressed him, but he left his hand where it was.

"Gotta make friends with the corpsman." Jones was startled. A white hand had covered his kneecap. The hand was an insolent thing, backed with whorls of dark hair, and between the fingers, with the yellowed scales of some virulent skin eruption. "I mean—in case of emergencies. I'm Joe Garbini." Jones took the hand, resticting his grasp carefully to the upper joints of the fingers. Garbini laughed.

"Uh—Andy Jones."

"Good. Good to see a new face." At this word, Jones first perceived the face of the man who had so freely touched him. It was a grotesque face. There were the craters of old acne scars, overgrown with dark hairs at the temples, high on the cheeks, even on the tip of his considerable nose. His cheeks were hollow, suggesting the absence of molars, and the teeth that remained protruded from his mouth, fanglike and yellow. But the forehead was his most striking feature: it was lined with three parallel creases nearly a half inch in depth, and the skin between bulged out in folds, the color and texture of a bird's wattle. It was as though the face had begun prematurely to seek its skeletal form. The eyes, isolated in this sunken face like sand bars in a retreating tide, seemed ready to drop from their sockets. Taken aback, embarrassed, Jones had difficulty responding. The face appreciated this and laughed.

"Nice to . . . ah, meet you." Garbini laughed again. He expected this reaction to his face, and, in men at least, it rather amused him.

"I saw little Horace bite your head off." He leaned close. "Don't let it get you. He's all right, better than most. Keep looking this way. When you get a chance, take a peek at his arm, the left one. The muscle snapped up, just like a window shade, when he was carrying a guy out on the Pacific side." Jones gazed toward the other bench. Indeed, Baxter's left bicep seemed atrophied. It was balled near the armpit. "There's a little tendon, ties the muscle to your elbow bone, so they say. He ripped it off. Don't bother him much when he eats or when he wipes himself, but he's a pitcher with Pittsburgh, was, anyway. Class double A. Right now he don't know if he can throw any more. But he's not a bad guy, otherwise. Just got problems. Take my advice, don't bug him and you'll get along fine."

"He's a pitcher, huh?"

"That's what he says, anyway. I looked him up in an old *Sporting News* but I didn't see nothin'. Well, we all got problems." He grinned. His teeth seemed to grin quite separately. "I bet even you got some."

"Where we goin'?" Garbini had a good ear: he heard the note of veiled apprehension in Jones' voice, and it made him laugh.

"Didn't they tell you?"

"Not much. They didn't tell me much."

"Maybe they didn't want to upset you. Think of that."

"Where we going?" Garbini laughed. Fat beads of sweat lay, like brooding hens, on the shelves of his forehead.

"Maybe it should be a surprise." Jones opened his mouth. He was annoyed and had prepared to shout at Garbini, into the roar of the jolting truck. But a glance at the IC's face warned him that he was being baited.

"Come on, Joe. Tell me," Jones said with forced easiness. "I don't dig surprises much as I used to."

"Well," said Garbini. He looked about him in mock conspiracy. Then he brought his lips very close to Jones' ear. His breath was warm and flecked with moisture. "It's a bread run, see: up to Captain Rodriguez' camp by Lake Negro. That's why we got all these supplies—medicine and radio parts and stuff. You'll love it. Over the hill and through the swamp to Grandma's house. With all the kids." He kicked the Camaguayan lying nearest him. The man smiled in his sleep.

"Through the swamp?"

"Uh-huh." Garbini grinned. "I been through twice. Takes two days to cross the damn thing and you can't see three feet in front of your nose. But I don't want to spoil it for you." He sighed. "Then up through the banana factories. Up through the highlands. Over the ridge and down to the lake. Oh yes, and back again. Ten days at least. The Camaguayan colonels here—they got three colonels for every soldier—I understand they didn't want us to go. Wanted to wait for helicopters. But Rodriguez can't wait and we're going." He laughed.

"Helicopters? Don't we have any?"

"Sure," Garbini laughed. "Six of them. Laying in pieces on Las Casas airfield. The Camaguayan guards weren't too alert last Tuesday. Alertness ain't their most famous quality, you'll catch on to that. They go to sleep on the john; on top of their women. I seen one go t'sleep on a bouncing Betty once." Garbini laughed. "They probably sleep in hell. Must drive the devil nuts."

"Shit," said Jones. "What happens if someone gets hurt?"

"You're asking me?" Garbini pointed at the red crosses, threw his head back, and cackled.

17

"No . . . I mean—" But Garbini was crippled by his laughter. Jones gave in: he grinned resignedly. But only for a moment. "If it's serious, I mean. How do we get them out?"

"They walk, friend. If, like you say, it's real serious, they drop dead after a few steps." Garbini grinned. "I guess we could leave them with the Indians. They're O.K.—real pro-American and they got some nice, sexy broads. But they're still a little backward: they think penicillin is an evil spirit." He poked at the red cross on Jones' left brassard. "That's why we need a good corpsman. Are you a good corpsman?"

"No," said Jones.

"I thought so. I thought so." Garbini cackled again. He slapped both kneecaps and then, for good measure, slapped Jones' left kneecap as well. "You got too many of them Red Cross things on. You look like a walking tic-tac-toe game." Jones' left knee was pounded again. But Garbini's enjoyment was so genuine, so enormous, that Jones, quite in spite of his annoyance, managed a weak smile.

"Sorry," he said amiably. "I don't care t'be a target, that's all."

"Oh—but that's just what you are. After generals, Jonesy, the Riffs like to shoot corpsmen best. They aim at the crosses." Garbini extended his fore and middle fingers, a compact Derringer, and sighted them on Jones' helmet. He made an explosive sound with the loose bags of his cheeks. "Take the damn things off, and when you get to the Negro, smear some mud on your helmet." Jones frowned, hesitant. But, with a sharp tug, Garbini ripped off the left brassard and tossed it over the side of the truck.

"Hey, man," said Jones irresolutely, touching the arm, as though it had been injured. Garbini, however, was not finished. He made a meaningful sign with his hand. Reluctantly, Jones tugged off the other brassard.

"That's better." Garbini took a long front tooth between thumb and forefinger. The tooth wobbled slightly in his grasp and blood appeared at the gum line. "Teeth're killing me," he said confidentially. "Listen. If things get hot, see, and you

18

hear some one call out, 'Corpsman! Corpsman!'—you know what you do?" Jones shook his head. "You don't do nothin'. You just sit right where you are and say, 'What's my name, please? What's your name, please?' And, 'Did Jesus Christ perform the miracle of Coogan's Bluff?' That's how they got Jo-Jo Knutson. He crawled out twenty yards in real heavy M30 fire and then got his throat cut for his trouble. *Capitsch?* The Riffs can sound like your old Aunt Molly." Jones stared dolefully at the other brassard. Then he threw it over the side.

"Don't worry about me," he said. "I ain't crawlin' out after nobody. Riff or Camaguayan or even you." Garbini smiled. "You're a man after my own heart, Jones. Inexperienced, but with all the right instincts. Oh-oh. We're going down."

The crest of the plateau appeared now behind them. Eroded by deep, snaking gullies, it looked, Jones thought, like a giant human brain. The wind died down as the truck dropped below the rim. A new heat swelled up, different from the brutal, direct parching of the plateau's surface. It was a claustrophobic, soft heat: the pressure of damp breasts. Sweat lingered on the skin, unable to fight free into the moisture-filled air; it choked the body's myriad tiny breathings. Jones raised his arms: streams ran down over his ribs on either side. They were a thousand feet above the jungle, a thousand feet above a simmering cauldron. Almost immersed.

Garbini had thrown his head back on the truck's railing. His mouth was open; Jones could see his lower teeth and a lump of whitish, lolling tongue. He snorted as he breathed out. Jones still wanted to talk. "Joe," he said, but Garbini didn't respond. Across the way Baxter was staring at Jones, but not, Jones thought, seeing him. The little man's childish face, in its intentness, appeared abruptly terrified. But then Baxter yawned; his lips opened out like a bud in sudden flower. Jones prodded Garbini lightly with his elbow.

"Uh . . . What is it?"

"Hey—are there any Riffs around here?" He pointed vaguely towards the red bush-spattered countryside. Garbini rubbed his chin.

"Jones. Listen. There are Riffs all over. There's probably two in this truck right now."

Jones looked down at the truck floor. He yelped, snapped his legs together like a schoolgirl foiling a voyeur, and leaped a full foot to his right, along the length of the bench. Garbini was laughing again. A Camaguayan, the cause of Jones' panic, opened his eyes and smiled at the sky. His rifle lay carelessly across his raised thigh. The muzzle had been pointed at the tender angle of Jones' groin. Garbini kicked the barrel away with his foot. The Camaguayan didn't stir.

"Don't worry, Jonesy. You can come back. He hasn't cleaned it—not since he used it to fish for quarters in the head." Garbini made motherly calming gestures with his hand and lips. Coyly, slowly, Jones inched back. "Now. What were you saying?"

"Ah . . ."

"Yeah—about the Riffs. You can stop shaking now, Jonesy. The Riffs . . ." Garbini flicked at the tip of his fleshy nose. "They're all over, but they're not always Riffs. Get what I mean? No? Well, that guy there. He was probably a Riff last Tuesday, or maybe it's only weekends when his mother-in-law's around. They don't take their allegiance too serious, you know what I mean. The same guy who saved your life a week ago, tomorrow he'll hand your balls to his girl friend."

"You're exaggerating," said Jones hopefully.

"Well, maybe. But it's not like over on the Pacific side around Camaguay City. All us IC's here were on the Pacific side. It's a war over there. Here it's still a game. Nobody—not us, not the Riffs—wants this stinking, mosquito-infested coast. And aside from San Pedro, that's all there is—that and the highlands where the Indians are. And everybody, but everybody hates the Indians. You die here, you're not killed in action, you just sort of passed away. They play it down. We just sweat and slap, sweat and slap. Until the Riffs get bored and shoot. Personally, I prefer Riffs to mosquitos and mosquitos to those lazy little pricks."

"You—you ever kill anyone?" Garbini beamed. Jones regretted his question at once.

20

"When it's safe. Women and children, if they've got gold fillings. You think this means something?" He rubbed his thumb negligently over the arrow and question mark on his lapels. "Not here, anyway. Just between you and me, Section 2's a penal company, pretty much. Baxter, there, he's been kind of testy about taking orders since his arm got snapped. Falk," he leaned forward to whisper, "that's the guy next to me. He's just a kid looking for his mother's tit—and that's anyplace but where the nasty guns are. Hall, the other guy, he's not too bad. Talks and shivers in his sleep. His hands shake pretty good too. He's got three weeks to go and he doesn't want to buy it now. As for Storch—" Garbini shook his head and then raised his pupils to the tops of their orbits. "He's something special. Oh, you'll like Lieutenant Storch."

"Shit," said Jones. Sweat dribbled into his eyes; there was nothing, not his fingers, not his sleeve, dry enough to relieve them.

"All we needed was a lousy medic," said Garbini. "And now we're all set."

"And what about you?" said Jones in irritation. "You're not here for your—" he had almost said "looks." Garbini's eyeballs swelled, anticipating the word, and seemed momentarily to roll free of their bony sockets.

"Jonesy." Garbini placed his impertinent hand on the corpsman's arm, on the dustless place where the brassard had been. "Jonesy. I'm the best of them, remember that. I'm just dishonest."

"Just?"

"Just." Garbini smiled. "Cheer up. There's always Sergeant Hook."

"That mother . . ."

"No. He's the main man. You watch Joe Garbini when we start through the jungle. I'm going to be so close, it'll look like I climbed in his pants. And if you're smart, man, then you'll be right behind me. That's where the safety is."

"Yeah? If he's so good—then how come he's in Section

21

2?" Garbini shrugged. He began picking his nose without embarrassment.

"There's such a thing as being too good." Garbini balled a strand of mucus between his thumb and forefinger. Then he placed it on a bluish lower lip. "That's the way I see it. He embarrassed the generals. That and the beard—he's got a skin thing, he's allergic to the sun, so the doctors don't make him shave. You watch Hook. He speaks Spanish and all the Indian dialects. The Camaguayans'll do anything he says. Sawed-off Sanchez, he hates him for it. Watch Hook in the jungle. He hears everything. The animals—damn it, I've never seen a mosquito bite him. It's kind of a legend around here. Watch him with an M16 in his hand. Oh, if he gets it, I tell you, we'll never get back to San Pedro. And it won't be the Riffs' fault —we'll kill ourselves." The truck swerved and Jones, sliding forward, clutched at Garbini's arm.

"I heard some things about him," he said, when he had pulled himself upright. "Even out there, out on the *Sting*. I heard he was crazy."

"The magazine article, you mean, the *Killer Priest* business? Yeah, that's what started his trouble. But he's not a priest—he just prays a lot. In funny places." Garbini chuckled wistfully. "The other part's right. He's a killer. That's why I trust him. I made Clarence Hook promise to take care of me." He looked at his watch. "Half an hour to the bridge. I'm going to sleep."

"Sleep? How can you sleep in this heat?"

But Garbini's mouth was already gaping. Jones stared at him: at the scarred flesh of his face with its mass of whites and pinks and light blues; at the folds of his forehead that wriggled gently, like drowsy worms. Jones was alone again, his isolation stressed further by Garbini's easy sleep. Baxter was asleep. Falk was reading a dog-eared paperback—*Congressional Medal Heroes of World War II*. (Jones could see his lips move.) Hall was asleep, though he stirred more than a sleeping man should. Two Camaguayans slept oddly, holding hands, their cheeks touching. A jet plane roared overhead, depositing a thin, then fat trail on the blue of the Camaguayan sky. The transport began to jounce. Jones noticed that trees had now sprouted on the landscape. Trees with curious leaves. Trees of a sort he had never seen before. Abruptly he turned and poked Garbini again.

"Joe."

"Mmm . . . What now?"

"I know my stuff. I got high marks at Great Lakes." Garbini looked at him, squinting through the sun's brightness. "I'm smart," said Jones. "I'm no fool. I been to college."

"So. What's the trouble then?"

"I—I don't like to touch things sometimes. That's all."

"Okay, Jonesy." Garbini shut his eyes again. "You're not so bad. We're none of us so bad."

Garbini stretched out his legs, shoving the slack Camaguayan bodies aside. Jones tried to sleep then, but the light on the inside of his eyelids dazzled him. He put his hand over his face: the hand was hot, choking. He cursed. Fifty yards away, behind Baxter, a red mound nosed out of the earth. There was a man atop the mound, the first man Jones had seen since San Pedro. The man wore a yellow sarape, belted, and a wide-brimmed hat. He watched the truck, and when its wheels, by merest chance, passed harmlessly over the antitank mine, the man threw his fist into the air. Jones thought he was waving. He waved back.

WRITTEN SIX WEEKS BEFORE: LETTER FROM PRIVATE HORACE BAXTER TO HIS AUNT MINNA, *in loco parentis.*

Dear Aunt Min

I got the socks and the SPORT magazines. And your letter was very nice too. I read it three times and its in my pockit right now.

Dont worry about my arm. It dont hurt me at all. And please dont tell anybody about it. I dont want the Pirates to find out.

They want me to get it operrated on here. Sargt Hook says the army will do it free and good. If he says so I guess it must be o.k. But it scares me. I never had no operation before. I got to think about it.

But dont you worry Im in San Predo now and its very safe here. Not like at C-City. I guess you know that from the Daily News. Its only four months now and Ill be out. If my arms no good maybe Ill go back to school. Im not sure. I got to think about it. Or maybe Ill join up here again. Would that make you very mad? Its not so bad except for the fighting. Even the white men from down South are real nice. And Im a pretty good soldier tho right now my arm is on my mind a lot.

Give my love to Rina and uncle Howie and to Atlas. I hope he isnt chasing cats anymore. I cant wait to see him.

Well I got to go. I hope you can read my writing. Say a prayer for me. Maybe Ill come to church with you when I get back. Would you like that? I feel older now and Im an inch taller. Dont worry. I dont. And no matter what happens Ill do you proud.

Love and Kisses, Your son,
Horace.

II

JONES CRIED OUT—a shrill, feminine bleat when the things began to drop on him. Then, to the Camaguayans' delight, he danced, stamping murderously on the foot-sucking earth, slapping at his own head and neck. For perhaps ten years the lianas above the jungle trail had grown leisurely, entwining themselves, falling dead in their own entanglements, making a capacious hammock of their intricate warp and woof. Into this net had fallen a decade's accumulation of things: some long dead, some just dead, some dying, and some now horribly alive. When the bell rope creeper grazed Jones' neck, the hundredth that had surprised him so, he had been furious. He jerked at it angrily and the whole rotten bag was torn open. It sssshed down on him in the semidark: blind reptiles, rusty salamanders, birds' eggs, hairy spiders, and pounds of decayed vegetable matter. Now Jones had stopped his dance. With a low moan he hurled his equipment—both packs, his helmet, his .45—into the jungle. When, for the third time, Hook made his way back along the halted line of men, he found Jones, his eyes shut, embracing the trunk of a sapodilla tree.

"What now?" But Jones did not answer. He was rubbing the side of his face rhythmically against the tree trunk. Hook reached up and knocked a sapodilla fruit to the ground. He looked at Jones, then at the brown, rough-skinned fruit, apple-shaped. Not ripe yet. "Jones," he said, as he kicked it aside.

"I want out," said Jones.

"There's no out," replied Hook mildly. He sucked in his lower lip and chewed the tuft of beard that grew just beneath it. "What happened?"

"I just pulled," said Jones. He stared at the ground, at his bootprints, filling already with dark water. "And it all come down. Spiders. Snakes. Little toads. Crawly things. On me. It all fell on me."

"Pull yourself together." Hook turned to smile at the Camaguayans, who were watching them with intense curiosity. They nodded eagerly and, to a man, returned his smile, exaggerating it. Jones pushed himself away from the tree. He began tottering in erratic circles. Hook bent to collect the corpsman's strewn equipment. "Don't touch the jungle, Jones," he said. "Don't touch it, and it won't touch you."

"Yeah? Yeah?" hissed Jones. "What about this?" He drove his right arm high, in front of Hook's eyes. His wrist and forearm were covered with fat, thin-skinned blisters. Hook pushed the arm away with a curt movement.

"A plant with spines—about four inches long. You must have touched it down by the river. It's nothing."

"Nothing? It itches." Jones slapped with uncoordinated violence at the heavy, slow mosquito that droned near his throat.

"Nothing. Poison ivy's a lot worse." He handed Jones his haversack and dropped his helmet over his sweat-flecked head. "Come up front with me. I'll send Garbini back."

"I'll be all right," said Jones truculently.

"Sure," said Hook. "Come along."

As Jones staggered forward along the file Camaguayans made way for him, stepping deferentially into the thick undergrowth that lined the narrow trail. They were interested in him: they knew there was trouble between the tall black man and Sergeant Master Hook. Jones wavered under the clumsy, unbalanced weight, shaking his head, trying to understand the echoes in his helmet. The volume of jungle sound was terrific; it persisted at a dozen distinct levels. The whine of things that penetrated the very convolutions of his ear; the unnamed stumbling thuds in the near underbrush; the falling things: fruits, branches, tired trunks; spider monkeys gibbering; the bleep of the frogs; the contrapuntal chatter and branch-shakings of innumerable birds—and, especially at midday, the

26

trilling of cicadas: an endless, unbroken chorus borne across the jungle like a marathon flame, undimmed.

"Fuckin' big crybaby," Garbini unlipped his yellow fangs and hissed into Jones' ear as they passed each other. Jones had dislodged Garbini from his position of safety. Something bounced off Jones' helmet, pinging. He cursed. A Camaguayan smiled. His calves ached from the minute, careful steps he had been taking, for the ground, obscured in the dull light, had constantly to be tested and retested. Jones was bitten three times in rapid succession on the side of his nose. Hands preoccupied, he gnawed furiously at the insect-filled and sodden air.

Despite his fearful revulsion, Jones was annoyed at himself. He knew a corpsman didn't belong at the point. He knew now he would be under Hook's constant surveillance. And he had given sufficient grounds for distrust. The first time it had been a snake: a big, lazy, yellow-and-black thing that had blundered across the path not two feet in front of him. They had stared at each other, and the snake's forked tongue had whisked out to pluck the sound waves of Jones' shout from the air. Finally Hook had come. He shouldered the heavy, coiling reptile as he might have a rolled rug, and without looking at Jones, who had drawn his .45, he heaved it into the jungle. Then the ants . . . The little Camaguayans ahead of him had gone under the fallen trunk easily, but Jones, more than a foot taller and without suspicion, had brushed against it, snapping off a square foot of rotted bark. Hundreds of furious, nipping ants had penetrated into his underwear through the gap at his belt line. The shock of their massed stinging was dreadful. Jones assumed, at first, that there was a bayonet between the joints of his spinal cord. He screamed. And Hook had had to come again.

At the point, Lieutenants Storch and Sanchez were seated on their haunches like children watching insects. Sanchez had his knife out: he was playing mumblety-peg and, for excitement, he used the tip of his own boot as a target. Storch stared ahead, appearing to ruminate at a place deep in his throat.

27

His personal retainer, Private Luis Ruiz, was hunched nearby, fanning the lieutenant with a copy of the Camaguay City *Herald*. When Jones arrived, Storch extended his right hand, palm flattened, as though to test for rain. Twenty yards ahead, Jones saw Sergeant Hook and an Indian on their knees at the other side of the trail. He started toward them, but Hook waved him back.

José Ix was disarming the grenade trap. Hook held the trip wire taut, as the Indian's long fingers probed into the overgrown mechanism. José Ix was a friend, a Mayan chief, an excellent soldier, and a man of great influence in the Camaguayan highlands. The Indian's tongue came out, touching gently at his thin lips, as his fingers touched gently at the rusted works of the trap. The Indians hated the Riffs, who had massacred nearly five hundred of their people during the previous dry season. The Mayans were eager to fight; they were intelligent and trustworthy. But the Camaguayans, and especially the colonels of their army, despised them—their loathing a product, Hook thought, of their three hundred years of successful oppression. José Ix shook his head.

"Is it a good day in the calendar for disarming traps, my friend the chief?" Though José Ix understood English, Hook spoke in the highland dialect, for he was proud of his fluency.

"It is a poor day for leaving the hut," the Indian replied. "A poor day for travel. A poor day for everything but long sleep and prayer. I am a fool to be here."

"It is the day of the unknown, is it not?"

"Yes." He looked at the American and smiled. José Ix's eyes were black and they were slightly crossed, a deformation cherished by the Mayan Indians. "I wonder at this. A white man who knows my religion and the traditions of my people better even than I do. We remember so little now, and it is all confused. The cross that you wear on your neck, the cross of Jesus Christ, is it also the cross of our four directions? I cannot tell any more. Like the man who lived with monkeys, it is easier now to swing in the trees." He sighed. "This was put

28

here before the rains. The pin will not go in easily. I will try now. You should go back, I think."

"I will stay." The Indian inclined his head.

"Someday soon, Sergeant Master, you will get your wish. I will be sorry for it."

He inhaled. Hook enjoyed seeing the intentness of his features. The large, bent nose with its wide nostrils, brought very close to the hands now, as though complementing their dexterity with yet another sense. The thin lips drawn even more thinly over the teeth. The long, richly haired skull, a hatchet's head pointing his concentration. A mosquito landed, settled to bite, bit, was ignored, bit again. Carefully the pin was inserted, but, as it penetrated the tiny mouth, a small branch snapped forward. The pin fell. The bomb vibrated, humming, on its wire. José Ix covered his face. And Hook, excited, stared in challenge at the ugly, corrugated shell.

"Cheez Christ," said the Indian. They both laughed exultantly. "I must be quick now. Soon my hands will be no good." José Ix grasped the pin and jammed it downward with a sudden, sure thrust. Hook leaped forward and began detaching the grenade from its perch at the tree's base.

"It's one of ours. They can't have many more. They only took fifty in that raid." José Ix stood up. He wiped his forehead with a green handkerchief. The fingers of his left hand flexed unwillingly; they were still shaped stiffly to fit the grenade's squat body.

"I don't think it would have worked," he said. "I think the long rains have killed it."

"Well. Let's let them find out." Hook looked at his watch. "It slowed us down."

"You did not turn your head away. I saw that."

"To die with a hole in the back. Is that better?"

"You were not afraid."

"I was very afraid."

"For me then."

"For you, yes. And for my own, ugly skin."

29

Hook signaled the others forward. Lieutenant Storch spat angrily, as though the delay had been a whim of Hook's. Ruiz folded up the fan and handed Storch one of the four spare canteens he carried. Storch drank. There was a tremendous crash. Jones fell on his hands and knees: a man auditioning for the role of a large dog. The others stared at him. Under his palms, the soggy leaf mold squirmed like tentacles of something slowly carnivorous. Jones leaped up and jammed a hand under each armpit.

"What was that?" he whispered hoarsely. "What was that?" "A tree," said Hook. "It fell down. Let's move. Please."

They moved out at a trot. Hook expected only harassment here. The Negro jungle was too inimical for either the short-handed RFN or the Americans to keep continually patrolled. It would be different in the highlands. Hook slowed the pace. The little Camaguayans, carrying both their own and Rodriguez' equipment, were beginning to lag. He looked back at Jones. Now and then the corpsman would stare upward, probing for some small portion of the sky. But there were only leaves: thicker here, thinner; nowhere did the sun penetrate. It was difficult, in this perpetual dusk, to judge the time of day. Had he thought about it, Jones would have guessed six o'clock, and he would have been three hours fast. But Jones was not thinking of time.

The jungle reminded Jones of an elevator—as a child he had been trapped in one for over six hours. In front and behind he could see perhaps ten yards; half that to his left and right. Hands reached down from above to caress his face and neck, like those sudden, invisible surprises in a Coney Island ghost ride. Exhausted as he was, Jones preferred movement. When he halted, he was transformed, he imagined, into an utterly vulnerable thing—to be crawled on, burrowed in, eaten. Jones was an extremely sensitive young man. He had once had a pedicure.

They passed through thick swirling nebulae of mosquitos, so teeming that they obscured the jungle walls in an opaque mist. Their concerted whine sickened Jones. The nape of the man ahead darkened abruptly with a sheet of sucking dots. Jones had ceased now to react. His face was swollen; his thickened eyelids moved with difficulty over the slick surfaces of his pupils. But the mosquitos, at least, did not follow their prey: they remained in their weird, wheeling orbits. Jones blew dead insect bodies from his nostrils and wondered how long he could keep up.

The rains had ceased only the week before. At the lowest parts of the swamp, the stagnant water was two feet deep, and beneath it lay a bed of strength-destroying mire. The effort required to extract the trailing foot drove his lead foot deeper into the mud. The Camaguayans, shorter, were in beyond their waists. Men fell and struggled to their feet, weapons spewing water. The web of mangrove root was impenetrable in places. Unseen amphibians ducked in and out of the root whorls, leaving rippled disturbances behind them. Jones had lost all sense of direction. Things (or things imagined) brushed at his calves beneath the water. He wanted to leap aside, but his balance was too precarious. The stench of putrefaction dizzied him. He breathed through his mouth, and insects settled there. He coughed them out at first. After an hour, he merely swallowed.

They halted, when they reached higher ground, to burn off leeches with their cigarettes. A Camaguayan sergeant named Raoul helped Jones, who could not bear to see the little sanguisugent lumps on his inner thighs. They began to climb subtly after that. The Indian trails tended to follow the line of ridges, but, since the war, the regular traffic had ceased, and the paths were thickly overgrown. Hook and José Ix wielded their machetes almost constantly. Jones had fallen twice, his clumsiness induced by exhaustion. He had a stitch in his side. Moreover, despite the oppressive heat, he had begun to shiver, and the unreasonableness of his body terrified him. Then, suddenly, they halted again.

The pit was six feet long and about four feet deep. José Ix dangled over it, his body still wriggling, despite Hook's firm hold, from the first instinctive reactions to his fall. Hook set him down as he might have a light satchel. Both men were silent for a moment, admiring the camouflage. There were sharp wooden stakes at the pit's bottom, and the bodies of poisonous snakes, now merely skeletons, were strewn between them. The pit smelled very strongly. Had a portion of the covering not collapsed during the rains, Hook doubted if he would have seen it in time. On the other side, as anticipated, they found two four-ounce antipersonnel mines at what Hook termed the point of reduced alertness: where a man, having circumvented one threat, will permit his attention to lapse. Garbini arrived at the point as Hook was disarming the second mine.

"Need any help, Sergeant?" he inquired from a safe distance. But Hook waved him back. "Ass kisser, suck up, brown nose," he growled at Jones as he started toward the rear. Jones, however, was jumping imaginary rope and did not hear him. Weary as he was, he had determined that the fewer things he touched —and that included the ground—the safer he would feel. "One, two, buckle my shoe; three, four, shut the door," he panted in a half audible undertone. Lieutenant Sanchez watched his shifting boots.

Garbini was dangerously irritated. He flailed at the jungle fringes as he made his way back along the line of men. His initial compassion for Jones had faded. In case of ambush, he did not care to be the only American in the midst of ten Camaguayans, spaced, five in a group, ahead and behind him. Garbini did not fear death, nor even injury; it wasn't his habit to consider such things. He merely resented the responsibility that would devolve on him in an emergency. As he walked, muttering vilely, he saw a fat, naked Camaguayan backside, hunched at the trail's edge. Armando was squinting, biting his lips, mimicking facially the compression of his intestines. He sighed. A large, soft stool began to emerge. With a lithe motion and an athlete's timing, Garbini kicked the man's upturned helmet under his bared buttocks. Armando shrieked and pummeled his belly when he saw how he had been made to befoul his own headgear. He held the helmet in his hand, shaking it, like a fat salesman hawking wares. But, by then, Garbini was back in place, greatly mollified, laughing.

With a muted sss-thwack, the blade drove itself into the ground between Jones' feet. He yelped, and, irrationally, slapped his hands over both ears. The handle hummed with its vibrations, then quieted. Across the trail, Lieutenant Sanchez shook his head slowly. "No more, please. Stand still. You are making me nervous, Mr. Black Man." Jones nodded. He nodded again. Then he bowed, backed like a discreet private servant, and nearly disappeared into the jungle. Sanchez retrieved the knife. He wiped the blade on his thigh. He sat on his haunches near Lieutenant Storch, who also sat on his haunches. Lieutenant Storch had not perceived the incident. He had found a sort of sweet grass that he particularly liked, and he was chewing slowly, green blades protruding over his flat lower lip.

Though nearly spent, the patrol proceeded another three miles beyond the pit before they were permitted to camp. Hook had used this particular site during the previous dry season, and he was reluctant to repeat his actions. But it was a good position: a high, grassy knoll with a wide stream to the rear. The M30 was placed at the knoll's apex, and fire lanes were cut in a fan shape away from it. He sent Baxter and José Ix on a reconnaissance of the camp's outer fringes. Then, despite their protestations, he made the tired men dig in, using the overgrown depressions of the previous encampment. Socks and shirts were spread out to dry; water was purified; the knoll was sprayed with insecticide in a futile attempt to discourage mosquitos and the deeper-biting sand flies that would appear at night. Hook had heard the uo, the small frog that heralds rain, but the first shower at least was brief and did not penetrate the leaf cover. José Ix and Baxter returned, having found no sign of Riff activity. Hook was worried, nonetheless; they were still three hours behind their schedule.

Jones sat huddled under his shelter half. The Camaguayan Sergeant Raoul had helped him again—helped him with the trenching and with the unfamiliar bits of equipment. Raoul

33

seemed a pleasant sort. He spoke English quite well, Jones thought, as he smoked his third cigarette carefully. The first two cigarettes had each burned a hole in his mosquito net, and Jones had begun to suspect that there were more insects inside than out. He had eaten nothing, though twice since they had halted he had drained his canteen. The thick, moist smell of the jungle suggested a giant female's groin. He moaned. The inhibition of his senses was disquieting. His untrained eyes could not function: the shapes of the darkening jungle overlapped, commingled. His nose and ears were sated with rich sensations, few recognized. And he dared touch nothing, not even his own tacky, swollen face.

But the Camaguayans were strangely unconcerned. They grouped together chattering, giggling, devouring too many of their scant rations. Once past the Rio Negro they had begun to relax. At that point their chief interest—desertion—had become impracticable. Though they ignored authority, they trusted it implicitly. They did not know where the patrol was going or why. The war itself seemed merely another irrational happening in a world that, even under better circumstances, they would not have bothered to understand. Their nonchalance was burdensome to their five IC advisers. The Camaguayans were, for instance, totally useless on watch: They would fall asleep at once or sound an alarm for whatever amusement it might cause. Lieutenant Sanchez and a corporal named Gutierrez with a missing left forefinger were the only two exceptions. Sanchez, however, reserved his excellent soldiering for special moments. On tedious marches he was morose, lazy, and, quite often, dangerous.

Storch had set up housekeeping. He directed Ruiz with gestures (he spoke no Spanish), tapping the man with a stick on the shoulders, on the thighs, as though patiently training a dog to obedience. Storch wore a silk pajama top with a Japanese dragon, coiled and smoke-exhaling, embroidered on the back. The dragon appeared to be defending something—perhaps it was the huge, white egg of Storch's cranium. The lieutenant had certain privileges, which he guarded jealously. More water: four canteens carried by Luis Ruiz and a capacious canvas water bag of his own. A special stove. In any bivouac of more than two days, a personal latrine. But most precious of all: Hook's reports, delivered to him four times daily. He said nothing, either of disapprobation or approval at these sessions, but Storch cherished them as reminders of his rank and power and of Hook's subordination. Now he belched: a triumphant, resonant sound. And from the stream, a bull frog boomed an answering call of passion.

Garbini rolled his yellow, phosphorescent dice on the blanket. Seven. Seven. Seven. These were his most cherished possessions (he had had them made to specification by the great Nick Papoulas himself). They glowed golden under the tiny blacked-out dots. Seven. Seven. Seven. Garbini clicked them in his fist: it was meant as a signal for Tom Hall, but Hall pretended not to comprehend. Garbini leaned forward in the dark, found the back, and poked it between the shoulder blades.

"I've got no money. And I don't feel like being cheated tonight, thank you. Go bother someone else."

"No money? So let's play for your wife. You don't want her anyway." In anticipation Garbini aimed the tip of his boot at the other man's back. Hall, exasperated, turned over suddenly as he had done several times before—he would throw only one punch, they both knew that, it was all that his now demoralized spirit had patience for. But Garbini's hard boot tip was waiting and Hall impaled his solar plexus on it. "Come on, buddy boy," said Garbini reasonably, as Hall collapsed. "I don't want to hit a man with glasses. Not again. Come on. You can't sleep anyway."

"Go to—" gasped Hall. "Oh just go." He clutched at his scrawny chest.

Tom Hall was thirty-one. He had a wife and three small children, all girls. His wife had taken his testicles away, or so Hall had once dreamed; she had put them in a box marked "spices" on the kitchen shelf. Isabel Hall was simply too beautiful for a man of her husband's physical and mental capabilities. He was five foot eleven and weighed only 140 pounds. He had hair on his chest, but it lay in a single trough between his nipples, and the rest of his skin, especially his back, was white with unseemly purple blotches. He wore glasses over watery eyes and on the bridge of an angular nose that ended in large miter-shaped nostrils. Tom Hall had joined the IC's to escape from his wife.

His three girls all resembled Isabel, red-haired, fair-skinned, already busy testing their sensuality—he could not find his contributive masculinity in even one aspect of their faces. Isabel had a trim, thirty-eight-inch bust and superb legs. (She had been Miss Enriched White Bread the year before their marriage.) Mornings, she and the little girls would saunter around the house naked from the waist down. The four pudenda seemed to grin at him, watch him, encompass him. Hall was obsessed with jealousy while being titillated by it: he was potent only with fantasies of his wife's infidelity. He had had three letters from Isabel in two years: he had written once. Now, as his hitch neared its end, he found himself experimenting morbidly with the trigger of the M16. Garbini tormented him at regular intervals, but it was Hall himself who had told Garbini about Isabel, shown him her picture. On several occasions during the last month, Hall had been quite clinically insane.

Jones was smoking his eighth cigarette of the night. He just discovered two inch-long fat blisters, one on the skin of either heel. He prodded them cautiously: the fat bags of liquid gave way under his finger tip. The pressure caused a slight, burning sensation. Jones was inclined to hypochondria, and, as the only child of prosperous parents, he had been conditioned to demand expert medical care. His first instinct was to call the corpsman (he had always done so on the *Sting*): then, remembering who the corpsman was, he thought it would be advisable to have someone more competent examine his feet, perhaps Sergeant Hook. He debated this matter for some time and decided, reluctantly, that such an action would

36

entail a considerable loss of face. He groaned and, for the first time, opened the stranger's medical pack.

He found a needle and sterilized it with a match. Then he inserted the point gingerly into the left blister at its base. He squeezed the warm liquid out, making gurgly sounds of distaste in his throat. He sterilized the needle again. But as he approached the second blister, a harsh roar exploded in the jungle, very near the camp. Jones punctured his Achilles tendon instead. The roar was repeated; there was a hoarse coughing. Jones felt his helmet move up and down, adjusting to his excited scalp. He opened up the second blister quickly, shook antiseptic powder over both feet, and applied Band-Aids. A monkey woke up and began to shriek. Perhaps, Jones thought, perhaps it's being killed. He peered toward the edge of the jungle. Here and there, little shining lights, eyes, he imagined, would gleam, change color, fade away, reappear. Jones threw himself back and pulled his blanket over his face. But, even through the cloth, he could hear the sound of Garbini's husky voice, punishing Hall once again.

"I tell you her boobs were like this. Like this. Can you see, Hall? No. Well, you just try to picture those chest fruits—three handfuls each and pointing up. I mean, she walked on her toes, like they were filled with helium and any minute, if the wind was right, they'd lift her up and she'd just float away. Long, straight blond hair. Beautiful lips, always wet and shiny. When she walked, her cheeks moved left-right, up-down. Oh, let me tell you, Hall—Hall? Are you listening? I don't want you to miss nothing. You got three weeks to go and you might want t'get married one day."

"Shut up. Shut up. Shut up," said Hall, but in a low tone and without vehemence.

"Eat it, prick. I'm talking. Where was I? Yeah—she's in the class ahead of mine. I's fifteen then—not so good lookin' as I am now—but my dork was twelve inches long by the time I was eight. Oh man, did I ever want to pop her little red balloon. One day, see, I'm standin' in the hall, around the corner, when I see her go by—to the girls' room, I think. So I

37

start tiptoein' behind her. Left-right, up-down goes her ass. What I'm gonna do, see, I'm gonna tap her on the shoulder, then, when she turns around, I'm gonna lay one right on those marshmallow lips. I'm just reaching out—you hear this, Hall? I'm talking for your benefit, buddy—I'm just reaching when she wriggles her butt once and lets out with a motorboat fart that rattles the windowpanes. I mean it was a ten-second shot and she kinda sighed when it was over. Took the crease out of my pants, it did. Then she wriggles her butt again and, bang, she's gone. And me standin' there gaspin' for air. Helium, shit, I know what her tits were full of. Hall? Hall? You hear me? That's what women are. Clap and stink and paternity raps." A ball of red mud and vegetable matter sailed over Garbini's shoulder and struck Jones' shelter half. "Sucker," said Garbini. "Sucker. Don't say I didn't warn you."

Jones emitted a tiny sound, half shriek, half whimper. Something, he imagined, had touched at his skin. But it was only the cool, sleek material of his poncho. He cursed methodically for several seconds, and this seemed to afford him some relief. Jones pulled his blanket off. A fluttering sound above. He looked through the netting. The fluttering again, and now a high-pitched squealing noise as of a small, unoiled hinge. Then, on the other side of the camp, he heard Baxter's voice. "Damn vampires!" Vampires. Were they kidding? He put his hands to his throat. Then he thought, while I'm at it, I might just as well strangle myself. A scratching on his shelter half.

"How's it going, Jones?"

"Fine, Sergeant. Fine." But the voice broke as he pronounced the second "fine." Hook sat near him.

"Feel like talking?" Jones grunted, shrugged. He could barely discern Hook's outline in the darkness. The squealing sound again, and a rustling flutter high among the leaves.

"Sergeant Hook—ah . . . There ain't no vampires is—are there?"

"Well . . . Just tiny ones. They don't drink much." He

38

laughed. "Might give you a case of rabies though." Jones was silent. "This isn't quite your cup of tea, I take it?"

"No. No, sir. It isn't," said Jones.

"Instructive, though," Hook went on wistfully. "Not so much for the flora and fauna and the local customs. It's a microcosm of life, speeded up like an old movie. By a microcosm I mean—"

"I know, Sergeant," said Jones quickly. "I know what a microcosm is. I been to college. I got my degree. I'm an educated man, Sergeant. I intend to be a lawyer some day."

"I'm glad to hear that," said Hook. "I was going to be a lawyer myself once. But that's another story. Yes. An archaeologist, too, once. . . . And other things." He touched at his collarbone with a tentative forefinger, and probed for the familiar shape that was hidden there.

"So, you see, sir," said Jones. "I don't really belong here."

"Well. I don't know about that. It requires intelligence of a high sort to fight a war like this. To fight and survive, that is."

"Maybe so," said Jones. He lit another cigarette. "Do you smoke, sir?"

"No."

"Do you mind if I tell you something, man to man?" Hook ran his fingers through his beard. "Do you, sir?"

"No—" said Hook. "Just stop calling me sir. It's beginning to sound like an insult." There was silence. "You were going to tell me something, Jones. Man to man."

"This war, Sergeant." Jones exhaled. "I don't think we should be fighting it. I don't think we should be killing innocent people. I think it's a crime."

"I see."

"That's the way I feel."

"Well," said Hook slowly. "This belief of yours. Man to man, now. It's not going to affect your performance as a soldier, is it?"

"I'm a corpsman, not a soldier."

"Don't quibble. Answer my question."

"I'll try not to let it."

"Try very hard, Jones. Very hard," said Hook mildly. "And, in return, I'll try to keep you alive. Fair enough?"

They were silent once again. Jones wished he could see the sergeant's face. The various tones of Hook's voice were deceptive: they seemed to express, at worst, a certain amusement. In the jungle a heavy object began to fall. Jones could hear the several stages of its descent through the thick foliage. It felt cooler now, almost chilly. He drew his blanket around him. The black silhouette of Hook's body was motionless, arms wrapped around shins. Jones felt irritable. He began speaking again.

"It's pretty hard. I mean, put yourself in my place. We weren't exactly rich at home. I had to work my way through college, and I got me a straight B average too. After bein' a second-class citizen all my life, I thought I's finally gonna be my own man. Now I'm back to go again. Takin' orders like some shoe shine boy." Hook hummed awkwardly for a few moments, but the theme eluded him. It struck him then that he was glad of the darkness: Jones' sullen features, he thought, would probably have irritated him. Hook did not permit himself irritation and realized that in the future he would have to be very careful with Jones.

"Your own man?" he said dubiously. "Did you really think so? At your age—what are you? Twenty-three? At your age even I wasn't quite that naïve. Do you know anyone who's his own man? Anyone who even wants to be? Did you take a look around while we were on the trail?"

"How d'you mean?"

"Let's call it a conceit of existence. I won't define the word for you." Hook stretched and then sprawled easily on the moist loam, hands flat behind his head. Jones, peering through the mosquito net, envied his body's casualness. "The irony of it. The ironies, rather. Parasites devouring their own life's substance. The trees are broken by the liana, and the liana gives life to the matapalo. Insects eat the matapalo leaves, and they are eaten by birds. A thing is born, and, as it begins to suck its life from something else, yet another thing, born a moment

40

later, is sucking on it. The life force here is incredible. Irresistible. Suicidal. Sometimes the pollen's so thick I'm afraid it'll take root in my brain. But teeming life exists only where there is teeming death. And here, besides, there are no civilized distinctions. No moments of death. No moments of birth. It is all death; it is all life. They are each other. If you died now, Jones, things would sprout from your body in less than a week. And, within an hour, you would be several kinds of food."

"Like you said, Sergeant. It's not my cup of tea." Hook sat up.

"No. Probably not. But it's the condition of your life. That's why the jungle is good. That's why war is good—if it can ever be called good. They inform you, in one way or another, of your own precious insignificance. It's healthy for the soul."

"I'm not insignificant."

"No. In one sense—"

"And," said Jones, interrupting him. "I don't have a soul. Or if I do, it don't seem to matter much." Hook rubbed his hands together.

"Oh. It matters. It matters. And it's here that you first know it. You know it or you despair. One or the other. Back home, life is a euphemism for itself. We try not to think about it—about death. But here, where the parasites are waiting, where the Riffs are waiting, then you have no choice. And it's good, believe me. When you have known death, you are alive—for that fragment of a moment, at least. There is a heightening in war, if nothing else."

"All this talk about souls, Sergeant," Jones said. "They tell me you're a religious man."

"They? Yes. It's no secret."

"A Christian?"

"Yes."

"You ever kill anyone?"

"I have had to. Yes."

"Uh-huh," murmured Jones. "I guess that proves it."

"Proves what?"

"Proves—" whispered Jones in a barely audible tone. "Proves that you're a Christian."

Hook opened his mouth. Left it ajar. Then he shut it with difficulty, pressing the teeth in admonition against the flesh of his lower lip. He was very glad, indeed, that he could not see Jones' face; that Jones could not see his. Cautiously, so that the gesture might not be noticed, he brought both palms together and clasped his fingers until the knuckles cracked. He said an orison for patience. And Jones, protected only by the thin net, waited nervously, excitedly, for the outburst that was to come.

"You'd better get some sleep, Andy," said Hook. The use of his Christian name infuriated Jones. It was Hook's only rejoinder. But when Hook stood up to leave, Jones became anxious again, aware of his surroundings again. He was afraid to be alone.

"Sergeant—"

"Yes . . ." Hook attended with curiosity. Jones' voice had become frail once more.

"How long does this keep up? The jungle, I mean." Hook nodded, giving confirmation of his own suspicion. Jones was scared; Hook understood this, understood how his fear might manifest itself in bitterness. And he pitied the man.

"We should reach the plantations by day after tomorrow." He leaned down and brushed off his pants legs. "Really—if you want the truth. We're safer in here. Once we're in the highlands it'll be different. The Riffs already know we're here. They'll be waiting for us when we come out." Hook smoothed down the corners of his mustache. "We'll be on the move by dawn. At least I hope so. Watch your water tomorrow. And, if it's all right, I'd like to have you at the point with me. Do you mind?"

"You mean you don't trust me. Isn't that it, Sergeant?"

"No. You can have your choice."

"The point."

"Fine," said Hook. "Well, I'd better go wake up the Camaguayans. The ones on watch." He began to walk away. Jones

42

listened as the oddly faint sounds of his footfalls diminished. Then Jones spat thickly, fiercely. But he had forgotten the mosquito net, and his saliva befouled only his own mouth and chest.

WRITTEN SIX WEEKS BEFORE: LETTER FROM PRIVATE JOE GARBINI TO HIS UNCLE, JOE PETRILLO, A MAN OF GREAT STANDING IN THE MAFIA.

Greetings Unk,

Well, I bet you never expected to hear from me again. Not after what happened. But here I am writing and taking the bull by the horns so to speak.

I been thinking a lot Uncle Joe. About what an asshole I was back there and about what my mother used to say. She talked a lot about you Uncle Joe. Did you know that? She said to me once, Joe (me) the world is full of skunks but you got one real freind and thats your uncle Joe. My brother Joe is an honest man. Now that may sound like a pile of horseshit to you but its the truth. I swear to god. I figure she loved you an awful lot. Thats why she named me after you. Dont believe that crap about her been crazy over Joe Dimaggio when I was born. My mother didnt know a home run from a jock strap and thats the truth.

I guess Im not a boy anymore. Been here in the jungle all the time surrounded by the Riffs makes a man grow up. Back then when you saved my skin I was just a crazy kid. I could kick myself real good. What say we let bigones be bigones, huh unk? Is there a chance for me? When I get back to the big PX I mean.

If I get back that is. Its real bad down here, Uncle Joe. Gee, the bugs and the snakes are all over and the Riffs got us outnumbered 100 to 1. Dont you believe what the papers say. Just last week I got shot up. Another inch and your nephew

43

would be dead. But I got the SOBs who shot at me. Three of them. The guys down here want to give me a medal, but I says the hell with it. All I want is to get back and prove myself to the boys.

So you see unk Im a diferent man now. That money I took. Gee whats $5000? If Id a had any brains Id a known there was more money just playing it strait. I was a 1st class asshole thats what. And what hurts me most is all the trouble I made you. They would been right to knock me off the way they wanted to. But you got them to let me join up instead. You paid them back all that money. That was real white of you. Ill never forget you for it.

I know you didn't mean those things about disowning me. I know you were just a little pissed. I know you wouldnt hate your sisters son, the one that loved you so much. Listen uncle Joe. Please. I get out in 6 months and 4 days. And I got nothing for me. No Job. No training—except for one thing. I can use a gun real good. I figure its a god given talent. And I think you should have all the benefits. Who else deserves it?

Youre a big man, Uncle Joe. The biggest. If you talk to Strezzi and Palumbo I just know theyll listen. Theyll let me come back. You just tell them Ill do anything. Please, Uncle Joe. It means a lot to me. Even the cops give a 1st ofender another chance.

Well I got to go out on patrol now. Looks real bad. Were surrounded by a whole division of Commies. I hope Ill be here when your letter comes.

    Love, Your sister Mary's son,
      Joe.

P.S. If they dont trust me with a gun, try to get me a job with the girls.

 # III

PRIVATE LUIS RUIZ was found dead before dawn the next morning. He lay at the jungle's edge, near the straddle trench that had been dug the night before. Jones had not been told; he had meant to relieve himself at the trench. When he saw the sprawled, bloating corpse, his fingers, already working the fly zipper, clutched at his tender parts in a painful spasm. The body was untended but for Garbini, who squatted easily nearby, finishing his breakfast. Jones began to back stealthily away, his hands still held flattened across his crotch. Garbini saw him, however; he began to gesture, shouting gleefully. Jones shook his head, waved both hands in front of his face; placed his forefinger over his lips; finally stamped both feet. But Garbini persisted.

"Hey, Corpsman. Yoo-hoo," he shouted. "Over here. This man needs your help. He's constipated something awful. He hasn't moved his bowels since last Tuesday. Matter of fact, he hasn't moved much at all lately."

Jones' lower jaw began to assault his upper jaw, biting, gnawing. His eyes crossed of their own will, and Garbini, waving at him, abruptly possessed four hands. Jones walked unsteadily toward Garbini, who was now standing near the corpse, and every movement of his legs seemed, for Jones, a tactless discourtesy to the dead man. The eyes were open and infested with wrathful, hissing flies that sucked at the drying juices. He had been a small man. Jones did not remember him. He didn't know whether the plump, bulging abdomen was his own or merely was the result of his agonized dying. The neck and the left side of the skull were grotesquely swollen, purple-blue. The man smiled against his own volition, as the swelling stretched his lips aside. His fists were clenched near his ears in an impotent furiousness. Blood, caked black now, had drained from his earholes.

"How? How—" Garbini belched and threw his C ration can into the trench.

"Snake bit him. Commie snake."

"A snake. But . . . Oh sssh—aaah!" Jones opened his mouth and then clamped it shut. A hot, bitter sensation had begun swirling up, along the passages of his chest. Jones thought it would emerge as a belch, but, when his lips came open, a caustic fluid gurgled out. He turned away from Garbini quickly —and vomited on the corpse's stomach.

"Some stinkin' medic," said Garbini, amused. Jones gagged, could not control the spasm, and puked once again. This time he managed to avoid the corpse. "Well," said Garbini, thumbing the furrows of his brow. "Well, he's dead, that's for damn sure. Only a dead man'd put up with that. I tell you, I'm gonna be a pretty sick pup before I ask you t'make a house call."

"It's the heat, I—" Jones wiped his lips vigorously on the back of his sleeve. "Why don't they bury him?"

"Well, Jee-sus. They can't bury him like that. Ain't you gonna clean him up a bit?" Helpfully, Garbini brought out a small pack of toilet tissues and tried to hand the pack to Jones. Jones shoved his hand away; then he looked at the corpse, looked at the jungle, growled, and began hurrying back toward the knoll. "Sorry, friend," said Garbini to the corpse. "My buddy don't like dead men. These minority groups, you know. Uppity." He followed Jones, a low chuckle bubbling up and down in the confines of his windpipe. A bird flashed across the clearing, a bright streak of green. It was, at its lowest, three yards above Jones' head, but he flailed up at it nonetheless.

"Jones," said Garbini. "You're a bad man. A real bad man. I'll say one thing for Billy Graham. He was a snob, but he never puked on his patients."

"It's the heat, I tell you, and the water. I don't feel good."

"Ain't you never seen a corpse before?"

"Of course, damn it." Jones made a gesture of irritation. Then he slumped to one knee on the slope of the knoll.

"Who? Your old granddaddy?" Jones looked up. "Just like I figured. That's not dead. Dead's when a man's trippin' over his own guts like a jump rope. Dead's when a man's head is where his pecker should be an' his pecker's comin' out of his left ear. Not some lily-holdin' department store dummy, made up so he looks better than when he's alive."

"Shut up. Where are the others? Why don't they bury him?"

"First things first, friend."

Garbini tapped Jones on the shoulder. Then he pointed toward the south and along the stream bank where, through the fringes of an early morning mist, they could see Sergeant Hook and fifteen Camaguayans coming slowly toward the knoll. Hook held the three-foot fer-de-lance in his right hand, the hand raised high above his head in a patent sign of triumph. The snake's ashy-gray body flailed and coiled, catching onto Hook's forearm and spiraling fitfully around it. The charcoal black diamonds on the back seemed to elongate, contract. The Camaguayans danced around Hook, delighted by the hunt, tormenting the prey. Hook paused beneath a ceiba tree. He stretched out his left hand, palm flattened. Eagerly Private Falk handed him a knife. As Jones watched, horrified, Hook lopped off the snake's head with ceremonial precision. An ebullient cry of joy from the Camaguayans. The snake's body contorted, leaped upward, as though seeking its amputated part. Blood spattered into Hook's beard.

"Jesus God," moaned Jones.

"Poor snake," said Garbini reflectively. He poked with the nail of his small finger between two blackened molars. "I'd hate to be around and guilty when old Clarence is handing out justice. He's a hard man. But the little toads lap it up. He's like a god to them. Catches the fuggin' snakes with his bare hands. That's pretty cool. Y'gotta admit that, Jonesy. Jonesy?" Garbini looked down. Jones was on his stomach, hugging the full length of his body to the ground.

"This God-damned war. This God-damned war. They're not gonna get me."

"Hey, Jones? Hey, buddy? What're you doing? Man, you're laying right on an ant hill." Jones scampered to his feet. He ran three yards up the knoll. Then he stopped and began slapping at his body. "Aaaaaah," he hissed. Then he stopped slapping. He stared at his hands, at his chest. . . . He was still for a moment, senses alert, but he felt nothing on his body. He looked at Garbini.

"Prick," he said solemnly.

"Now. Now. No ethnic remarks. I'm thinking of you. What would the Navy think—a corpsman crying like that?"

"I wasn't crying."

"No. But you will." Garbini grinned. "Here comes old Clarence. Just wait'll he sees how you puked up his fancy funeral."

Walking deliberately, in long, measured strides, Hook led his followers toward the trench. The snake's body, its nerves not yet dead, danced and squirmed, ejecting squirts of blood that dribbled down Hook's forearm. The Camaguayans laughed, shouted; they pounded each other between the shoulder blades. Falk, just behind Hook, held the open-jawed head gingerly between thumb and forefinger. He grinned and, alternately, swallowed deep gulps of air. The sun had risen. It found a crevice in the leaf cover, and the small troop now cast long shadows before it.

Hook remained impassive: his face perhaps vacuous, perhaps serene. Jones saw him for the first time without a helmet. The long hair, jet black, was drawn away from his forehead; it invaded the nape of his neck. He had huge ears. The lobes were shaped like the bowls of dolls' spoons. His nose was oddly delicate, seeming inadequate to the mat of heavy beard surrounding it. Black commas were painted on his cheekbones (to reduce the glare), but these were suggestive as well of savage face paintings, and they lent his eyes a gaunt intensity. The sun glinted from his forehead. Jones admitted reluctantly that Hook presented a striking figure. Garbini spat, seeing what

Jones saw, and, by inference from it, seeing also the terrible degree of his own ugliness.

"He's seen it. He's seen it. He's seen it." Garbini chanted. He jabbed boisterously at Jones' left bicep. "He's seen your puke and he knows it's yours. He knows."

Jones sidled away from the tell-tale jabs, but Hook, he decided cheerlessly, had no doubt already guessed. The sergeant was kneeling before the corpse. He raised his eyes and, with deliberation, scanned the encampment. He saw Baxter, Hall, and Gutierrez, the men on sentry duty at the jungle's fringes. He saw José Ix, and smiled as he watched the Indian bathe his muscular legs in the stream. Sanchez was cleaning his guns, sighting along the barrels, sighting occasionally toward Hook himself. Storch had just wrapped his tenth Band-Aid around his tenth toe, and he panted with the effort. Since Ruiz's death, such menial tasks had devolved, once again, on him. He was supremely annoyed at Ruiz. Hook looked toward the knoll. Garbini, at its summit, answered his stare with a grin. Then Hook saw Jones. With bogus interest, Jones was watching a log as it bobbed downstream. But he was aware of Hook's scrutiny, and his subconscious betrayed him. He wiped his mouth just once: Hook nodded resignedly. The Camaguayans didn't mind the vomit. Nor did they particularly resent their comrade's sudden death. The snake and the ritual to come had already flooded the shallow capacity of their imaginations. Hook understood this. He knew that their innocence was as often a glory as an impediment. His concern was solely for the man who had died.

He began very gently to wipe the belly clean with his handkerchief. As he pressed on the swollen mound, the corpse began to hiss through its clenched teeth. The Camaguayans fell silent, perplexed for the first time. But they recovered almost at once, and commenced replying profanely to the dead man's terse remarks. Fat Armando shook his finger at the deceased, reminding him that he was dead and suggesting he no longer had the right to hiss at them. There was some laughter at this sally, but Hook ignored it. He closed the eyes and tried, with little success, to compose the arms and legs and to straighten the clothing. Then he became still. The snake's body writhed lazily against his ankles. Garbini, watching yet, knew that Hook had begun to pray. He spat again. Then he shrugged.

A grave had been dug. The body was covered with a poncho and placed beside it, one recalcitrant fist protruding. Hook knew the dead man's family: he had no wife, but a mother and two sisters were dependent on him. Hook had removed the man's effects (those that had not already been stolen), and he was thinking, as he spoke, of how much money he himself could afford to put in the shabby, cracked billfold. The Camaguayans lined up attentively, glad of an excuse not to resume the marching. Prayers were said and responses elicited. They sang hymns, mostly of the Christmas season, for those were widely known. Hook's baritone resounded heartily in the pleasant morning air, and Sanchez, once again, drew a wishful bead on him.

Jones' stomach rumbled as he sat, his head on his kneecaps. Garbini rolled his dice desultorily. Birds, sensing competition in the joined voices, began to twitter and shriek busily. The stream rushed, roaring against the stony obstructions in its midst. Lieutenant Storch filled two of Ruiz's canteens, threw two away. Finally the singing stopped. Hook began to address them in Spanish.

"Our friend is dead now and we are all sad." But the expressions on their faces were not sad at all. Expectant, dull, eager, indifferent. Surely not sad. "Yes," repeated Hook, "we are all sad. Are we not?" Something, they realized, was demanded of them. They frowned, grimaced, practiced various unlikely mimes of dejection. "But we should not be sad. No. We should be happy for our good friend Luis." The frowns quickly dissipated. It was easier to be happy. In fact, they rather envied Luis his dereliction of responsibility. Someone would now have to carry his supplies as well. Yes, they had never really trusted Luis.

"Think of a prisoner, think of him locked in a tiny cell that has no windows. Five feet long here. Five feet long there.

Very dark. Very cold. A straw mat, a broken chair, a pail to do his business in. And this prisoner, he is sentenced to live there all his life. A terrible thought, is it not? All his life?" There were nods. "To him, to the prisoner, this is the whole world. He knows nothing else. He says, my room is beautiful. The floor is the earth. The ceiling, it is the sky. My walls are high, high mountains and I—I am a great king. The emperor of all this world. But we know better than that. We know better, do we not?" Heads nodded again, but they were less certain now. "We know that he is no great king.

"You and I—we know many things. We know that there are other rooms than his, better rooms. We know there are green fields outside the prison. We know there are oceans and mountains and jungles and cities. Yes, we laugh at him. We are so wise." Someone did just that; someone laughed nervously. "But we should not laugh. No." The man who had done so slapped his hand hastily across his mouth. "For we are just like that man. We are stupid prisoners. We—you and I—we live out our lives in a tiny prison room and we think that this is all. And our lives are no bigger, no brighter than that stinking, filthy cell. No." Hook spoke softly. "Our friend Luis, lying here before us, he knows that now. And he is laughing at us." They took him literally. They leaned forward to peer at the shrouded corpse.

"There are worlds beyond this little world and they are beautiful to see. The worlds that Jesus Christ promised us. And we will go there. We will. Life is nothing. Death is the key that will open our prison door. And we will be free." A man said, "Aaaaah?" Someone struck him smartly on the back of the neck. "Let us go now," said Hook. "Let us do the job we must do. But not afraid. Never afraid. For there is nothing to fear. We will be free. Today perhaps, as Luis is free from prison today. Tomorrow perhaps; perhaps fifty years from now. But free. I promise you that."

"He sure talks a lot," said Jones, yawning. "What'd he say?"

"How should I know?" Garbini was scratching the scales on the back of his right hand. A thin, white flurry fell between his legs. "*Muerte*. Death, I guess. He always talks about death —beats me why."

"He's crazy. That's why."

"Could be." Garbini stood. Luis had been placed in his grave, and, alongside him, as was fitting, the head and body of his murderer. The Camaguayans had begun to shovel dirt over the corpse.

"Another late start. Another stinkin' hot walk with no breaks. Hey, Jones." Jones looked up. "Hook say anything about who's at point today?"

"Me." Jones thumbed his chest apologetically.

"Ahh," sighed Garbini. "I like you, Jonesy. But I'm afraid this can't go on. You're interferin' with my comforts, man. You're interferin'."

Twenty minutes later the patrol moved out. It was already hot; the birds had become quieter, and, as though to compensate, the cicadas were gradually augmenting the shrill whine of their call. Mosquitos, flies, tiny hopping insects rose out of the high grass at the stream's edge as the men's feet disturbed it. Hook spoke with Sergeant Raoul. Then he looked upstream, wary of the logs that might come hurtling down on the small Camaguayans. But there was only the decomposed body of a tapir; it bobbed on its back, four legs stiffened. Lieutenant Storch made a grunting noise. The Camaguayans were overburdened; there was no one to take Ruiz's place. Behind them, Sergeant Raoul nodded to Jones, and then headed back to his position near the end of the file. Halfway there, he tossed an empty C ration can aside. It bounced once, then it settled at the base of the knoll.

Rifles raised high above their shoulders, the men stumbled across the cold, strong current—thigh deep on the Americans, hip deep on the Camaguayans. A few moments after the last man, Baxter, had passed into the heavy undergrowth on the far side, a single figure stepped cautiously out, into the abandoned encampment. He wore a poncho, faded green shorts, and an American Army helmet, much battered and holed by bullets twice over the left temple. He put his rifle down and examined the C ration can. The piece of paper inside had been folded many times. He opened it, read, and nodded just once.

Dear Lucky Luke:

Of all the nerve, man, you sure got balls. 4F! That's a good one. Just proves those army doctors aren't fit to prescribe a roll of toilet paper. Imagine inducting a guy with my brains and letting a pinhead like you go scot free. I always thought your toes were funny looking, but not that funny, brother. Not that funny. 4F! I can't get over it. Man, there is no justice in this world. Nothing personal, Luke boy, but this really gets on my wick. Of all the fucking luck! You always were a first class cop out, but you really outdid yourself this time. 4F. Sure, Luke. We know. And it hurts real awful when you walk.

Listen, you tell those SAS guys I'm through. And all the rest of those creeps too. I joined the Navy and that's that. It's none of their business and you don't have to defend me to nobody. I'm here because it's safer on the Sting *than it is in Camaguay. Safer than it is on campus. That's why. That's the only reason why. Not as safe as you are, Luke boy, hiding behind your cockeyed feet, but safe enough. I'm finished with that revolution shit. From now on I'm taking care of me and nobody else.*

Things are patched up pretty good between me and the old man. After I got arrested in that second takeover he was pretty pissed. But this Navy business hit him right where he lives. Ma says he goes around bragging about all the risks I'm taking for my country. Risks! You bet. I risked getting the clap six times last month, and that's about it. Anyway—good news— he's going to buy me a Mustang before I go away to law school. Hang around, hammer toes, I'm going to make up for

53

*these three years taking orders from Uncle Honky. You better
be real nice to me.*

*Do me a favor, will you? Ellen Rosenfeld's birthday is the
seventeenth of next month. Send her two dozen roses (nice
ones, none of your cheap shit). Her address is in the telephone
book under Sam Rosenfeld. Yes—I know she's white, Lucius.
But her daddy is immensely rich and she just loves my licorice
stick. Haven't I told you? I'm going to be on the Supreme
Court some day and you, buddy boy, will be my chauffeur.
I'll send you the money. No. Better yet, have my daddy give
it to you. Make up some story, like you did for the draft board.
He wouldn't want to know the truth, it'd scare the poor man.
Don't forget now. And just put "from A.B.J." on the card. I'm
counting on you.*

*Don't worry Lucius. I'm not going to volunteer for anything.
I'm very delicate, and all the officers here know it.*

> *Be good you lucky prick,*
> *Andy.*

Imperceptibly the patrol climbed from the floor of the Negro Valley toward the highlands. By following a low ridge that
wound deviously, sometimes doubling back on itself, sometimes veering sharply away from the objective, they added a
few feet of altitude every hour until, at two o'clock, they were
three hundred feet above their previous night's encampment.
Pure sunlight appeared at distant intervals now, through the
gap made by an occasional fallen tree. But the heat had not
diminished, nor had the disconcerting onrush of sound, and,
but for Hook and José Ix, the change went unnoticed. These
two saw new birds, passing visitors from the highlands, and
the first pine trees that had taken root to stifle the undergrowth
with acid droppings. The ground was surer: naked rock
pushed through the ubiquitous carpet of vegetable matter. But
the mosquitos had not relented, and, for nearly all the men,
it was this private conflict, now a matter solely of endurance,

that formed the strict limit of their vision, their hearing, their attention.

Hook was at point, too many yards ahead of the patrol's main elements. José Ix, just behind him, knew this, but had said nothing. He understood from their long experience together that the sergeant's mind was now held in a peculiar, anxious balance: his instincts intently alert; his reason distanced, recalling the fer-de-lance and young Luis' death. José Ix watched the sergeant's agile body—crouched low, weaving, striding softly despite his weight. Hook breathed stentorously, not from exhaustion, but rather, as a dozing man snores, from the deep concentration of his faculties. José Ix thought of an angered jaguar's skull, the sharp ears folded back, seeming oddly naked and as purposeful as a fired bullet. He felt secure behind the sergeant. "But," he said to himself, "he will lead us too far. He is afraid of nothing. If even Ek ahau himself, the black lord of death would appear: he would try to crush him to his breast."

Sanchez was just behind José Ix. As he jogged, head down, he chatted to himself in a news commentator's voice of heroic acts performed by one Lieutenant Ulysses Sanchez, or, projecting his fantasies, by one Colonel Ulysses Sanchez. There were insistent fingertips at the outer angles of his eyeballs, forcing the pupils inward and toward his nose. This and a painful tingling in the extremities were symptoms of a chronic hypertension. Lieutenant Sanchez needed to fire his guns. The harsh explosions were as relaxing to him as the strong blows of a masseur. And only then did he forget that he stood not even five feet tall.

Lieutenant Storch had gas; he nearly always had gas, for he ate in rapid gulps. As he trotted, he would make a fist and pound himself firmly under the heart. The gas pocket, when struck expertly, was dislodged in a resonant belch. Storch had convinced himself that Hook was responsible for Ruiz's death; responsible, as well, for the lieutenant's present discomfort. The ten Band-Aids, clumsily applied, had come loose and were now an unpleasant adhesive jelly in his boot tips. The extra canteens jiggled on his hips, taunting him with the sounds of cool, running water. There were three inflamed boils on the back of his hairless neck, and Jones, close behind him, watched these eruptions for whole half hours at a time. Whenever Storch slowed, Jones, mesmerized by the boils and the rhythm of his own footfalls, would bump into the sweat-soaked, noisome back. Jones apologized each time. But Lieutenant Storch only grunted, chewing his lips with a detached and bovine indifference. And Jones willingly kept close to that broad back; it would, he hoped, absorb the full brunt of any Riff surprise attack.

There was a group of five Camaguayans behind Jones; Private Lancelot Falk was ten yards behind them. Falk was nineteen. His hair was blond, curly, and thinning already in two symmetrical coves above his temples. His skin was very white, mole-spattered, with a tendency to redness. He smiled often, but the innocence of his smile lent to his otherwise strong features a quality of indecision, effeminacy. Falk picked his nose a great deal, chewed his nails, and played constantly with his private parts, as though satisfying a deep curiosity. At night sometimes he sucked his thumb, running the edge of his forefinger over or around his snub nose. Of all the IC's, Hook perhaps excepted, he was most comfortable with the little Camaguayans, although, unlike the sergeant, he understood nothing of their language.

All that morning Falk had recalled excitedly Sergeant Hook's barehanded capture of the fer-de-lance. Falk came from Tennessee, from an area where hunting prowess was especially respected. His own modest skills had been eclipsed by those of his brother Clay, who had been killed in Vietnam two years before. His father, Falk suspected, blamed him for his brother's death. Clay had been powerful where Lancelot was merely strong; brilliant where he was of average intelligence; handsome where he was only good-looking. They had been much alike in their tastes, this likeness due mainly to Lancelot's emulation. Lancelot remembered now how easily his brother had killed woodchucks at a hundred yards. He remembered the young, pretty girls for whose attentions he always had to struggle with Clay's. He remembered the post-humous award for valor, and his own pathetic skulking during the battle for Hill 408. And then he thought of Sergeant Hook and was consoled. Hook was a new idol. One he would not have to share with his father.

Five Camaguayans marched between Falk and Garbini, and among these was Sergeant Raoul. Raoul heard a parrot squawk; he smiled. The soldier just in front of him tripped and fell heavily; he smiled again. A mosquito bit him on the ear; Raoul smiled once more. The Camaguayan sergeant had very long, muscular arms; they reached to a point just above each bowed knee. His stride was that of a small ape and his body, as though to give this likeness further credit, was remarkably hirsute. Hair flowered in profusion from the neck of his shirt and from his cuffs. There was hair in his ear holes, on the tip of his nose; long strands protruded, bedewed with mucus from his nostrils. His eyebrows joined and, together, reached out at both sideburns. Raoul was strong, but incapable of using his strength. He abhorred violence. At that moment, moreover, he was too obsessed with the consequences of his recent traitorous act to be of much use at all. A monkey chattered, the report of a toy machine gun startling him: and Raoul smiled. He had begun smiling at everyone, at every event and at every abrupt sound soon after he had tossed the C ration can aside.

Raoul was not an idealist. He sympathized with the RFN for purely pragmatic reasons. General Amayo, the military dictator of Camaguay, had expropriated his father's flourishing trade in pornographic pictures. Raoul, as heir to the family business, was bitterly resentful. Besides, he had loved the profession. It had been his boast that he knew more women of questionable morals than any other man in Camaguay. More-over, he had derived a superb and irreplaceable titillation from having himself photographed with women (and with men, with children, with animals, with literally anything that offered an aperture for penetration). Pictures of his magnificent genitals, if not of his face, rivaled in circulation even the official reproductions of General Amayo in full uniform. Garbini, trotting just behind him, sneered malevolently at the powerful, stooped frame. Garbini suspected Raoul: not of collaboration, but of nearly all other disreputable habits. The week before, in San Pedro, Garbini had lost two hundred dollars to Raoul in a poker game. Since Garbini himself had used a marked deck, he was naturally distrustful of the sergeant. But Raoul had other worries. He knew there would be an ambush, and he doubted whether the Riffs would be able or willing to spare him. Raoul thought of death. And this time he did not smile.

For the Camaguayans this was the most critical time of the day. They had been conditioned by ancient custom to sleep when the sun was at its zenith. The five men ahead of Hall, and the four ahead of Baxter, who guarded the rear, were now stumbling forward in various degrees of somnolence. Two, Baxter noticed, held hands as they marched; they giggled and winked, leaned close to whisper. After each five-minute halt, the IC's had to kick the Camaguayans awake, set them on their feet like so many mechanical dolls. These were known as the killing hours. The Riffs, who could discipline their troops more convincingly, endeavored to attack just after noon when the reflexes of their enemy were least responsive. Hundreds of Camaguayans had sighed, pillowed their heads and dozed, only to pass, without rousing, into an irreversible sleep. Baxter was aware of this; he had seen it happen a dozen times. At the first shattering sounds of an ambush, he knew, the Camaguayans would begin to totter about in crazy circles, and he would have to shove, to tackle them to the ground before he could protect himself or return the fire. Baxter carried his rifle in his right hand, favoring the injured arm. There was no pain; there never had been any pain. Even when it happened there had only been a subdued popping, more auditory than felt. But Baxter was not used to the constant reflection on life, on fate, on his future, that he had experienced since the accident. That morning, borrowing words remembered from tiresome

Sunday School sessions, he had even tried to pray for his recovery. And this attempt, demonstrating, as it did the extent of his own concern, had troubled him perhaps more than the physical fact of his injury. The man ahead of him slowed to a walk, then stealthily goosed his partner. There was laughter and further hand play. Baxter grimaced. Without favoritism, he hit each a stunning blow in the kidneys with the butt of his M16.

It was insufferably hot. Though the temperature never climbed higher than eighty-five degrees, the humidity remained at an uncompromising 100 percent. The dew of the morning had evaporated lazily, risen, condensed on the undersides of leaves, risen again. Flat layers of mist floated in the still air. Every surface was damp and faintly glistening. Globules of sweat dangled and fell, dangled and fell from the tips of noses and chins; globules ran down their sides, igniting a series of unrelievable itches. Insects landed on their faces and became glued there, fluttering tiny, useless wings. And yet they continued to move, intelligences drugged by the rhythm of their limbs and by the sodden air. While they jogged there was at least the semblance of a breeze. When they halted, however, the heat settled upon them in its full fury, burrowing deeply inside their humid pants legs and helmets and sleeves. It waited just above and behind them like some vigilant, hugely amorphous carrion bird.

The mosquitos attacked, lingered on the unresisting flesh, and left sated and drunk with blood. A blizzard of tiny feather-shaped seeds descended on them, causing sharp, repeated sneezes, depositing an acid taste on the backs of their throats. They were forced to detour around a thick mesh of thorn-covered hedge, through a massive colony of chaco spiders—their bodies pink and white and mounted on long, slender legs that covered the area of a small saucer. The chacos had coated every bush, every clump of undergrowth, even the high branches of trees with their golden cartwheel-shaped webs. At the point Hook judged that they had made up perhaps three-quarters of an hour, but the men were flagging, and twenty minutes later they crossed gingerly over a seething carpet of reddish ants in migration. A halt was called so that each man could brush the nipping, persistent bodies from the legs and back of the man ahead of him. Raoul, who had a large rent in his pants leg at the shin, was badly infested. While he slapped at his thighs, he hissed, "Amayo, Amayo, Amayo," as though the general's name was the worst blasphemy he could think of.

The dictator was not well liked by his soldiers. All but four of the Camaguayans in Hook's patrol had been inducted suddenly, arbitrarily, and for an unspecified length of time. Some had not seen their families for eighteen months—leaves were too often the means of desertion. General Amayo had been dictator for twelve years. The upper classes supported him, for previously they had endured two decades of economic and political chaos. But, though the country had prospered somewhat, little had been done for the poorer peoples, except occasionally as the price of continued American aid. The farmers were exploited; the slums of Camaguay City were an abomination; the Indians were ignored by the government and hated by everyone, even the poorest Camaguayan peasant. Then, two years before, the war had broken out.

The RFN was based in Valencia, a small, infertile country to the north that had undergone a successful Communist revolution some few years after General Amayo had consolidated his rule. The guerrilla army was comprised of as many Valencians as Camaguayans, and a considerable percentage of career revolutionaries from South American, European, and even Asian countries as well. The fighting was ferocious on the rich Pacific coast of Camaguay, especially near the capital. General Amayo, surrounded by a numerous bodyguard, directed operations from an underground bunker in the foothills around Camaguay City. He had not made a public appearance since, eight months before, he had been stabbed through the left thigh by a young man with an ice pick (an ex-lover, not a Riff, as it happened—the general was a discreet homosexual). The young man had been summarily dismembered. Amayo could be ruthless when necessary or when provoked. The RFN, adhering to the Communist definition of terror, were ruthless with or without reason. Now, shaken by dissension and Riff atrocities, Amayo's regime was preserved only by the American military presence. The soldiers in Hook's patrol, with a few exceptions, would have hated both—the general and the RFN —had they not been constitutionally incapable of sustaining any emotion for more than a few hours.

They marched for five miles beyond the river of ants, proceeding less efficiently, their motions awkward and self-defeating. Hook realized that the fine edge of his own alertness had become blunted. He was no longer able to distinguish the several parts of the jungle. He was not seeing individual vines; not seeing soon enough objects that might conceal a booby trap. Reluctantly he called a halt and, when he had done so, was surprised to find that the others had fallen so far behind him. The line had become perilously elongated, the Camaguayans grouped together and separated by long intervals from the Americans ahead of and behind them. The Camaguayans drank at once. They held their canteens high, and Hook knew, from the angle of their holding, that he would have to find water before they camped.

He opened his own canteen and poured water over the backs of his wrists. The shadows had deepened. There remained no more than two hours of usable daylight. A squadron of bees droned past. Hook saw José Ix, who loved wild honey, follow their flight with longing. Sanchez and Storch squatted. Jones stood, bent over, his hands on his knees. He was coughing, bringing up heavy phlegm methodically from his throat. Hook inhaled. He pressed his hand to his forehead. Then he stepped into the undergrowth and vanished.

Hook knelt to pray. As he always did now, he focused on the woman, her visionary anointing remembered. It thrilled him, and he feared his exultation. Leaves touched at his shoulders as though to calm them. "Judgment is near. Caesar has taken what is his. So much of me. Have I been wrong? Such is my failing as a man, oh my God, that I can no longer trust my own intentions. We are warned, and with reason, to beware of visions. The devil has power to assume such pleasing shapes as these. Teach me. Use me. God of sacrifices, you who, in love, gave your only Son for our redemption. Take me as well. Take my soul to damnation if it answers your will. In his name, make me a more perfect instrument. I would serve you." Unconsciously, Hook had begun to pray in the Mayan dialect. Now he was silent in his mind. He probed inward, voiceless, egoless—emptied by the fierce, swinging pendulum of his meditation. And the mosquitos circled, haloed about his head, whining in their strange frustration.

The Camaguayans were already asleep. Jones envied them. A large, bulbous, yellow flower nodded sensuously at the trail's edge. It was four inches across and as deep as a pint bottle, seeming both top-heavy and inebriated as it jiggled on its thick stem. Dead insects, oddly shriveled, were strewn in a crude circle around it. Jones growled and kicked out. The flower's head popped off, disgorging insects like a lamp bowl after a long summer. There was a turgid liquor and a musky scent of putrescence. Jones gagged. He sat gingerly on the far side of the trail. Raoul appeared, moving in low, bowlegged strides, and, when he neared Jones, he bowed hesitantly, as though in deference. Then he handed the corpsman a yard-long section of green vine. Jones, acting out Raoul's mimed indications, put the vine to his mouth and sucked once; a spurt of cool water surprised him. Raoul laughed. He was pleased with his gift. As he turned to go, he nodded once slowly—to acknowledge some imagined bond between them. But Jones did not understand the gesture.

The rabbit, a female, had been blinded by the hairs of a malignant liana. This had happened three hours before, and the rabbit had already long outlived the expectations of its maimed state. She was pregnant for the first time: a small, gray, sinewy animal. Panicked now, she stumbled accidentally onto the trail and against Jones' ankle, nudging it with her forehead. He, terrorized, leaped aside while pulling unsuccessfully at his .45. The animal was startled by his abrupt movements; it huddled down. Jones did not perceive the rabbit's blindness (it would have repulsed him), but he knew that this at least was a familiar animal. He supposed its awkward actions to be a sort of friendliness. He grinned. Then Sanchez's knife severed the rabbit's left rear foot.

The rabbit began to hop in circles, blood jetting from the tip of its foot. Now and then it would pause, dazed by the inexplicable pain, and begin to search blindly for the injury. Then, horrified by the strangeness of its own limb, it would limp clumsily away, as though to distance the agony. Jones put his hand to his mouth. The knife hissed again. Now the other rear foot was bloodied. Sanchez had begun to laugh; he chattered, exhorting himself in a low, shrill tone. The rabbit was quite crazed, dancing on its stumps. Jones made a sound, groaning for it. And Sanchez knelt once again to retrieve his knife.

Hook's heel came down swiftly on the hand and pinned it there. Sanchez yelped. He tried just once to draw his hand out, but the pressure merely increased when he did so. Hook rolled his heel backward and forward, crushing the fingers trapped, as they were, between the knife's handle and the hard undersurfaces of Hook's boot. Sanchez stared up. He was in considerable pain, but, after the first yelp, he made no further sound. Hook matched the lieutenant's stare. His face was placid, the eyebrows raised, as though to express a fleeting interest in the event. The brown eyes and the black eyes researched each other. Then Sanchez smiled grimly. With deliberation he bit into Hook's thigh just above the knee.

Sanchez's wedged, rodential teeth were good for biting; even through the sturdy cloth they found purchase in Hook's flesh. Jones watched their struggle, incredulous. He watched as Lieutenant Storch, no more than two yards away, yawned and cleaned an ear, as though he were alone in a small, shadowed room. Hook's expression did not alter as the areole encircling Sanchez's mouth began to darken. He even noticed, approved when José Ix broke the rabbit's neck with an easy and compassionate motion. Skin and fabric came loose as Sanchez, not content merely to bite, began worrying his prey. But the absence of any reaction demoralized him. He threw his head back. Blood had been smeared grotesquely about his lips: it was the mouth of an old female impersonator, Jones thought. Sanchez looked up at Hook. Hook was already looking down at him, his expression unchanged, even to the degree of elevation in the eyebrows. Then Sanchez bit again. But now not out of vengeance, now to distract the pain in his hand.

It was a silent tableau. Yet, in Jones' imagination, it borrowed sounds from the jungle like a movie, insanely dubbed. A monkey's crazed chattering exploded when Sanchez stared, bloody-mouthed at his adversary. And when the dogged jaws worked at Hook's thigh, crumpling the material of his pants leg, a pompous frog began to guulmph, guulmph, guulmph. Hook pressed down on Sanchez's fingers; an insect crackled busily. Even the sweat that dripped from Sanchez's ear lobes was given sound by the heavy plopping of sap among the leaves. Lieutenant Storch belched—and, as though this were an agreed-upon signal, Sanchez released his grip. "Enough," he said. He said it in Spanish to disguise the objection of his capitulation.

Hook raised his boot dispassionately. Then he walked away, turning his back on the little Camaguayan. Sanchez shoved his hand against the warm angle of his groin and flexed it there. He glanced at his knife, now half-buried in the moist soil. He made a quick motion toward the gun on his left hip, but the act was aborted.

"I'll kill you," he said quietly. Jones stared at Hook. But the sergeant was already too many yards ahead. Jones swallowed; Sanchez was speaking to him. The lieutenant clutched at his knife and Jones, instincts abruptly made aware, covered the vulnerable parts of his abdomen. "I'll kill you," hissed Sanchez. "I'll kill you, Mr. Black Nigger Man."

64

Dear Daddy,

*I'm doing real fine down here in Camaguay, don't you worry
a bit. I'm holding up my end, just like you told me to. I'm sure
glad you wrote me all those things about Grandpa Falk at
the battle of Shiloh. I guess he was a real brave man. Well, I
don't think I'll never be as brave as Clay or Grandpa Falk,
they were something special, but Sergeant Hook says I got
nothing to be ashamed of. He says I'm the best man in the out-
fit right now.*

*It's real hot down here and the mosquitos bite something
awful. I spend my free time reading the Bible and those
pamphlets Rev. Muskie sent down here. I'm not smoking or
drinking and I don't even look at them funny foreign
women. You don't have to worry about me marrying one.
That's real silly. I want a nice American girl, not someone
that'd embarrass Mom and you.*

*The soldiers here are real nice and I've got lots of buddies.
I'm well liked, the way Clay used to be. Even the niggers
seem friendly. I don't socialize with them much, because I
know they're different, but, just the same, Daddy, I don't think
they're half bad, the polite ones at least. And I don't notice
that smell you said they had. What's it supposed to be like?
Maybe it's just I'm not smelling right. Anyhow, we all stink
pretty much down here.*

*It's real crazy being in a place where hardly anyone speaks
American. I remember what you said that time you and me
and Clay was down in New Orleans—you know, about people who spoke foreign being stupid and sneaky. It's funny, now
sometimes people look at me like I'm stupid and sneaky and
just because I don't speak Spanish or what ever that crazy*

65

gibberish is. I feel real strange. I wish sometimes you were along to show me what to do.

But I'm all right. And I'll try like you said to get one of those commies for Clay. They're pretty darn tricky, but Sergeant Hook's pretty tricky too. You know I found out Sergeant Hook reads the good book. Why I bet he knows almost as much about it as Rev. Muskie himself. And he's got a big, black beard. Not because he's a hippy or anything like that. No sir. He's got a skin thing is all. But it makes him look real fine.

Well, I got to go. I can't wait to get back home. I'm feeling fine and I put on ten pounds—all muscle. You tell Ma that, and all the people at the bank, and the kids at the drug store if you happen to get by there. Maybe, when I come home, maybe you and me could go hunting. I'm a real good shot now. Yes sir. You can even bring your bank friends along to watch.

Love,
Your son Lance.

IV

ON THE MORNING of the third day they reached East One, the largest of the American Fruit Company's banana plantations. Eighteen months before the company had been compelled to abandon its workings when the Riffs, in their first concerted assault on the Gulf Coast, had sunk an American banana boat and burned the wharves and warehouses of Gros Michel Port, the company's private harbor. Two miles of the single-gauge railway track had been torn up; all the rolling stock had been burned or derailed. In the village of East One a hospital, two schools, and a convent were leveled. All the native personnel had been efficiently rounded up and herded into Bolivar Park. There twenty-four men had been liquidated by machine gun fire. Families were spared, for the Riffs, drawing on fifty years' experience of Communist terror, had learned that deaths were better remembered when mourning relatives remained behind. The Americans were left uninjured, that the Camaguayans might loathe them for being still alive.

The entire area seemed derelict, haunted—as if it had been abandoned a century, not merely a year before. The laboriously cleared plantation was now a chaos of interwoven plant growths. Recently a storm had blown over a good many of the tall, fragile banana plants; insufficient drainage and alternate periods of aridity had sterilized the remnants of the crop. The rusted tracks of the railroad disappeared bravely into the green, wavering inferno, the banana leaves, especially, seeming some surrealist's conception of cold flames. And a broken wire fence surrounded it all, as though incarcerating the rebellious land.

67

There had been reports of Riff activity in East One. The patrol entered the village in a poor semblance of readiness, but there was no resistance beyond that of a large sow, which leaned playfully against a Camaguayan private, bowling him over. Two years before the village had had a population of nearly three thousand, as many Indians as Camaguayans. The company had transported most of the Camaguayans back to San Pedro; the Indians had simply returned to the surrounding hills. About two hundred people remained, cultivating a few tiny gardens in Bolivar Park at the village center. The windows in the long, rectangular blocks of company-built housing were uniformly broken, and birds flitted freely in and out. Hook made a temporary camp in the hospital's gutted foundations. Then he and Sanchez and José Ix began the usual, futile interrogations of those few inhabitants who would allow themselves to be found.

Jones and Garbini huddled in the sparse shade of the hospital's rear doorway. The walls on either side had been reduced to a four-foot height, but the metal door frame remained and, on it, a heavy door (once marked "Fire Exit" in two languages) was suspended crazily by a single hinge—as though still clumsily asserting the building's wholeness. Hook was reporting to San Pedro GHQ on the radio. He and Falk, whose responsibility the radio was, knelt on the tiled remains of a spacious lavatory. Raoul squatted nearby, ostensibly repairing a boot lace. But as he sat, knotting and unknotting the lace, flicking his cigarette nervously into a broken toilet bowl, he eavesdropped on the static-blurred, sometimes contradictory commands of Colonels Smith and Hernandez.

Though he might have looked out through any breach in the flame-blackened wall, Garbini made a point of kicking the door open with his foot. It complained bitterly, threatened to tear itself free of its one flimsy support. The plantation began about fifty yards from the doorway. The foliage was inert, shriveling in the heat of high noon to prevent the escape of its precious moisture. Garbini poked the sole of Jones' boot with the tip of his own.

"Want a banana?" he asked. He indicated the doorway with a shrug of his right shoulder. Jones leaned forward and peered toward the green turmoil.

"I don't see nothing."

"There must be. Someplace in there."

"It's a long walk." Jones leaned back and tipped his helmet down over his forehead. Garbini slapped at his own abdomen, evidently admiring its flatness. A large red blemish had appeared on the day before on the tip of his nose. This afternoon it wore a rakish white cap.

"I like bananas," said Garbini confidentially. "Nice bananas, full of vitamins. And when you're finished then you can smoke the skins. Ever try it?"

"No," said Jones irritably. "You?"

"Yeah. Matter of fact I did."

"So. What's it like?"

"Like smoking your old man's jock strap, if you want to know. Them hippies're crazy."

"Beautiful," said Jones. "Beautiful."

"You're in a bad mood." Garbini made clucking noises with his tongue. He broke down the M16 and began cleaning it.

"Yup. Yes sir. I took one look this morning. 'Man,' I said, 'my friend Jones is in a real bad mood today.'"

"You better believe it."

"Things could be worse. I mean, suppose you owned all them poor banana trees. Must be a billion dollars gone up in weeds."

"They ain't trees," said Jones. "They're herbs," he continued in a pompous monotone, "grow like a stalk of celery. Eighty-five percent water."

"Jesus. You don't say. Jesus. Eighty-five percent water. Jesus. What a thrill."

"I told you," said Jones. He stared at his own feet. "I went to college. Took botany. I remember things."

"Yeah," said Garbini. "You're a gem. A real fourteen-carat, diamond-studded brown ring." He lit a cigarette and inhaled deeply. The skin of his sallow face appeared, wraithlike, through the curling stream of smoke. "You know—I was going to college. Had it all set." Jones snorted derisively. Garbini threw the exhausted match in his direction. "Cut out the comedy, Andy boy. I mean—we're pals—but just don't get on my wick."

"Sure, Joe." The corpsman smiled. "Just clearing my nose. That's all. Got a little congestion."

"Well. The next time pick it with your finger like a man."

"What college was it?" he said placatingly. "Where were you gonna go?"

"Hell. I didn't have any special place picked out. We didn't get that far. My Uncle Joe, see, he's with—ah . . . this big corporation." Garbini chuckled. "They need accountants all the time. So Uncle Joe put in a word for me, and I had a scholarship all set up. It was in the bag." He exhaled, and tongued a smoke ring. "All I hadda do was get myself out of high school, but I run into some women trouble. It was this lady biology teacher." Jones grimaced, but Garbini chose to ignore his expression. He frowned, as though the act of remembering was partly physical; the fat, pink ridges of his forehead slithered, nestling together.

"She was about forty, I figure. Very, very serious type. Biology class was a gas. She'd answer any stupid question, so long as you asked it real sincere like. 'Miss Pucker, why is it human beings have two feet?' And she'd tell you. I mean, man, like everyone don't know—if you didn't have two feet you'd fall flat on your ass. I could kill a whole class that way. She'd go on and on, twittering like a bird, tellin' you about evolution and dumb things like that. Then, when she'd finished, I'd put my hand up and say, still sincere, like a man askin' his wife if she come good, 'Gee. That's real interesting, Miss Pucker. I never thought about it that way. But why not three feet? Why not? Then we could sit on the third one, like a camp stool.'" He guffawed. "Oh, man, and she'd take it serious." He went on in a fluttery falsetto, rolling his eyes. "'Well, Joe,' she'd say, 'you have a really questionable mind. Three feet. Well, can anybody answer Joe's question?'" Garbini slapped his thigh.

He laughed again. A cuckoo landed on the broken foundation wall; it regarded him with suspicion.

"But man, I wasn't doing so hot in bio. Just couldn't cut up them animals. Human beings, sure, but not animals. I like animals. They don't get on my wick." Jones cursed. He suppressed an acid retort. Then he considered getting up, but the heat quickly dissuaded him. "I figured I'd have to try something special. One of those abominable snow jobs. See, she wasn't really Miss Pucker—it was Mrs. Pucker, only her husband had gone bye bye. I couldn't blame him. She was a mess. Dyed her own hair black, guess she didn't even want her hairdresser to know. I could tell, 'cause sometimes her forehead and the tips of her ears'd be black too. She drove this cool Mustang, shifting like crazy, even when the car wasn't movin'. I mean, she was no prime rib. She had big, sloppy legs with them little blue veins. What do you call them?" Jones wanted to ignore him, but the temptation was too great.

"Varicose," he said.

"Glad you're still with me. Wouldn't want you t'miss nothing. Not a word." Garbini grinned. "Anyhow, one day I make believe I'm real interested in this science book—one I know she's got at home. Well, she gets all silly about me improvin' my mind and about how I'm really smart, even though the highest mark I got to date was a booming 32 percent. So off we go in the Mustang. I can see it like it was yesterday. We pull up in front of her house and I say, 'Miss Pucker. Reason I'm not doing so good in bio. I just can't concentrate. You see I—I—I . . . I'm in love with you, Miss Pucker.'" His hands slapped together with a resounding pop. The cuckoo disappeared.

"Jones, you shoulda been there. She jumped across the seat and almost impaled her whatsis on the stick shift. She lands me a smacker on my lips, deep, like she was going to give me a home tonsillectomy. Man, my life passed in front of my eyes. I swear it." He shook his head. "Worse yet. Trouble with bein' a biology teacher, you gotta go fishin' in that formaldehyde all day long. She'd grab my hand and my hand'd start stinkin'. She'd grab someplace else and that'd start smellin' like some dead pig's abortion. I tell you, Jonesy. If she dropped dead tomorrow she wouldn't need no embalmer."

"Jeeesus," said Jones. "Are you for real, Garbini?"

"No. No buddy. It's just something you ate." Garbini belched expressively. "Well, to make a long story more repulsive, she gets me up to her bedroom. That's where she keeps the books, she says. But I don't see nothin' 'cause right away she pulls the blinds down so its blacker than a—blacker than—" he looked at Jones, "anyhow it's real dark in there. I start playing with myself right away, 'cause I figure, man, my biology mark's hangin' right there between my legs. She's got herself naked in about three minutes, sweatin' like a stevedore and, brother, if you think formaldehyde stinks, try a forty-year-old bitch what's just lugged off ten pounds of girdle." Jones made a gagging sound. Then he tipped his helmet until it covered his face entirely. "There we are. Got the picture? Me on top, wondering if I really want a high school diploma. She's on the bottom, squishin' and squooshin' fit to beat the band. I says, 'I love you, Miss Pucker. I love you, Miss Pucker. I love you, Miss Pucker.' And she says, get this, 'Joe, dearest, call me Miss Fucker. It gives me goose pimples.'" He cackled. "Hey, Jones. You awake in there?"

"Yeah. But, man, I don't believe this. Not a word."

"Oh, it's true. It's the story of my life. I tell you, Jonesy, I attract them like flies." Garbini shook his head in mock dismay; spit flew from the corners of his mouth. "Where was I? Yeah, I's on top of Miss Pucker, thinkin' horny thoughts so's I won't lose my prong. Well, I figure, see, I'll play with her titties. I grab the left one and I suck on it, tweak it, tickle it, pull it out, push it in, the works—and, all the while she's moanin', 'Give it to me, Joe. Keep talking. Use bad words, Joe.' So then I reach down, still cursin' like a trooper, and I grabs for the right boobie. Only I can't find it. Nowhere. Only some funny stuff what feels like Saran Wrap. I got a little scared then. I leans over on the other side figurin', hopin' maybe the left one's the right one and the right one's in the outfield someplace. But there's nothing. Just a big hairy armpit." He

72

whistled. "Boy, Jonesy, did I get nervous. What the hell, I thought maybe she's gonna blame me for losin' it. I start feelin' all over. I even grabbed the tip of her nose, 'Joe,' she says. 'What's the matter?' 'Nothin'. Nothin'.' I say, 'Just some equipment missing. Keep talkin' and I'll find it.' 'Oh, Joe,' she says in a real squeaky voice, 'I had to have surgery. I hope it won't spoil it for you.' 'No,' I says, 'no. I'm left-handed anyways.' Got that, Jonesy? I'm left-handed anyways."

Garbini began to sputter, gobble, cluck like some lunatic fowl, squirming from side to side, his elbows pressed against his stomach. Jones, amazed at the variety of these noises, lifted his helmet to peer at him. He saw Garbini's Adam's apple as it bobbed—a lumpy tonsure against a mat of escaped chest hairs. Then Jones saw Hook's boot. Then Jones saw Hook.

"Jones. Come with me. And bring your kit."

"Aw, Sergeant," groaned Garbini, "I was just getting t'the good part."

"I bet." Hook smiled. "You're a born fungiphile, Joe. Probably the reincarnation of a truffle hound. Come on, Jones." Hook turned and started to walk toward the hospital's main entrance.

"Aw, Sergeant," Garbini whined. "Hey, Jones. College boy. What's a fungiphile?"

"Someone who hits baseballs. Left-handed. What else, Joe?"

Jones slouched as he walked, scuffling debris aside with the edges of his boots. His own odor had become offensive to him: he tried now to avoid the fetid, warm gasps that issued from the shirt at his neck. He was, he knew, on the edge of a dangerous anger. The sergeant's slight command had annoyed him beyond reason. Despite nearly two years in the service, Jones resented having to take orders: once before he had been severely reprimanded for his intransigence. As he passed Falk, the young private handed him the receiver of a defunct hospital telephone. "It's for you," he said. The corpsman tossed it aside. Falk, who had begun to laugh, hesitated, then grimaced. Jones had offended Falk, who seldom spontaneously shared his humor with Negroes. Jones sensed this; it didn't disturb him.

Outside, on the hospital's wide, shattered stoop, he saw Hook standing with Sergeant Raoul and a woman who held an infant clasped in her arms. Jones frowned. The child was perhaps nine months old. A scrawny thing: Jones saw the sinews of its neck, outlined like rubber bands in batter. But it was the child's head that repulsed him, that caused his frown. The scalp was shingled with shiny white-yellow scales; these had destroyed the sparse hair and were reaching down now, over its forehead, to threaten the eyebrows as well. The woman spoke to Hook: her tone was lowered, but Jones understood a truculence in the flow of strange words. Hook replied. She shook her head. Hook pointed at Jones, apparently asked her to wait, and then came quickly toward the corpsman. Jones retreated into the building's gutted half-doorway.

"I think maybe we can do something for the child." Hook smiled effusively as he spoke, his large teeth very white against the dark fringes of his beard. "I'm no doctor, but—hey, Andy. Try to look a little more cheerful. Please, she's nervous enough as it is. Doesn't exactly care for us gringos—"

"Sergeant—"

"Cortisone might do the trick. Can't hurt anyway. Bill always kept a big tube in his kit. I'll hold the child and talk like a Dutch uncle, and you glob the stuff on its scalp."

"No," said Jones. He shook his head: two wide, emphatic arcs. The woman gasped, uncertain what this terrible negative might mean. Hook roared with laughter. He pounded Jones exuberantly on the shoulder, then, swiftly, he drew the corpsman to his side in the terrific embrace of his right arm.

"Smile, Andy," he said. "She'll think the baby's dying." Jones complied: he stretched his lips until the teeth were visible behind them. "Good boy. Now come." But Jones' body resisted the forward pressure.

"No," he said. "I ain't touchin' that mess. Not if you paid me. Not if you order me. I don't want no jungle rot like Garbini has." Hook laughed again, but the stiffness of Jones' body

74

against his arm was augmented then by a spasmodic quivering. Hook dropped his arm. He glanced hastily toward the woman. The child was crying, for she had clasped him convulsively to her bosom. Raoul spoke softly to her, but she was inattentive, her eyes fixed on Jones.

"This is different, Andy."

"You ain't no doctor—you said so yourself."

"Well, look . . . I'll put it on. You just stand by. She knows the red cross on your helmet."

"No."

"The baby deserves a break."

"I don't know nothing about it." He handed Hook the medical pack. Then he smiled very broadly. "It's all yours. If you want to make a big hit with those creeps, fine. But do it yourself."

Hook studied him. Jones blinked a dozen times under his scrutiny; the uncertain corona of his smile wavered, reasserted itself. He crossed his arms on his chest, for they, too, had begun to shake. Garbini laughed: behind them, somewhere in the ruin, Falk had handed him the telephone receiver. Raoul called out and Hook nodded, but the nod was meant rather as an appreciation of Jones' unwillingness. He began undoing the flap of the kit. The sun flashed from the tube's silvered top and the woman, mistaking this for some unfamiliar menace, began to retreat awkwardly down the steps. Hook followed her.

Jones intended to remain there. He honestly doubted whether Hook could perform the act, so dreadfully abhorrent was it to his own senses. Raoul ascended the stoop, grinning, shrugging, shaking his head, as though partaking fully of Jones' cynicism. The woman had stopped. She answered Hook volubly, her words seeming interrogative; there was a black gap where her front teeth had been. Jones felt Raoul's fingers on his elbow. The sergeant had produced a perfect yellow banana from his pocket and jammed it, point forward, into the palm of Jones' hand. Then he gestured, indicating that they should re-enter the ruin, but Jones did not follow him. He stood, arms still crossed, watching. He meant to represent judgment, but with the banana protruding over the crook of one elbow, he seemed rather the image of some dark, lowering god of fruitfulness.

Hook unscrewed the cap. In the manner of a magician demonstrating his sleeves to be empty, he presented the cap and the tube, one in each hand. Hook depressed the tube and a curved worm of the white ointment slithered up. The woman started. Hook flicked the worm off with his fingertip and rubbed it ostentatiously into the skin above his nose. He smiled cheerfully. Then he produced another worm, decapitated it, and approached the child. The woman shook her head again, but at that moment the infant's hand struggled free, searching for the place above its ear where there were already bloodied scabs in the shiny pseudo-skin of the disease. And, though she continued to shake her head, now as if the gesture were a talisman, not a negative, Hook's ministrations were suffered without resistance.

Jones lowered his eyes, stared at the banana, which he noticed now for the first time. Scales had begun to sprinkle down in a thick, floclike cloud; they adhered to the tips of Hook's boots as he vigorously massaged the scalp. The child, afraid at first, now began to coo happily. It pressed its head upward like a cat meeting its caresser's hand, glad of the vicarious scratching and the relief it gave. Hook spoke soothingly throughout the operation, using a primitive English when he addressed the child. Finished, he bound the hands gently on the infant's chest with his own handkerchief and then gave the woman the tube and a small packet of vitamin pills. The mother leaned close to his face. She smiled, and Jones thought she was going to kiss him. He cursed. But she did not. She spat instead. Three times, with increasing vehemence. And then she hurried away.

Hook did not move. He blinked his eyes several times, for they had been fouled with her detritus. Then he reached for his handkerchief, but he had given it to the child, and his fingers fumbled confusedly in the empty pocket. He inhaled profoundly. The woman had already disappeared, trotting swiftly around a building's corner. The baby, sensing its mother's agitation, had begun to wail. Its voice, disembodied, could yet be heard. Hook raised his sleeve, pressed it to his forehead, wiped it twice across his beard. Then, sobered, he began to climb the steps. Jones was waiting there; and, for some reason, inexplicable even to himself, he had the gross temerity to smile.

"Bad day for us Samaritans. Huh, Sergeant?" Hook hesitated. There was silence between them for a prolonged moment. Jones saw nodules of saliva embedded in the dense mesh of Hook's beard. He felt strangely elated, as though enthralled in a strange challenge he could not understand. The sergeant nodded, cleared his throat, touched at the cross beneath his shirt.

"You mean the spit? She had reason to spit, I suppose. But the child will be better, perhaps. She'll give him the medicine."

"You like that. Being spat on by some old hag?"

"Well," Hook shrugged. "No. But one thing. At the very least it cleanses the act. Of pride, of self-righteousness." He dabbed at a thread of spittle on his pocket flap.

"Cleanses, my foot," said Jones. He discovered himself to be laughing: soft knuckles of sound at the back of his throat. "I bet next time you see a sick kid—you'll think twice about bein' a goody-goody."

"Oh?" said Hook. He stared intently at Jones, tempted to anger, then bewildered by the corpsman's odd self-destructive manner. He began to roll up his right sleeve. Jones' heart pummeled his chest; he mistook the action for some preliminary to violence. There was a very fresh, four-inch-long scar on the inside of Hook's forearm.

"So? So what?" stuttered Jones. He had not yet recovered from his apprehension.

"Nothing. I got off easily this time. No stitches." He rolled the sleeve down. "With my own knife she did it."

"Man. Don't you catch on? These people hate us."

"Yes. Some of them do. I know that."

"Well. Do you blame them?" Jones' voice cracked; its harshness disconcerted, alarmed him, but he persevered nonetheless. "You go through this place with a gun in one hand and a pill in the other. When that kid gets old enough, you'll shoot him in the back."

"Calm down, Andy."

"I'm calm. I'm calm."

"Keep your voice down then." Hook nodded toward the ruin. Mildly, he said, "If they hear you, it'll compromise my authority. I'll have to do something then, and I don't want to."

"Why not? Or don't you have no jail to put me in?"

"That's one consideration." Hook smiled. "But the main thing is—I can't bring myself to blame you. The officer who sent you here made the mistake. You can't cope, that's all. The Navy should have known that."

"That's right, man. I don't fit. I ain't no killer and I don't want t'get knocked off by no half-wit jungle woman."

"You don't want to get killed?"

"No."

"How very unique of you." Hook put out his hand to touch Jones' shoulder, but there was cortisone under the fingernails and Jones shied away.

"Don't touch me."

"How did you get to be a corpsman, Andy?"

"I had high marks is why. I was first in my class. I got brains, that's why."

"Yes. You do have brains." Hook closed his eyes, inhaled. "All right. Just try and hold out until we're back in San Pedro. Then I'll see to it you're sent back to the *Sting*."

"Sure. That's the way. Get rid of anyone who won't agree with you." Hook laughed.

"Well. What would you prefer?"

"Oh. I want out. You better believe that. But, long as I'm stuck here, I want to figure you, Mr. Cool. I want to see you mad. I want to see you scared and crying. From here on in,

Sergeant Hook, sir, I'm gonna be watching you. Right now, I don't quite get the picture. But I will." Hook raised his eyebrows. He nodded.

"Fair enough, I guess. A challenge is good for the soul. Maybe I am too complacent. Maybe we'll both learn." Hook wiped his hand on his pants leg. He looked up at the sun. Pensively, he said, "I wonder who you are, Jones. I wonder who you really are."

Hook turned. He walked into the hospital. Jones cursed bitterly, preferring even this dangerous confrontation to his aloneness. He picked up a fragment of brick and hurled it across the deserted, weed-sown street.

WRITTEN TWENTY-THREE DAYS BEFORE: LETTER FROM PRIVATE TOM HALL TO HIS NEXT-DOOR NEIGHBOR, PROFESSOR ALFRED H. HOOPLE, JR.

Dear Professor Hoople,

I guess you're surprised to get this. I guess you are. We never got to know each other too good, except for hello and goodbye and that day we burned our leaves together. Do you remember that? I always admired that nice, pointy beard of yours and the way you kept your shoes so shiny. I never thought you were snooty, the way Isabel did, because I was a working Joe and you had all those degrees. I never did. And I always wanted to know you better, but I just never got around to it, I guess.

Well, you're probably saying, what's this guy after? I'll get right to the point because I know your time is pretty valuable. It's my wife, Isabel. You know her, I guess. I mean, you've seen her around. She's a very striking woman, professor. You'll agree to that statement, I think. With that red hair and those good legs of hers, any man would agree. That's the trouble, Professor Hoople. That's the trouble.

She doesn't write to me. It's been almost two years since I left Calderwood, and I got only three letters from her so far. You can see how upsetting that would be. Will you please help me? I know you don't want to get involved in things like this. But please, professor, none of my friends will tell me the truth. I'm a desperate man right now. Otherwise, believe me, I wouldn't bother you like this.

You know that patio of yours, where you read books in the summer and wave at our kids sometimes? It looks right down on our house. No one can get in the front door or even the side door without you seeing—if you were that kind of guy, I mean. With a pair of binoculars, a cheap kind, you could pick up a pair for five dollars tops at the Army-Navy store on South Street—with a pair like that, you could look right into our bedroom. Not that you ever would. Or does she always pull the curtains? It's funny. I don't really remember now.

Well I guess I'd better call a spade a spade. Is my wife seeing other men, professor? Thats what I want to know. Please, I can take it like a man. It's the uncertainty that's driving me crazy. You must have seen something. Delivery trucks outside. Men going in and coming out with their ties loose or something. You're a man of the world, professor. You know hanky-panky when you see it.

I want you to know something, because this letter sounds pretty crazy I guess. I love Isabel and my little girls. I wouldn't do anything no matter what you tell me. I'm not much of a guy. I never could figure why Isabel married me. I wish her the best always. But please, I got to know. Write to me soon, at the above APO. I'll always be grateful to you.

 Sincerely,
 Tom Hall.

They left East One just after noon, traveling northwest toward the highlands and the lake. Source of the Negro River, Lake Negro nestled in the angle formed by a fifteen-hundred-foot-high, pine-covered ridge that jutted erratically toward

the southeast, joining at one end with the north–south range
of the San Barnabas Mountains. The lake itself was sacred to
the Mayan tribes of Camaguay. A ruined ceremonial city, ignored even by archaeologists, stood on an island at the upper
end of the lake. Opposite the island, on the eastern shore, was
the Camaguayan village where Rodriguez and his troops
would rendezvous.

Between East One and the spur was a long, broken inclined
plane, the farmland of Indians since primeval times. From a
distance, the steep fields, terraced against erosion, seemed as
neat and complex as a shingled roof. But they were untended,
the ubiquitous, hearty weeds pushing through the stubble of
another season's crop, like worms through a nearly un-
fleshed skeleton. This was the area of most frequent Riff in-
filtration. In places where the *milpa* system of cultivation had
long been in use, the red earth was disfigured by miniature
Grand Canyons. *Barrancas,* gullies, ten feet deep, gouged out
by the fury of a single titanic thunderstorm, had to be circumvented. It was an ambusher's terrain.

There was a searing heat, but, unlike the heat of the jungle,
it was dry and direct. The sun could at least be seen. For a
time, the men derived comfort from their unimpeded view
of the blue-white sky and the towering cumulus clouds that
bulked about in it. But their pleasure was soon vitiated by the
monotonous pulling in their calf muscles. The underfooting
was uneven, treacherous, always uphill. The sun's glare drove
their eyes down until they were inextricably engaged in the
appearance and reappearance of their own dusty boot-tips.
Dark groves of pine, mahogany, and ironwood, some quite
considerable, brooded down on their passage presenting, to
the IC's at least, a continued menace. For the first time the
Americans became anxious.

But the Camaguayans were not concerned. The open country
reminded them not of danger, but of desertion. They were
restless. They grouped together as they walked, giggling,
chatting, pointing at objects that piqued their interest. They
aimed their rifles at birds, at comrades. The two lovers picked

little bouquets of wild flowers for each other. Again and again, tired of marching, the men stepped out of line, ostensibly to urinate, and had to run, shouting, to catch up. Baxter, Hall, and Falk were placed in the rear to discourage stragglers. Falk, however, was too easy-going; the Camaguayans merely smiled at his unassertive commands. Hall had developed a blister on his heel and was not unsympathetic to delays; moreover, as the country opened out, he became more and more introverted, hardly speaking to anyone. Baxter was last. The Camaguayans admired him because of his height and color, and because he was willing to hit them on occasion. They were a submissive people, and they distrusted as fools those who would not take advantage of their submissiveness.

There were two Indian villages within the first fifteen miles of their march. An odd, expectant forlornness pervaded both: there were no young men among the huts with their low mud walls and steep, four-cornered thatched roofs. Yapping mongrel dogs were virtually the only animals, for nearly all the pigs and sheep, as well as personal property, had been cached in the wooded hills. The patrol halted for a short time in each village. The women and children greeted the IC's with jubilance, but avoided the Camaguayan soldiers who, in their turn, spat whenever an Indian approached. To Jones it seemed that all the women, the old and the young, knew Hook and were flirting with him. The children inserted their fingers deep into his beard, caressing it, as though it were a holy fetish.

Most of the young men were with Rodriguez, north of Lake Negro, preying on the Riff supply trails that led down from Valencia. The villages, bereft of their manhood, were terribly vulnerable. The American command had offered to evacuate the women and children, but the Indians did not care to be bullied and oppressed by the Camaguayans in San Pedro. They judged their peril with a fatalism that perhaps only Hook, of the Americans, could appreciate. José Ix, a descendant of the *caciques* who had ruled the country in pre-Columbian times, had relatives in every village and was revered, partly because of his American allies, as a young and powerful patriarch. He and Hook questioned the villagers. Things had been very quiet, they were told. The Riffs feared the Americans. All would be well. Hook nodded, seconding their enthusiasm, but he was concerned for them.

Garbini excepted, the other IC's had begun to avoid Jones, aware instinctively that he was not one of them. Now Sergeant Raoul and he sat together, hands between their knees, in the shade of a great hammock-bestrung mahogany tree. Raoul was continuing a long monologue of his persecution. During the march he had chatted, walking just a pace behind Jones, now and then touching of the corpsman's buttocks in emphasis. Jones was irritated; he did not acknowledge Raoul's complaint. As in the first village, Sergeant Hook had appropriated Jones's medical kit. The children were now lined up in front of the headman's hut, and Hook, who sat in the doorway, would take each in his lap like some dark, department-store Santa Claus. He examined them, popped vitamin pills into each opened mouth, talked heartily in the Mayan dialect. Evidently, the Indians missed the other corpsman, Graham. Jones noticed female fingers that were pointed in his direction, and, above the fingers, shaking, doubtful heads. Raoul poked him in the side; Jones had apparently ignored him more than was permitted. In penance, he offered Raoul a cigarette. The sergeant snatched it eagerly, vociferating his gratitude, though, as Jones knew, he had almost a carton secreted in his pack.

"—Is it not?" said Raoul, as he lit the cigarette.

"Damn right it's hot," replied Jones, misunderstanding him.

"No. You have not been hearing me, I think. Is my English so bad?"

"It's good," said Jones truthfully. He wiped his forehead. Fat, black ants tended to drop from the tree's branches to thrash, stunned, in their laps. But they did not consider moving.

"I say. It is always us, the little men, who must fight their wars. Is that not so? That is how they keep us silent." Jones did not regard himself as a little man, but he was too tired to demur. He decided, chiefly on the strength of this remark, that he did not like Raoul. His hairiness, his near quadruped stance, suggested some ersatz, fabricated human being. Like the dwarf who always bobbed up and down, gibbering by Bela Lugosi's thigh. "Down, Igor," said Jones half-aloud. He grinned, but Raoul was asking insistently again, "Is that not so?" Jones nodded obediently; he flicked an ant from his knee. "When we make trouble, bang, into the Army. And then we die, while they stay home and rape our women. Yes. Are you afraid for your woman back home in the slums? I have heard what they are like, the slums of America."

"I ain't got no woman;" said Jones. There was Ellen Rosenfeld, of course, but then you could never tell if those crazy civil rights whites really gave a damn for you. They had too many problems of their own. Raoul sighed.

"You are lucky, my friend. My wife and four children, they are in Camaguay City. I worry. General Amayo did not like my father. My father, he was a famous photographer."

"No kidding," said Jones, but he could not have cared less. Hook, he saw, was now squatting in front of the hut, conversing with a withered old man, the shaman of the village. They ate a pasty substance from decorated gourds, scooping with their first two fingers.

"A very famous man," said Raoul. "A very rich man. He did fashions—for the magazines, you know. But my father was too brave. A brave fool. He said what he thought of that stupid, old queer Amayo." Raoul clapped his hands together. Jones looked up, into the branches: he wondered why the ants kept falling down. "One day soldiers come to my father's studio. They take him away, and all his equipment. Thousands and thousand of pesos that equipment cost. For months we did not know if he was dead or alive. They starved him, my father. They whipped him with sticks. His back was covered with shiny scars, like worms."

"That's tough," said Jones piously. He grimaced: a remnant of his previous meal had become lodged behind a wisdom tooth.

84

"You know what they wanted from my father?" Raoul paused, challenging the corpsman to answer.

"Uh—" began Jones. He repressed a flippancy that came to mind. "Can't guess."

"They wanted the names and addresses of all my father's models. Yes. The general wanted to examine them for gonorrhea. Personally." Raoul cursed in his own language. "One by one, they took those poor women from their homes. One by one the general's men enjoyed them. While he watched. While he watched!"

"Oh," said Jones. "So your father told them, huh?"

"Have you ever been whipped, my friend?" Jones shook his head. "My father is still alive, a broken man of sixty. And one of those girls—I was to marry her."

"But you have a wife."

"Yes . . . this was some time ago."

"Oh," said Jones. "You found another woman. Kind of fickle, no?" Raoul paused then. He studied Jones' face, wondering suddenly whether the corpsman had been mocking him. But Jones blinked his innocence several times, and Raoul decided his own unfamiliarity with English nuance had been at fault. A naked female child came and stood, hands behind back, staring at Jones. Her navel was distended, resembling an embryonic thumb. The red cross had attracted her; other men with red crosses had given her food. But Jones did not understand. He saw only the navel and the dirt encrusted on her thighs. He looked at Raoul intently and for the first time. The child went away.

"Ah me," said Raoul. "And now I am fighting for General Amayo. Fighting against my own people." He plucked at the hairs that blossomed from his shirt collar. His hands were pink and delicate, though a black watershed of hairs lined the upper joint of each finger.

"So," said Jones. "Why do you do it?"

"I don't want prison. I don't want to be like my father."

"Yeah," said Jones.

85

"In Harlem, I hear, there is bad disease and barbed wire fences with soldiers. Is that so?" Jones shrugged.

"I don't know. I don't live in Harlem."

"No? But do not all black men live in Harlem?"

"Not all. Just the stupid ones."

"Still—you were very poor."

"Uh-uh," Jones grunted. "My daddy owns a big furniture store. Pay on time. Fifteen dollars a month for the rest of your child-bearing life. He really milks the spics around our way."

"Spics? What is that?"

"Uh—" Jones smiled. "You wouldn't understand. But listen, Sergeant, you come up North some time and give me a ring. I'll drive you around in my new Mustang. We'll do all the hot spots." Raoul frowned, puckered his lips, spread them tentatively, then produced an expansive grin. He began to chuckle.

"I see. I see. You are pulling my arm. If your father is a big man, how is it then they have take you away from your home?"

"They? The Army, you mean? Hell, I wasn't drafted. I joined up."

"You . . ." Raoul's lips were drained of their pink brownness as he pressed them tightly together.

"You think we're gonna move out soon? Huh?" But Sergeant Raoul was on his feet. Without answering Jones, he ducked under the crude native hammocks, and began to stride disconsolately toward a group of sleeping Camaguayans. "That's it, Igor," muttered Jones. "Don't go away mad, just go away."

The shaman's thin, blotched hams wavered slightly as he squatted. He was ninety-seven years old, and Hook knew now that his mind often wandered. His harelip, the emblem of a prowess in matters supernal, was withered, appearing almost undeformed, for the teeth that had once forced the split wide had long ago dropped from his jaws. Hook ate slowly, nodding; for the last few minutes, the old man's conversation had been totally disordered. Talk of birds and snakes; talk of old wives;

talk of the wretched state of his own bowels. The shaman started suddenly, as though awakening.

"Eeee. The eyes. The eyes." He raised his forearm, as though protecting his face from some imagined glare. "I am afraid. They see through my chest. Go. Now. Go."

"What eyes, father?" But the old man had buried his face in his hands: the monkey who would see no evil. "Go back to the hills. Go back. We have nothing to give you here. We have nothing."

He groaned deeply. The groans became a sort of snore. Hook waited patiently, respecting the man's madness. And soon the shaman lowered his hands. He began eating voraciously. In time he spoke again of his bowels and the women he had outlived.

"Now she's right pretty," said Falk. He indicated a girl of about seventeen, who sat cross-legged, weaving a geometrical red-and-yellow pattern at a small loom. Garbini growled, revealing his jagged fangs. With expert stealth, he slipped a silver amulet into his cuff. A moment before Garbini had extracted it from an old woman's pocket while giving her a tin of his C rations. Garbini watched Falk surreptitiously. The young private, it seemed to him, was too honest for his own good; moreover, he would do anything to make a favorable impression on his idol, and Hook had already twice reprimanded Garbini for similar acts of petty larceny. But Falk noticed only the sheen on the smooth red-brown skin, the slight curve of bosom. He sighed.

"Now what would your daddy, the colonel, say?" Garbini laughed in relief; his dexterity had been successful. "You makin' eyes at a brown whore like that."

"My daddy's not a colonel. I told you that. And shame on you, Joe—telling Sergeant Raoul that my daddy was a rich chicken pot pie maker. You're a big kidder. I caught on to that." Falk winked, assuming an air of masculine wiseness that was not endorsed by his freckled pug nose and dull, wide eyes. "Anyhow, my daddy always said, 'Lance, prejudice don't have no place in bed.'"

"That so? Tell Corpsman Jones that. He'd like to hear it. Maybe he's your brother." Falk considered this suggestion seriously.

"No. I don't think so. Mr. Jones comes from the North. My daddy don't ever go north." Garbini spat accurately, dousing a beetle. Falk smiled. "You're a real funny guy. I heard some of your stories. But I don't think you're half so bad as you make out."

A filthy, ancient sheep ambled past them. It saw Falk with a bleared eye, snuffled happily, and approached to rub its coarse and yellowing fleece against his thigh. Falk was delighted; he laughed without constraint. Nearby, a pack of children, attracted by the sound, sidled cautiously closer. They imitated the example of a dark, slim girl of about nine, stepping when she stepped, smiling when she deemed it safe to smile. Falk took off his helmet and placed it on the sheep's angular head. The animal bleated, then seemed to hic-cough; its eyes became absurdly crossed as it peered up at the darkness that had descended upon it. The girl giggled. The children, encouraged, made various, rather sobered, chuckling noises.

Glad of the audience, Falk got down on his hands and knees, ignoring balls of dried dung, and began to imitate the befuddled animal with a remarkable deftness. Garbini cursed. Even on all fours and with an expression of ovine stupidity, Falk was, he knew, quite sufficiently handsome. The nine-year-old's smile had altered in a subtle manner: from amusement to a kind of coquetry. Garbini appraised her admiration: he cursed again. Falk stood then and tossed the children some fragments of chocolate. They stopped laughing and began to jostle each other with an increasing roughness as the bits were snatched up and mouthed.

"Dirty little savages," said Garbini.

"Hells bells," replied Falk. He retrieved his helmet. The sheep was now trotting in circles, peering at the sky for the source of this sudden and capricious darkness. "Hells bells,"

Falk said again. "What'd d'y'all expect? They ain't never had nothing. That there chocolate's something special."

"Jeesus. You sound more like Preacher Hook every day. That what you're doin' on your knees? Practicin' your brown ring position?"

"Ah, excuse me," Falk said mildly. "You wouldn't be wanting to fight, Mr. Garbini? Would you now?" Garbini's eyes opened wide; sharp glints of a baleful light illuminated the protruding, yellow orbs. He did, indeed, very much want to fight, and he knew just what parts of Falk's fine facial anatomy he would destroy. Garbini was a devastating and unprincipled street fighter. The condition of his own face freed him from any self-concern he might have had. As a rule his terrific commitment to brutality demoralized his opponents before they could usefully defend themselves.

"No kid," he said with reluctance. "Do you?"

"No—not in front of these people here. We're Americans and we ought to stick together. Some other time." He grinned. "How's about we play some dice instead?"

"No more penny ante. It ain't worth my time."

"Aw heck. Don't you never do things fer fun? Well. Sergeant Hook says I shouldn't play with you. He says them shiny dice of yours're loaded. Are they, Mr. Garbini? Joe?" Garbini shrugged.

"If Hook says so."

"Yup. He's smart. But you've been around a bit, too, I reckon," said Falk, knowing, despite his youth, the effectiveness of flattery. Garbini patted Falk on the shoulder, leered at him.

"Don't I look it? Huh, kid? I mean with this face?"

"Now, you can't tell by that. No sir," said Falk with well-intentioned sincerity. "There was a guy, a garage mechanic, back home. Hank Dorper. A real pal, he was. A straight arrow. Used to take me fishing an' all. And he was more ugly than you. Honest, Mr. Garbini— Hey . . ." Garbini had spat on Falk's cuff.

"Tit sucker," he said. "Go fuck yourself. Please." Garbini turned, spraying dust on Falk's boots, and walked away.

Hall wiped his glasses with deliberation. The opaque smudge of sweat and skin oils shifted under the prodding of his moist handkerchief from the lower corner of the lens, to dead center, to the top left corner, to the lower corner again where it assumed the shape of a nippled breast. Hall began to hum: the sublimation of his furious impatience. He put the glasses on hopefully, but his vision was still blurred, seeming now a mistiness in the eye itself.

Hall hummed more loudly: a chant of his grammar school days, "Oh, they don't wear pants on the sunny side of France. Oh, they don't wear pants . . ." He steamed the lens as though with a sigh. He polished once more, but his thumb slipped and left a print—the mark of a moist lower lip on the rim of a drinking glass. The two smudges now orbited each other, separating, coalescing, aligning themselves like two plump buttock cheeks. "Oh they don't . . ." Hall blotted one cheek viciously. Then he took thumb and forefinger and, with patient thoroughness, smeared both lenses until they admitted light no more freely than two crumbled bits of waxed paper.

In the streaked, clouded range of his vision, Hall saw Baxter reassembling the M30. His small hands worked deftly and without hesitation. A Camaguayan in a pose of careful observation stood nearby, but he yawned, scratched, his attention frequently lured away. Baxter instructed him in pidgin Spanish, proud of his own dexterity. The clack-click of metal parts resounded across the village, contradicting the heat and the lazy bodies that wallowed in it. Tears came to Hall's eyes. Though he had not thought of it before, he hoped very much now that Baxter's arm would be all right.

Lieutenant Harry Storch found a leech on his inner thigh. He was sprawled, splay-legged, in the shadow of the shaman's hut, his pants around his calves. "Ug?" he said when he saw it. A fly touched down on his flat, bald head, seemed self-conscious there, and buzzed instead onto the rim of his ear. Storch did not notice it. He knocked the ash from his cigarette and then inhaled until the tip was a furious orange. The leech undulated once, perhaps in anticipation, perhaps in sheer blood surfeit. The butt approached it, held between fat, yellowed fingers. On the animal's back little sensory pimples seemed to have a separate aliveness. The leech contracted, appeared to hesitate between alternatives, then held firm.

Storch puffed. He applied the hot cigarette ember again, this time to the animal's other extremity. The leech came loose, its underside pinked with the lieutenant's blood. It rolled between his legs, made helpless there by its own rotundity. Storch frowned: the blood had suggested a sort of simple justice. He smiled. His heavy eyes sparkled with mischief as he peered about him. No one was watching. He picked up the leech, and, like a man with a handful of cocktail peanuts, he popped it into his mouth.

WRITTEN THREE MONTHS BEFORE: NOTE FROM LIEUTENANT HARRY STORCH TO COLONEL FRITZ (FATTY) ARBUCKLE, HIS ONLY FRIEND

Fatty boy—Hook's applying for a transfer again. I just got wind of it. You see his letter gets filed in the you know what. It's worth a case of your favorite scotch.
  Thanx,
    Harry.

V

THEY WERE ATTACKED just five hundred yards beyond the village. A single shot pierced through Lieutenant Storch's water bag, and drove it, spurting, twice around his neck. They dropped to the ground: the Camaguayans slowly, awkwardly, with explosive grunts. There was a retrospective silence, punctured only by the harsh gulpings of Lieutenant Storch, who drank the escaping water furiously, a finger in one hole of the wounded bag.

"Pretty good shot," said Hook, surprised. "He's in the hut."

They had been crossing a farmer's abandoned maize field, between two high slopes. Fifty yards to the right and slightly ahead stood a hut, gutted by fire the season before. The thatching was gone; only a few blackened rafters remained of the roof. The mud walls were intact in front, but breached at the sides and in the rear. Hook saw the rifle's muzzle move, left-right, protruding three inches from a triangular chink in the wall as might an anteater's probing snout. The muzzle flashed: dust spattered behind them on the far slope.

"That's more like it," he said to José Ix. "The first shot was lucky. Let's flush him out of there."

Hook crawled back to Sanchez' position. A sporadic return fire commenced along the line: Baxter and Garbini and Gutierrez. The majority of the Camaguayans, having attained their prone positions with such effort, now lay inert, some facing away from the fire, some with their hands over their ears. Sanchez smiled when Hook approached. The tip of Hook's beard was reddened with the dust of the arid field.

"He is a dead man," said Sanchez gleefully.

93

"Let's try to take him alive."

"No."

"Yes. He may know something."

"But he will not tell. And you will not use my methods. And we cannot bring him with us."

"Let's try. The ditch there. Follow me."

Another bullet was fired. There was a shrill scream, but the Camaguayan had merely been startled. Hook signaled to the IC's and they began to crawl up and down, kicking, prodding, slapping the line of torpid bodies. The man in charge of the M30 and his partner were in an absurd state of panic. They had forgotten how to assemble their weapon and were now sprawled amidst a confusion of spare parts, extra barrels, and ammunition, shrieking and throwing dirt at each other. Baxter pounded each on the helmet top, and, cursing laconically, shoved them away from the M30. Hook grinned.

"Jones," he shouted. "Get ready to follow us in."

Jones said "Shit." Then he wrenched off his helmet and began to spit carefully on the cross. Having done this, he patted dust onto the spit, but his handiwork was not effective, seeming to make his head more conspicuous than less. Hook and Sanchez were crawling toward a shallow irrigation ditch that led to a point about fifteen yards south of the hut. They sidled forward like great iguanas, crushing the maize stubble under their lowered chests. Jones took out his .45 and released the safety. He looked upward abruptly then, for some reason expecting a darkened sky, and he was amazed to see the high, cirrus clouds floating like bits of shell against the white-blue. A breeze tossed the branches in a distant copse of balsa. Jones' heart was thumping; the pulse-filled arteries at his wrist and throat seemed hugely tumescent. It was a beautiful day. He had never seen a day so very beautiful. The heat, the insects no longer existed, or, rather, were beautiful as well. Another shot was fired from the hut. Jones picked up a clod of earth and crumbled it as though it were a vial of rich perfume.

The ditch was too shallow. Though little Sanchez' body was concealed, Hook's helmet and shoulders and buttocks presented an excellent target. Abruptly, the sniper sensed their purpose. He fired twice at the ditch, but his bullets struck home harmlessly on the far side. The hut stood in a slight hollow; betraying his inexperience, the Riff continued to shoot high. Hook and Sanchez had now nearly flanked the hut. The sniper fired once more; he had adjusted; dirt spattered onto Hook's back. But then Baxter leveled the M30 and drove a furious stream of fire into the wall. The muzzle was quickly withdrawn. Jones saw that José Ix and Gutierrez had begun crawling to the left. Cautiously, Jones aimed his .45. He squeezed the trigger. Dirt showered down from the cross on his helmet. Jones cursed.

Hook and Sanchez rose together, firing. They raced toward the doorway, Hook in the lead with his long strides, Sanchez, scuttling behind, shoving at Hook in his anxiety to reach the prey. José Ix shouted. Jones saw an arm, then a vaulting leg appear at a breach in the left wall. Hook had reached the doorway. He seemed to hesitate; then he fell, firing his M16, knocking Sanchez to the ground. The arm, the leg went limp and slipped, as though reluctantly, back into the hut.

Jones crossed the field. The rate of his body's reactions had diminished rapidly, leaving him in a state of fearful depression. He was nauseated and strangely unable to get his breath. His legs shook: they could barely cope with the slight unevenness of the ground. The inordinate clarity of his vision had become an inordinate distortedness. The hut doorway, preternaturally dark, leaped and wavered before his eyes. He touched the skin of his forehead lightly, and his fingertips acknowledged the vulnerability of that thin tissue covering. The doorway was very near now. Jones dreaded, to the degree almost of frenzy, what he knew must lie behind it.

The sniper had been a boy of fifteen. Hook was kneeling, his head sharply inclined at the neck. Sanchez sat on a pile of rubble; a cigarette was jammed in the corner of his surly grin. Jones glanced toward Hook. He saw a bare, grimy leg, strewn at an angle no living body could long sustain.

"Where's he hit? Where? Where?" But he did not step forward. He stared down instead at a red, battered, wide-brimmed hat. A relic of their enemy.

"He's dead," said Hook in a monotone. "I won't need you."

Some aspect of the hat bothered Jones. The smallness of the band, perhaps; perhaps the angle at which the edge of the brim had been bent upward. He held his breath, afraid of odors, and looked down over Hook's shoulder. The sniper had been an ugly child—fat-faced with an incipient growth of mustache. His tongue protruded from between his teeth, bitten there, and two vertebrae protruded from the nape of his neck where the bullet had broken free after its lethal drive through his throat. He wore an undershirt and khaki shorts belted with a cord. Streams of blood, now already skinned with their clotting, had run from his nose. Jones gasped. Hook shut the book he had been reading and turned, startled to find the corpsman still standing there.

"Jones? What is it?"

"Good God. A kid. That's all he was. A little kid."

"Yes," said Hook.

"You killed a kid. You. You killed him." And then Jones saw the book: a small edition of the book of Common Prayer, a thin, gilt cross on its leather cover. "Are—are you praying? Is that what you're doing. Are you praying, Hook?"

"Yes," said Hook. He gnawed his lower lip. Then he turned once again to the corpse. "I'm praying. Would you let me have a moment alone? Tell Baxter to have a grave dug."

"You're praying." Jones shook his head, incredulous. "You goddamned murdering hypocrite. I hope it's you next. I hope it's you and I hope it hurts."

But Hook did not hear him, nor did he notice when Jones ran, stumbling out into the field. He touched the dead boy lightly on the forehead.

"My God, take, I pray, this soul to its eternal life. Forgive him his sins, not for his own sake, but for the sake of Jesus Christ who died for us as we die—in suffering and in fear, but yet the Son of God. Our kingdom, His kingdom is not of this world. Nor can it ever be. Make this child Your own. Grant him his true kingdom now. Please, my God. Please."

And Hook wept.

The Camaguayans were enthralled by the sniper's violent death. They laughed as they walked, crouching suddenly, rifles brandished, shouting, "Bah! Bah! Bah! I'm Sergeant-Master Blackbeard. Budda—budda—bah! You're dead." They talked of their own deeds, of their wondrous marksmanship, of their imperturbable courage. And no man would contradict another, for they were all heroes vicariously in Hook's heroism. Sergeant Hook, it was said, had never lost a battle. Hook was invincible—did not even the mosquitos fear him? And, indeed, General Camillo Hernando Illoy, commander in chief of the RFN, had put a price on Hook's head: a gold Benrus man's watch, once owned by the American ambassador to Valencia, and inscribed, "To Bernie from Jane. Best wishes on your new appointment."

Private Hall was driven nearly frantic by the Camaguayans' shrill and homicidal pantomimes. He cherished his present dullness, this absence of all desire; it was a manifestation, he presumed, of his own imminent death. In annoyance, Hall wondered why, at the edge of annihilation, his blistered heel should ache so insistently; why his bowels should be loose. These little torments seemed unnecessary, anticlimactic. He thought of the sniper whose head and shoulders he had carried while Garbini, laughing profanely, had carried the legs. There was that between them, between Garbini and himself: the unbridgeable void between dead things and those that live. He was already incomprehensible to the others. Yet they acknowledged his differentness, as they would acknowledge his death when it came. A Camaguayan raised the muzzle of his M16, brushing Hall's arm, and Hall knocked him sprawling with a blow behind the ear. The man got to his feet, dizzied, and began walking in the wrong direction. Baxter, just behind, turned him around, talked to him patiently for a

few moments. Hall cursed when Baxter caught up with him.
"Tom. You don't have to do that."

"Leave me alone." Baxter continued to walk, silent, beside
him. Trees had begun to cast long shadows, and birds, ex-
hilarated by the coming of night, chirped, flittered in low
formations of three and four. Baxter felt a chill and welcomed
it. They would have to camp very soon. He cleared his throat.

"You're a pretty good soldier, Tom. I been watching. You
know what it's all about."

"No. Not any more."

"Don't get pissed at those little guys. Not that pissed, anyhow. They *no comprende*—it don't matter how much you hit
them." Hall looked at him.

"What is it, Horace? What do you want from me?"

"Can I help, that's all? I don't like t'see a good man down."
Hall laughed.

"You got your own problems. Don't mess with me. There's
no sense in it. I'm not coming back from here."

"No?"

"No."

"How is that? How d'you know?"

"Because I don't want to. It's nice up here. Quiet. I'm looking for it, Horace. I want it. So stay clear. Don't be around
when I find it. Please." His voice, naturally thin, was broken
by that last word. He began to trot. Baxter, left behind, spat
just once, for he knew no more appropriate gesture.

An aroma of pine droppings was wafted down from the
hills. Fifteen miles distant now, the ridge they would have to
cross was clearly silhouetted, the sun's bright, burnished paten
resting on its summit. Hook, isolated again at point, was very
thirsty, for Lieutenant Storch had commandeered his canteen.
Hook was grateful for the discomfort; he bent and augmented
it once with a handful of red dust. Three rabbits, flushed by
his approach, bounded from a patch of maguay plants, and
raced, kicking up tiny spurts of dust, toward the ridge. The
patrol crossed a field of calf-high wild anise, crushing out
fragrance with their boots. A flock of swallows swooped down,

turning on themselves, as though their formation were a great cloth billowed and folded by the wind. Hook knew he loved the country and yet his love was stymied, as all human loves are, by an immitigable fear. Every flower-clotted gully, every scented stand of pine and sapodilla, every depression was potentially suspect, a threat. And Hook marched, clutching his M16, as though he held the land itself at gunpoint.

Sergeant Raoul watched Hook. He cursed then in two languages. Jones, just ahead, was walking, tranced, head inclined at the neck. He had again remembered the sniper's neck with its raw, bared vertebrae, and in this memory was implicit the fragileness of all necks and throats. The false enormousness of life, promulgated by the brain, sanctioned by self-desire and the senses, seemed to him a very precious lie—one he feared he could never wholly believe again. Raoul came close and touched his buttock.

"You see him? Hook. He is happy. He has killed a man." Jones grunted, only half aware. "A man? No. A child playing with a toy gun. You saw it yourself, did you not?"

"Didn't look like a toy. Not to me."

"Bah." Raoul spat. "What did he hit—the stupid one's waterbag? Should a man die for that? Did you see his other shots? He was harmless, believe me that. These are not professional soldiers like your Sergeant Hook. They are children, fighting now to save their country from Amayo. Why is it—why do you Americans love dictators?" Jones did not answer. "Too bad. It is too bad."

They walked in silence. Ten paces ahead Lieutenant Storch was experiencing a crisis of will. He would reach for Hook's canteen with his left hand, then slap his own wrist severely with the fingers of his right. Little yelps, bits of dialogue, could be heard by those just behind him. But his left hand was incorrigible, and it had powerful allies. Storch raised the canteen quickly and drained off the last two ounces. He belched, and began looking avidly behind him for other canteens. He beckoned Armando forward, but it was a futile gesture: Armando had drunk all his water before noon.

99

"It is not true," blurted Raoul. "I know that. It's not true. You do not have a car. I know a nigger cannot have a car." Jones turned on him.

"Nigger? Nigger? Crud, you ain't so lily white yourself. Can that nigger stuff." Raoul smiled uneasily.

"Excuse please. No offense." He fingered his thick lower lip. "Yes, you are right. There is dark skin in me. It is the same with all of us in Camaguay. Negro skin. Skin of conquistadors. For that reason we have no prejudice. We are all alike. We are all poor."

"So," said Jones. "How come nobody likes that guy José whatsisname? How come you spit all the time, when them poor Indians get too close? How come?"

"Yes . . ." Raoul shrugged. Then he smiled. "The Indians are different, you see."

"Yeah. I figured as much. I been different all my life."

"No, please. Don't get me wrong. The Indians support the Americans, they support General Amayo. They fight his battles for him." Jones slapped his forehead.

"And what about you? You out here for a picnic?"

"But that is not the same. Not willingly. I do not do this willingly." Jones laughed. Raoul became impassioned; he pressed very close to Jones. "You will see, my friend. When the time comes, you will see."

"What's that supposed to mean?"

"Well." Raoul frowned. "Well, I have said enough."

"Too much, brother. I don't like you bein' so close. Beat it." Jones increased the pace of his walking. Raoul began to scurry after him, legs bowed, long right arm outstretched. He grasped Jones by the belt.

"Only a joke. Only a joke," he said with forced cheerfulness. "You are too serious. We are brothers. Always. I promise." He winked. "When the battle comes, then Raoul will take good care of you." Jones halted in his tracks.

"What battle?"

"Soon. There will be a battle."

"What battle? Where? When?"

"Please. Don't stop like this. They are looking at us." Jones started forward reluctantly.

"What battle? How come you know so much?"

"I—I know nothing. But it is obvious, is it not? The Riffs must attack soon. Before we reach the hills, before we reach the thick forests."

"Yeah?" Jones chewed the corner of his mouth. He looked toward the ridge. In the diffuse light of dusk it appeared distressingly near. "And what then? The Riffs attack, what then?" Raoul shrugged.

"I do not want to die."

"No," said Jones thoughtfully.

"But we are friends. I hear what you have said to Sergeant Hook. I know you are on our side." He patted Jones on the shoulder. "Now tell me. This is not true, is it? You do not have a car?"

"No," said Jones. He stared at the ridge once again. The sun's disk had been halved by its edge, seeming perhaps a portent of menace. "No," said Jones again. "I don't have no car."

They camped for the night in a basin at the crest of a long, gradual rise. Polygonal boulders, the artifacts, apparently, of a huge and primitive hand, formed a rough circle fifty yards in diameter. In the lower corner of the basin a spring sputtered, filling a tiny pool, the excesses of which, in their turn, fathered a small stream. The sky was clear but hazy; a full moon shone with a bright, blurred corona about it. Stiff breezes blew and prevented the mosquitos from gaining secure purchase in the air. But for the men on watch it was a difficult time. The sounds of the rillet and the rushing air, the weird, agitated shadows compounded of moonlight and the strong wind— these either induced an exhausting alertness or dulled all senses utterly.

Garbini's dice flickered as he and Falk played craps. Despite his losses, the young private laughed, whooped, called out silly conjurations: "Come to papa, baby needs shoes." "Seven,

seven, send me to heaven." His enthusiasm disgusted Garbini, who growled and locked the furrows of his brow in a massive striation. Around them, the camp was very quiet. The Camaguayans were nearly all asleep, but for the two young lovers, who indulged now in a boisterous homosexual play within joined tents. Strange bulges appeared from time to time in the canvas, as though the tents had become oddly, capriciously pregnant. Another man hummed sadly, varying a single indistinct phrase.

Jones had not yet learned to rest easily on the unyielding ground. He wandered about the encampment, shivering and whispering quietly to himself. He drank from the icy pool, then followed the stream until, in a small, noisy waterfall it cascaded down into the valley they had just ascended. He gazed ahead. There was an extensive, dark grove of trees across the valley: branches wavered in a breeze, sending out suspect shadows, retracting them again. Rocks and bushes on the valley floor, twenty yards behind the lip of the basin, seemed to harbor menacing pits at each base. Just below, propped against a rounded boulder, Jones recognized Baxter by the now characteristic flexing and unflexing of his left arm. Jones let himself down between jumbled, broken rocks.

"Horace. It's me. Andy." Baxter lowered the M16 with apparent reluctance, permitting his aim to search Jones' belly for a long moment. "Horace? You on guard? Huh?" There was no answer. "Nice night. Chilly, but nice. Big moon up there. Think the Riffs're around?"

"What is it, Jones? What can I do for you?"

"Look. What it is—I come to apologize. See, I had this big chip on my shoulder. But I was wrong. I should never've taken things out on a soul brother." Jones smiled shyly, biting his lower lip; it was an expression with which he had often cajoled his mother. "You gonna forgive me? Huh? I mean, you and me, we gotta stick together."

"Oh? Why's that?"

"Color, man. Color."

"I ain't yellow, Jones. If that's what you mean." Baxter turned away. He rested the barrel of his M16 atop a leveled outcropping of the rock. Then, with a show of busy alertness, he scanned the terrain. Jones cleared his throat harshly.

"I'll forget you said that."

"Don't bother." Jones laughed. He slapped his own thigh. "Man. I don't figure you, Horace. I mean you sure get down on a guy quick. I talk a lot. Sometimes I talk crazy. That's all. Other times, man, I'm with you all the whole way. The whole way." He paused, moved closer to Baxter. "How old are you, Horace?"

"Nineteen."

"Nineteen. Son of a bitch." Jones felt better; he was nearly twenty-four himself. He placed a patronizing hand on Baxter's right shoulder. "What you gonna do? I mean, if you can't throw no more?"

"I can throw."

"Sure. Sure. What I want to say—see, my father's got a big furniture store and next year he's gonna open two more. That's big business. Top money, even for a guy what don't have a real good education. You got a high school diploma, Horace?"

"No."

"Well, then, hell—this'd be just the thing. You could pitch, too. My daddy sponsors a team and he even pays money—if a player's real good, that is. Jones's Movers. They come in second place last year. I played left field when I's a kid. We could use a pitcher. Why don't I put in a good word—"

"Not that kinda pitching," said Baxter angrily. "Not no more. I had enough of that. I'm a professional."

"Yeah—okay. You don't have to pitch. But I'm gonna own them stores some day, and, what with bein' a lawyer an' all, I'll need a good top hand. Now you could—"

Baxter spun around, rifle readied on his hip. Jones inserted himself hastily between two boulders. A few pebbles landed at their feet, and then Sergeant Hook appeared as a dark, anonymous form just above. Jones had leaped to safety so suddenly that it was only with complex contortions that he managed to squeeze out of his hiding place in the rocks. Baxter suppressed a laugh.

"This is your sergeant speaking," said Hook. "Don't shoot. I'm coming down."

The three soldiers stood in a small weed-grown pocket among the rocks, their bodies touching at the elbows and hips. Hook inspected the position critically. He sighted along his rifle, drawing a bead on various points in the valley. Then he grunted.

"Anything out there, Horace?"

"No sir. Not that I can see."

"They won't attack from this side, not if they can help it. A diversion, perhaps, but nothing more than that. What's the quickest way up from here?"

"Over there," said Baxter. He pointed to a small natural staircase in the rocks.

"Yes. That looks good. You must be tired. I don't feel like sleeping just now. Why don't you sack out? I'll take your watch." Baxter considered this offer, then decided it would be proper to accept.

"Thanks, Sergeant. I'm pretty bushed. Wake me up if you get tired. G'night, black brother," he said to Jones, placing an odd stress on the adjective. Baxter began to ascend.

"Remember what I told you," said Jones. He thought Baxter laughed, but he wasn't certain.

Hook prepared himself methodically. He kicked a shallow depression in the topsoil for his feet. Then he coated the muzzle of the M16 with a dark grease taken, Jones thought, from a shoe polish tin. He ran his fingers through his beard, massaging the skin of his face, composing his senses. After a moment, he carefully inspected the terrain. He divided it into fairly regular sections and then expertly memorized the trees, the configurations of rocks and bushes in each section, so that any alien movement would seem conspicuous. And all this while, he knew, the corpsman was watching him.

"Why not get some sleep, Jones? We've got a long walk tomorrow. You haven't slept much since San Pedro."

"Yeah—it's the hard mattress with me. What's your problem?

Guilty conscience maybe?" Hook turned toward him. Jones drew a cigarette nervously from his pack.

"I forgot. It's the politics of confrontation. You'd better not light that here." Jones took the cigarette from his mouth and cursed. "I know," Hook said. "War is inconvenient."

"Yeah. Pretty inconvenient it was—for that poor kid you shot."

"Ah," Hook nodded. "Yes. Thanks for reminding me." He rubbed his forehead: its square expanse, turned upward then under his helmet's rim, seemed abnormally pale in the moonlight. "Thanks. But I haven't forgotten."

"You didn't need to kill him, Hook. I saw. He was trying to get away."

"I don't know," said Hook thoughtfully. "You may be right. I think he probably was. But when I came through the door he swung around and . . . well. The light wasn't good." He tapped the stock of the M16 with his fingertips. "I wanted him alive, but my animal reflexes won in the end. It won't be the last time. It isn't the first. We still protect our own bodies. No amount of reason can teach the hand not to block a sudden blow."

"Hell," said Jones belligerently. "You prayed for him, didn't you? That made up for it. That did him a real lot of good, didn't it?"

"Now that you ask," said Hook mildly as he scanned the valley, "I think it did. It may have done him a lot of good. It was too late to help his body."

"Man, you're something else." Jones rubbed his hands together, then blew on them. "Tell me. Why are we here? I mean all of us? Do you think General Amayo's hide is worth saving?"

"No."

"Well, then . . . Is this war helping the Camaguayans? The ones that ain't already dead?"

"Do you mean is it making them richer, healthier, safer? Is that what you mean by help?"

"Sure. There ain't no other kind of help."

"In places I guess. Amayo will have to hold elections now. We're spending a lot of money. There's more food and more

105

medicine. But no. I don't think so. Not yet. Not for a long time, I'm afraid."

Jones was not certain how to proceed against Hook's easy yielding. He laughed and gnawed the side of his forefinger, the finger a substitute for the cigarette that had been denied him. An owl hooted: it was a long, sad, whirring noise. Hook listened carefully, then decided the noise was genuine.

"You didn't answer me, Sergeant. Why are we here? Why are you here?" Hook sighed.

"For the saddest of reasons, I suppose. Strategic reasons. The Communists are in Cuba and Valencia and Nahuatan. If they win here, they'll move south pretty easily, I think. Down below, right to the continent, there aren't any brutal, crude dictators. At least they're not brutal or crude enough. Amayo is strong, whatever else he may be. We have a chance here."

"It ain't no business of ours."

"But it is, my friend. Our way of life is in jeopardy. Right now. Right here."

"Our? Our? Your way of life. Whitey's way." Jones pulled up his collar with a sharp jerk. "That's what really gets me, Hook. All this money. Billions and billions of dollars, and meanwhile my family's starving in a ghetto. Man, if Whitey had to live with rats and roaches and junkies—then you bet he wouldn't be throwing his money away like this. We need some help. Us first. Not these foreign creeps."

"That's kind of uncharitable, Jones." Hook examined the disk of the moon. "Is your family starving? Really? Have you had a look at the slums of Camaguay City? Or even San Pedro? Ask anybody there if they'd like to swap ghettos with you. Find me three men back home with an annual income of four hundred dollars. That's the average here."

"Yeah. Figures don't mean nothing. There ain't no Mr. Cohen robbing them for every loaf of bread. Things're cheaper down here."

"Oh yes." Hook laughed. "Yes indeed. In C-City they pay three cents a pail for the water they drink. That's damn cheap. And the water's only a little contaminated."

"Well. They're animals, anyway. We can't take care of every primitive animal in the world."

"Sure. America for the Americans." Hook sniffed the breeze. "Showers tomorrow, I think."

Jones huddled down against the boulder, his hands deep in his pockets. He wondered, as was his habit from earliest childhood, how he would fare in a fistfight with Hook. Jones had only once been in a fistfight; he had lost, and the experience had made an irradicable impression on his mind. Hook was the same height, but at least twenty pounds heavier. And experienced. And strong. Jones thought he would probably lose; and the thought made him even more irritable than he was.

"What does it matter? Like you say, we ain't doing no good here. As for the American way of life, Hook. I hope America gets it in the neck. And gets it good."

"She may." Hook cleared his throat. "She may very well. The barbarian hordes are closing in. We've been poor, prideful stewards of our good fortune. Sometimes I think it's God's plan. But I'll try the last. There's nothing else I can do."

"I don't see it, Hook. What's in this for you?"

"Well. Let me try to explain." Hook spoke carefully, as though with an enforced patience. "I cherish two things only in life. My religion and my liberty. I am those things. In every one of its forms communism has suppressed Christianity and, with it, all human freedom. Suppressed with a ruthless and programmatic brutality. To my own way of thinking there can exist no more mortal enemy. It means to destroy me. I mean to resist it—at whatever personal cost. Is that clear enough?"

"Too simple," said Jones. "Redneck simple."

"In a sense, I suppose." Hook ran his fingers over the rock surface, probing for crevices with a strange interest. "But I was in Valencia when Illoy made his march down from the hills. I was there by chance. A student on holiday. I saw them hang two Catholic nuns up, naked, by their arms in Bolivar Square. That was simple, too—it took them a night and a day to die. A week later Illoy was hanging Valencians. The rich first, of course. The educated next. The middle class. Then just anyone at all. Simple. They tortured the man I had lived with. They imprisoned his fourteen-year-old son. Simple. General Amayo would have been embarrassed. Illoy made him look like a Sunday School teacher. He still does, believe me."

"I've heard them torture tales before."

"I see," said Hook. "Yes, they get tedious after a while. I think that was the cleverest thing the Nazis ever did—killing six million Jews after they killed the first one. No one could believe it. They say truth is stranger than fiction. I don't think it is. Fiction is stranger, but truth is tasteless and vulgar. That's the difference. We expect order from art, even in the midst of its worst enormities. Truth repeats itself: the same brutality followed again by the same brutality. It's numbing and senseless and stupid. And tyrants understand this—that one murder has the same value as a thousand in the human mind."

"So—you think Amayo is better?" Jones' teeth chattered as he spoke; he seemed to be nipping his words off.

"Better?" said Hook. "No. But a dictator like Amayo leaves little mark on his people, no matter what he may do. He's just an ego working out its will. He will die. But communism is an idea that transcends its tyrants. It destroys human minds. Amayo can't do that. For one thing, he's not clever enough. For another, he simply doesn't want to. He's out for his personal ends, that's all. For power and money and all the little boys he can defile. He's ruthless, but his ruthlessness is without purpose. He hasn't closed the churches because he doesn't think they threaten him. He doesn't burn books because he's merely a man, not the instrument of an idea. He's evil, but his evil is a pathetic thing."

Hook straightened up. He took off his helmet and the wind pushed at his long hair, tousling it. For the first time since he had begun to speak, he looked at Jones. The corpsman was sneering, crouched, as he was, in the rock's shelter. Hook saw the sneer. He thought Jones was cold.

"Man. It don't cut. It still don't mean you can kill anybody you want. Don't God say, 'Thou shalt not kill?' Ain't that the big Christian word?"

"Ah," said Hook. He nodded. "It's a terrible question. I've wrestled with it—God only knows I have. But there comes a time when the sanctity of one's life, the strict purity becomes self-regarding and sinful. Paul says, 'Respect the spirit of the law, not the letter.' I've thought about this. If, merely to keep my conscience clear, to comfort myself in a display of my own moral perfectness, I permit others to suffer and be killed—then I have killed as surely as I killed in that hut. And I believe in damnation, Jones. In heaven and hell. In eternal punishment and in eternal joy. It may well be that I have damned myself by these acts. I have to accept that. But better to lay down one's soul for another than to sit isolated, preparing for my own sterile and loveless salvation. That is what I believe."

Jones straightened. He stamped his feet. Then he blew on his hands, producing a loud, ugly raspberry—meant as a refutation of all that Hook had said.

"Well, man. You're beyond help. I can see that. It's time I went to bed. This Christian shit makes me sick. My mother was a Christian, brother, and she was an idiot twenty-four hours a day. Only difference between you and her—you're a dangerous idiot."

"As you please."

"As I please," snorted Jones. "Sure, Mr. Cool. Put up with me. Be patient with me. Don't use your rank. Only you can't keep it up. You'll crack soon, and I just hope I'm around for the party."

"I'll send you an invitation."

"Promise me, Sergeant. Promise me." Hook smiled sadly.

"I promise," he said.

WRITTEN THE NEXT MORNING: LETTER (NEVER SENT) FROM CORPSMAN JONES TO HIS FRIEND.

Dear Luke:

I'm in Camaguay now. That's right, in Camaguay. Some stinking Navy foul-up. If I knew how to desert, I would. I don't care what they'd do to me. I've been shot at and I've seen men get killed, and it just isn't right. I don't like it. I don't like it at all. A man shouldn't die like this. They should make old men fight, not people like me. All that college—all that work—they can't kill me now. It wouldn't make any sense.

Man, I must be crazy. Why am I writing to you? What do you care?—huh, Luke boy? Sitting up there on your fat ass, thinking, "Poor Andy." You prick. You fucking cop out. No. I'm not going to send this letter, Luke. If I did you'd be real pissed at me. Because I'm going to tell it like it is, buddy. I'm going to tell you what I really think.

I think you should be here. Not me. That's what I think. You great big fuck—you haven't got a brain in that thick skull of yours and you know it. It's a god-damn crime, me being here while you, a high school drop out like you, can sit safe on your fat behind. You're a nigger Luke, if there ever was one. A discredit to the black race. A stupid step-and-fetch-it, with your big, slobbering lips. Why? Why? Why not you instead of me? You'd probably like it. You're too dumb to be afraid.

I don't feel so good about things, Luke. I'm not the same guy I was. Sure I wasn't much fun to be with before, but now—now nobody better mess with me. When I get back, brother, I'll make you all pay. Uncle Honky and the system and my father and you Luke—especially you. You're all my enemies. I hate you. Oh God, do I hate you. I want

The letter ends here. Jones would no doubt have written more, but the point of his pencil snapped off. He threw the pencil then high and far over / at the highlands of Camaguay.

VI

HOOK STOOD and then stepped quickly away from the radio. The sun had just emerged from the Gulf, now more than a hundred miles behind them. Its level, distinct rays probed at the wooded ridge and the blue-purple flanks of the distant volcanos beyond it. Haze lolled in flat layers that ascended the valley like the steps of a disordered staircase. Hook pressed the side of his hand to his temple. One of the layers, he thought, seemed grayer, more substantial. Smoke . . . Hook stepped reluctantly toward the place where, isolated from the Camaguayans, isolated from the IC's, José Ix had passed the night. The Indian smiled cautiously. Then he understood Hook's face and the smile dissipated. José Ix stood up.

"Is your uncle in the hills with Rodriguez?" José Ix glanced quickly toward the northwest.

"No. I do not think so. What is wrong?"

"A recon flight. Last night it flew over your uncle's village. There was a hut burning and bodies the pilot thought . . . many bodies."

"Aaaah," said José Ix. His face responded very slightly. The eyebrows were raised and inclined, as though in mild astonishment. The nostrils opened out. The dark eyes did not shift, yet their pupils became abruptly depthless, flattened black disks. José Ix shaped two fists, the genesis, it seemed, of some more violent gesture, but the fists only ground their hidden fingers one against the other. "We must go. Quickly, I think."

"Yes. But carefully." He placed his hand on José Ix's shoulder. "We are soldiers. The Riffs are out there. This may be a trap."

111

"Yes," said José Ix. "But quickly. Death is not strange. I have known it in the soft, dark folds of my mother's dress. But the pain—we must go there quickly."

"We will," said Hook. "José . . . of all these people. It is you only I understand."

"Understand?" He formed the word uneasily, in a kind of anguish. "No. We do not understand each other, Sergeant Master Hook. That we can never do. Never. But perhaps we understand the same things. Please. Leave me now. I must think. I must get ready now." When Hook left him, José Ix was standing, fists opened, staring at the ancient, indecipherable writing in his calloused palms.

The patrol moved out and into a morning as beautiful as any of them had ever seen. Swarms of tiny white butterflies cavorted in swirling spirals above the high grass. Freighted already with pollen, clumsy bees bobbed, barely airborne. Dewed spider webs enthreaded the grasses and glistened in the morning light. To their left a chorus of red-headed woodpeckers rattled out robust and percussive polyphony in a stand of pines. Bird life seethed in the sky: tanagers, orioles, a dozen sorts of thrush, two dozen sorts of sparrows, parrots, parakeets, cuckoos, and insubstantial, insect-seeming humming birds. After a mile they paralleled a boiling stream. Fish slapped the water with glossy sides, falling from high surges. The sun had sheared off the haze, but one layer, as expected, had given resistance, leaving still a few curling fragments in the placid air. The smoke, for now they all knew it to be smoke, was yet two hours' upward march away.

Raoul had told them; he had passed from one soldier to another, deriving joy from the impartation. The Camaguayans were perplexed by Raoul's news; they had little capacity to conjur horrors from their own imagination, they were frankly more interested in the bright sunlight and the scuttling, long-tailed lizards, yet they knew that something was expected of them and they were vaguely troubled—was it sympathy, alertness, concern, was it all of these? They could not be certain. And the march was unimpeded, dulling still further their responsiveness. There was no ambush; the flanking parties reported no evidence of an enemy presence; there were no mines or booby traps buried in the path. It was as though the Riffs would allow no mitigation of their imminent dreadful surprise.

And then it was raining. A pride of black, renegade clouds rose up over the ridge. They could see the rain coming; they could hear it coming. It approached slowly like a breeze-blown, hissing veil, and, even as it struck a long expanse of blue appeared, foretelling its end. The path became a spillway; its currents in places covered their boot tops. The Camaguayans were delighted. They laughed and romped, water cascading from their helmet tops: they reminded Hook of the dancing toadstools in *Fantasia*. José Ix, beside him, began to hum a low, dissonant chant, and Lieutenant Storch marched with his head back, his fat tongue protruding. Hook had reported to Storch, playing out the farce of the command; there had been no order; Storch had merely wet his cracking, flat lips. The rain passed. The sun, jealous of the interruption, burned with the first real heat of the day. Sodden uniforms began to steam, as though each man had reached his kindling point. And now the rise on which the village stood could just be seen.

Baxter tried to keep up, but the men in front of him had been balky all morning. He could see the point now, but, where the grass grew hip-high or when they entered an eroded, meandering *barranca*, he was left alone with the four Camaguayans. Baxter was concerned: sufficiently concerned that he now held the M16 in his injured but more dexterous left arm. After the first withering volleys, when the Camaguayans, stunned by the sheer mass of explosive sound, lay prone and useless, the Riffs, he knew, would charge the rear. It was a standard tactic. Unless Hall could make his way back in time, Baxter would have to hold them off alone. He fingered his grenades for a curve ball, for a slider, for the new knuckle ball he had been practicing. Oddly, Baxter had been less worried about himself since the injury: less worried about wounds and death. But he did not want to be left alone. The four Camaguayans were walking arm in arm, supporting themselves in a tableau of helpless intoxication. Baxter prodded each in the kidneys with his rifle butt.

"You want to be dead?" They giggled and nodded enthusiastically. "Probably be a good thing," he said in English. They laughed, for they were fond of him, and one puckered his lips—an amiable mockery of Baxter's sphinctering mouth.

Garbini spat through split lips. His face ached from sun and wind burns and from several infected, pustulent insect bites. The rash on his hands had begun to inch beyond his wrist joints, and he could no longer wear his watch. He had a sore throat; the rain had ruined a full pack of cigarettes. Moreover he, too, expected an attack; he, too, was made uneasy by the Camaguayans' habitual laxness. Death did not concern him in the least, it was too intangible a concept, but Garbini fully expected to be inconvenienced, and that was irritating enough. The men in front of him were in charge of the M30. The very men who had panicked during the sniper's attack. In an ambush they would, he knew, feign wounds, groaning and holding their injured limbs. Garbini would have to do all the work. He would have to be a hero once again. It always happened; someone always exploited his good nature. He kicked a stone: the low missile struck a man ahead in the calf. The man limped but did not dare turn to look behind him.

Falk whistled as, in his imagination, he re-created their dialogue once again. At dawn, while they awaited a confirmation from San Pedro, he and Sergeant Hook had talked. During the last few weeks they had had many such conversations. Though Hook participated willingly, each was initiated and managed by Falk himself. Invariably the dialogue went something like this:

"You think I'm better now, Sergeant? You think I'm improved?"

"You're my best soldier now, Lance."

"I can use a rifle real good now, can't I?"

"Real good."

"My Daddy's gone be surprised. You know, I was all ready

114

to go in there. All ready—I wasn't scared at all. Like you said —what's there t'be scared of?"

"Nothing."

"'Course now, I don't want t'get my face messed up. I wouldn't want that. When I get back to Wickins Falls, I figure I'll wear my IC uniform a bit—for a few days anyway. The girls'll go crazy. Huh? Don't you think?"

"Like picking grapes off the vine."

"I think I've got a pretty good face."

"Wish I had it."

"And I'm more mature. Don't you think I'm a lot more mature?"

"An old man, Lance. An old man."

Hook signaled a halt. The village was no more than a half mile above and to the right of their present position. The Camaguayans sprawled, some in headlong dives, under the shade of a small sapodilla grove, for the morning breezes had faded, and it was extremely hot. The birds had been silenced by the heat, and there was only the torrid sizzle and chirrup of insects, sounding more like the complaint of a great, electric machine than the emanation of natural things. There were no clouds, but the blue of the sky was too brilliant to be seen; the sun left an angry white imprint—a soundless explosion— on the retina. The path meandered upward, a slight depression that crossed steep, terraced fields, gullies, clusters of rock, disappeared from view, and reappeared to cross another, similar expanse of terrain. The rise on which the village stood was clearly visible, but the first huts were still concealed behind its crest.

Hook handed his binoculars to José Ix. The lack of movement above was ominous: ordinarily, he knew, the activities of the village spilled over the rise, toward the small fields below. A long crescent of pine woods that flanked their ascent was portentously dark and expectant. If the Riffs were there, then certainly the patrol's arrival had already been noted. José Ix cried out, a voiced sigh. Hook glanced toward the village. Three black specks rose clumsily into the sky. Carrion birds.

Unable to meet the Indian's eyes, Hook rose hurriedly and signaled his men to their feet. Then he passed among them, talking seriously, checking each man's equipment. The Camaguayans were subdued: Hook's attention, his critical proddings worried them. It seemed now that he was busy preparing a sacrifice and, to a man, they peered at the forest, selecting places where they might safely hide.

Lieutenant Storch did not care about the village: just then he had something else on his mind. Lieutenant Storch couldn't be sure, but—if the report of his senses was accurate—he had gone in his pants again. This had happened occasionally before: not incontinence really, rather a kind of absentmindedness. He attempted to curse, but the dry tissues of his throat supplied merely a harsh croak. His walk became bowlegged in the extreme. It was no good. He'd never make captain, not if they knew he crapped in his pants. But who was to know? Meanwhile, with Hook as his aide, Lieutenant Storch's record became daily more impressive. There was a tacit agreement between them: in exchange for authority, Hook would not claim any credit for his successes. It had worked very well. Storch's hemorrhoids now began to burn, irritated by the freshly released acids. The lieutenant, propelled by angry afterburners, began to waddle very swiftly, past Jones, past Hook, to the point itself. Jones was surprised: he would not have accused Storch of such courage. Hook had great difficulty restraining the lieutenant lest, in headlong flight from his own body, he draw the patrol into a waiting Riff ambush.

Now, as they ascended, a few thatched roofs were visible. Confused by his anguish, José Ix crossed himself once: a furtive, unfamiliar gesture. Hook saw and prayed, remembering the woman of his vision. Heat radiated from the roofs in wriggling waves, as though the village were slowly consuming itself. There were no sounds. Then a small, spotted puppy appeared at the edge of the rise. It sat complacently to watch their approach. After a moment it yawned, tongue furling and unfurling in its mouth. José Ix touched his eyes with thumb and forefinger. To harden them.

"All dead," he whispered. "All dead."

And they were. An overpowering odor of putrescence, half sweet, half suffocating brooded over the village like a wide, hot canopy. Flies wallowed, sizzling, in black blood and dried juices. A dozen vultures rose as the patrol appeared, their wings flapping with the sound of shook dusty blankets. José Ix gasped, but resisted covering his nose—lest he offend the spirits of his dead. Behind him, the Camaguayans halted, hesitated, and, as one, turned their backs on the village. Corpsman Jones was stunned, not recognizing the fetid odor, not comprehending what he saw. Three hairy fruits (some sort of coconut, he thought) lay near the first of the huts. They were of regular size and shape, but the third, Jones saw, was turned at a different angle. It had a nose, ears, a row of tiny teeth, and a tongue dangling, half severed between those teeth. "Heee-ads," he whimpered. "Huu-man hee-ads." Then he swiveled with the first military precision he had shown and began striding down the hill, toward the distant Gulf.

Garbini chuckled. He alone promptly followed Hook and José Ix into the village. There was booty, and Garbini knew his success would depend on his swiftness. The bodies belonging to Jones' three heads were heaped in the village center. These had been girl children; the crevices of their genitalia were grossly enlarged: gaping maroon splits, alive with insects, that joined groin to tiny rib cages. Garbini counted three dozen corpses. To his left, the body of a young woman, one round breast unmutilated, sat, sprawled in contemplation of her fingers, which lay strewn on the ground about her like the petals of a daisy. "What a waste," he said. "What a waste." Garbini stood reverently before her, picking at his teeth.

José's uncle awaited them at the north end of the village street. He hung by his wrists from the branch of a ceiba tree— a tiny man, made yet less substantial by the emptying of his abdominal cavity. His body swayed slightly, turned left-right, as though executing an aborted obeisance. José Ix apologized; then he sliced at the branch with his machete. The body

117

dropped, but Hook caught it by the chest and let it gently down. He signaled toward Sanchez and Storch. They came forward reluctantly, Storch poking at his buttocks, Sanchez with a gas mask held to his face. A few Camaguayans followed. And on the hillside, invisible to those in the village, Corpsman Jones sat with his face buried in the bowl of his stiffened palms.

The hut was dark. Garbini waited impatiently for his eyes to adjust. In time he saw a *metate*, a loom, a heap of maize, the corpse of an ancient woman. There were a few pesos in the rigored fist. To release these he had to smash the knuckles with his rifle butt. The woman wore an amulet around her neck, but it was tin, not silver, and he rejected it with a curse. Then Garbini got down on all fours and began to poke through chicken bones, pig dung and broken pottery for the evidence of recent digging.

"Anything here?" Hook pushed through the low doorway. Hastily Garbini scrambled to his feet.

"Nothing, Sergeant. Nothing. One dead is all."

Hook knelt and examined the body. He touched its broken fingers, but said nothing. Then he crossed himself and began to pray. Garbini stood politely aside, playing with a bunch of dried peppers that dangled from the rafters. He had often seen Hook pray. Once, on the Pacific side, the sergeant had crawled through teeming machine gun fire to pray over a dead Riff private. On the basis of evidence supplied by his own nature, Garbini suspected that all men were at least partly insane. This postulate was apparently confirmed by Hook's actions; and Garbini was as tolerant of them as he was of his own less wholesome aberrations.

"Carry her outside, will you? We're digging a grave to the south."

"Okay, Sergeant."

"Did you get anything?"

"Get, Sergeant?"

"Souvenirs. Anything you might want to show me."

118

"Nothing here, Sergeant. These poor bastards, they don't have nothing at all. It's a shame."

"Yes. A shame."

Hook stepped out of the hut. Six Camaguayans were digging near the crest of the rise. Among them, by far the most urgent shoveler, was Corpsman Jones. A brown torrent of dirt cascaded over his left shoulder. Hook smiled sadly. The hut next to the old woman's had been burned to the ground. For a few moments he wandered through the ashes but uncovered no sign of its owner. Then Hook stared toward the wooded flanks of the hill that overlooked the village. At least there had been no ambush. But one was imminent: the Riffs would attack them before they reached Lake Negro.

"This is bad, Sergeant. I don't rightly like t'see this." Falk pressed a handkerchief to his nose. He pointed at the body of a once-pregnant woman: her womb had been scraped clean and the bloody, unformed fetus now lay beside her head.

"No," said Hook, inarticulate.

"What I don't figure—it's about me." Falk spoke nasally as he pinched his nostrils together. "Back home, if I'da seen something like this, even in a picture show, I'da closed my eyes. Why, I couldn't even bait a hook back home. Now I look at this like—I don't know . . . like they weren't human beings. Is that what they call experience, Sergeant?"

"It is," said Hook angrily. "Experience means you can get used to any kind of evil if you can just live with it long enough. Experience is hateful."

"I guess that's right. But one thing for sure: I couldn't do it. I couldn't. That's what I can't figure—the kind of people that'd do a thing like this."

"They're different." Hook put his hand on Falk's shoulder: Falk welcomed it. "That's why it's so hard to fight them. They're from another age. It's like playing poker with a millionaire. You don't dare to call his bluff. They can risk so much, so easily—things that are precious to us."

"We'll win, won't we, Sergeant? No matter what they say at home?"

119

"Even if we lose," murmured Hook. "Even if we lose."

Hall and Baxter carried bodies. They found bits of blanket and colorful woven shawls—inadequate shrouds that lent a transient dignity to the butchered forms. They worked in silence, patient with each other's hesitation. Flies rose in furious swarms at their approach. Carefully they tried to place the right heads with the right severed necks, the right fingers with the right stump of palm. But these things rolled free in the wide, common grave, thwarting their unacknowledged kindness. Sweat poured from cheeks and nose tips. As they staggered, an unwieldy, stiff shape between them, each would stare, for distraction, at the other's face. Together they made seventeen trips to the grave. By the seventeenth trip they had come to know and respect that other face. And for each that face, as long as they knew one another, would recall the agony of this day and their quiet, shared determination.

The shaman's hut was smaller, set somewhat back from the village, surmounted by a cross, the symbol of the growing maize. Cautiously, Hook bent and entered. He stood, waiting. As his eyes accustomed themselves to the darkness, he gasped, then crouched, then shied away, terrorized by what he saw. "Lord Jesus God . . ." he hissed. During the long moment reality was substanceless. Hook felt at his own throat, and the sinews there reconstituted first his body, then the hut—then the woman's corpse. She was nude to the waist, and her nakedness was of a dread familiarity. Long, thick brown hair; eyes wide and still vivid, unmutilated; palms blossoming out like pale flowers. She lay as though the event of her death had not been resisted. Hook went to his knees, strengthless, reverent. He prayed without coherence. Shyly, he knelt forward and touched the right hand; its texture was remembered. Then quickly, shamed by the temerity of his own eyes, he drew a piece of burlap across her naked breasts. Hook backed, staggered toward the daylight.

The sun smote him viciously. Hook thrust his hand into the mat of his beard, then discovered his mouth and entered it, bruising his fingertips on the edge of his lower teeth. He saw

Garbini and rejected him; saw José Ix, Hall, Baxter—and judged these men to be wanting as well. Falk stood, his helmet off, the sunlight glittering on the many blonds of his hair. Hook walked toward Falk, the earth oddly pliant and uncertain under his feet, but when he was near the young private, he found himself unable to speak.

"Sergeant, I—" Falk blanched. "What is it? What is it? You gonna get sick?"

"No." He touched Falk's bicep, then, interested, began to finger it with intense curiosity. "Lance. In that hut over there. A woman. She's dead." He touched his own cheek. Falk, disconcerted, moved, pressed the fingers of Hook's hand more closely to his arm.

"Yes, Sergeant?"

"I want you to bring her out. Carefully. To that tree over there. Her body . . . It's—keep her covered. Please. Do it yourself. Do it gently."

"Gently? Yes, sure, Sergeant. Gently."

"Give me your trenching tool." Falk did. "By the tree. Behind it. Do it now."

Hook walked toward the tree. It was another ceiba, gnarled and stooped, as if to spread its shade more fully over the ground. Green moss carpeted the earth beneath it. Hook heard his heart thumping, and he was afraid of it. He began to dig urgently, striking at roots and small stones with the edge of his tool. It was tedious labor, but Hook was grateful for it. The implications were terrible and obscure; he did not know if this, her death, were the climax or the anticipation of his visionary experience. A voice had called his name. The Camaguayans, he saw, were gathered at the village center, pointing to the north, talking shrilly, gesticulating.

Twenty-five yards from the last hut, where the path turned slightly left as it meandered upward to the ridge, Hook saw a remarkable sight: an old man coming toward them, seated on a burro, a green umbrella held open above his head. The umbrella and the burro's slow amble created a serene, a holiday air about both man and animal. The oddness of this apparition had affected the Camaguayans. They began to back away as the burro approached, shoving the bodies of comrades in front of them for protection. Lieutenant Sanchez alone held his ground.

The old man was not aware of his commotion. He was naked but for a loincloth, his skeleton precisely articulated. As his body moved, undulating slightly with the burro's gait, the tiny wrinkles in his skin opened out, closed, rippled, became pocked like the surface of a rain-pelted pool. His stare was undistracted; it acknowledged neither the village nor the men grouped within it. And the rigid stick of arm, the arm that held the umbrella, was exactly perpendicular to the line of his shoulders. The burro slowed as it passed the first hut. And then Sanchez moved: he leaped forward, pinioned the animal by its mane, and halted it abruptly.

"Who are you!" Sanchez shouted, made frantic by his own uneasiness. "Who are you! Where do you come from? Answer me!" Sanchez buffeted the burro's neck. Then he brought his face very near the old man's face. This was a tactical error. The face disconcerted Sanchez at once. The eyes were arid, fluidless, and of a smoldering, amber glint. The bald cranium had been completely reforested by some fuzzlike growth, the return of an infantile hair. His nostrils were wide and deep, as though already decomposed to cartilage. The old man drew his lips back; then, without blinking, his eyes rolled upward until only the lower rims of his pupils were visible. "Get down!" Sanchez shrieked, rallying his determination. "Get down!"

The old man seemed to waken. His head nodded, as though in vague affirmation, and for a moment Sanchez hoped he was senile, senseless. Then, with deliberation, the old man switched the umbrella from his right hand to his left. He slapped Sanchez across the mouth. It was a powerful blow, driven through a short arc, and the little man staggered backward. But, even as he fell away, Sanchez was unholstering his guns.

"No!" shouted Hook. He interjected his broad torso between Sanchez and the burro. But the two long muzzles, he saw, were already impotent, sagging in Sanchez' hands, aimed at the earth. Unperturbed, the old man had restored the umbrella to his right hand. Hook turned away from Sanchez and spoke soothingly in the Mayan dialect.

"We are sorry. Terrible things have happened here, and we are not ourselves. It is an evil day." The old man stared at Hook, and his head commenced again the irrelevant nodding. He gnawed at the insides of his mouth now, as though he meant to detach the flesh.

"Aaaah—rrrgh." It was an awkward, expectoral growling. Hook wondered if he were unused to speaking, if his vocal cords had forgotten their discipline.

"You will forgive us then?"

"You," said the old man in sudden animation. "Again."

"Again? Have we met before? I do not remember, old one."

"'Old'?" And then the man cackled, jetting saliva. A Camaguayan, horrified by the sound and the fierceness of this hilarity, slapped his hands across his ears. "'Old'? Who is 'old'? The nut or the tree?"

"I do not understand." But the man merely growled again, as though these few phrases had injured his throat. He struck the burro sharply. The animal moved ahead, and Hook did not obstruct it.

The burro began to trot. The old man's body attained his former rigidity—the umbrella fully hoisted, bobbing slightly as it answered the frightened animal's gait. The Camaguayans began to chatter in a confused simultaneity, and Hook, his brow furrowed, stared intently at the diminishing figure.

"He'll be killed. Going around like that. Doesn't he know there's a war on?"

"He knows," said José Ix. "But I heard the things he said. I heard."

"Yes. And what did it mean? Tell me."

"You know that, Sergeant Master Hook," said the Indian.

"I do not. But it makes me afraid." Hook would have answered, but he saw Falk then and remembered. He glanced toward the tree. His spade was there; only that.

"Lance?"

"Sergeant, what hut did you mean? I been lookin' all over."

"That one. The first one."

"Yeah." Falk grinned, embarrassed. "I was afraid of that. Listen, Sergeant, there ain't nothin' in there. An old piece of burlap, that's all." Hook moved toward him.

"Lance. Don't—" But he saw Falk's seriousness, and, in his eyes, the embryo now of pity. "Are you sure?"

"I'm sure."

"Nothing?"

"Nothing, Sergeant. There isn't room t'hide a baby's body in there."

"Jesus God," Hook cried under his breath. "Please. Not now. Don't drive me mad. Not now."

WRITTEN FIVE DAYS BEFORE: LETTER FROM PRIVATE TOM HALL TO PROFESSOR ALFRED H. HOOPLE, JR.

Dear Professor Hoople:

Well, you didn't write to me after all. Thats OK. It bothered me for a while, but I got everything figured out now. As usual I was real slow on the uptake and you can see now what a lemon Isabel got stuck with. It took a long time, but then I remembered how your wife and you were divorced, and how handsome your pointy beard is, and all the languages they say you can speak, and the big Continental and how strong and hairy your legs looked when you went off to play hand-ball on Saturdays.

Believe me, Professor, I hope you and Isabel are very happy together. I never deserved her. I don't have a college degree or any chance of making the big money. And besides, you're a mature man, a man of the world. She can look up to you and

124

that's good for her and its good for the girls too. I can't tell you how happy I am for both of you. It takes a big load off my mind.

Please don't worry about me. I won't make any trouble. And please don't spend any big money for divorce lawyers. You see, Professor . . Can I call you Al? I'd like that. And anyway I guess we're related now, sort of, so it'd be all right. What I was going to say, dont bother with a divorce. I'm not coming back, Al. I'm going to be killed. I feel it. My time is up and even if the Commies dont get me, you and Isabel wont have to worry. I know how to do it for myself. And I will. It'll be easy. I promise you.

Just a few things I want to tell you. I've got ten shares of Panhandle Pipe Line in my strong box (its in the cellar, in the workshop unless Isabel moved it). I didnt buy at the right time, but you'll probably know what to do with them right away. Also you'll find a savings bank book with three hundred dollars in it and a sapphire ring of my fathers which is pretty nice and which I'd like you to have. All the rest is in Isabel's name anyway.

Well thats all I can think of, Prfessor. I wont write again. I promise you. This is for the best and I only wish I'd got to know you better. But thats all right, you'd have found me pretty much of a drag. And it just couldnt be nicer for Isabel. You've got big money and a deep mind and I guess you know all those European ways to make love which I never could figure out. Take good care of her. Be a good father to the girls.

> *Love,*
> *Tom Hall*

Hook and José Ix disappeared at dusk. Soon after that the patrol, led by Lieutenant Sanchez, set out toward the north. An hour later, when night had fallen, they about-faced and returned to positions prepared that afternoon on the northwest rim of the village. This feint was executed clumsily.

The moon did not rise until ten o'clock, and night maneuvers of any sort terrified the Camaguayans, who, under the best circumstances, did not trust Sanchez' leadership. They grasped each other by the belts as they walked, chattered noisily to support their courage, and were rendered inert and helpless by any unexplained grouping of shadows. Two men, left behind in a gully, fired off their rifles until Baxter returned for them. As a reward for this consideration, they put a bullet through his haversack. When at last the patrol had reached the village, everyone was jumpy and irritable.

Jones was sitting, a blanket swathing his shoulders, on the edge of a shallow foxhole. He was exasperated by the evening's activities and smoked despite an explicit prohibition. Jones did not understand what had just happened: he was uncertain whether they had meant to return or whether their objective had been thwarted by the Camaguayans' incompetence. The absence of Sergeant Hook disturbed him. Jones, too, distrusted Sanchez, who was surly with the IC's and tyrannical with his own countrymen. He shivered. Since the afternoon Jones hadn't felt well; he suspected some sort of jungle fever, and this thought exacerbated his shivering. He had prescribed himself four quite different antibiotics during the day, and now his stomach was upset as well.

Moreover, Jones had cut his fingertip. A thin piece of metal, the side of an old varnish can, had intruded on his shoveling earlier that afternoon. It had been quite solidly buried, and when Jones bent to pull it out, the metal resisted, slashing the plump bulb of his middle finger. It was a fairly deep cut: under ordinary circumstances, with an ordinary corpsman, one or two stitches might have been taken. Jones had gingerly given himself a tetanus booster; he had disinfected and dressed the wound hourly. He loathed it, but he could not bring himself to take needle and thread to his own skin. Clean now, it gaped at him like the curving, open gill of a fish. It seemed to Jones to be the abstract and microcosm of all the dreadful wounds he had seen that day. With this very important difference: it had happened to him. He fingered the neatly sliced edges of the gash. He pushed the edges together until the tiny, grinning mouth was closed. His finger throbbed; the cut gaped again. Jones saw, not merely his own skin, but his inner meat as well: his subcutaneous vital layers. This distressed him, for he recognized the meaning of it: that all he had seen in the village—the dangling organs, the parted, red sinews—all these things his own body could not be exempted from. He fingered the cut once more, saw his own soft mortality, and was bitterly indignant.

A breeze blew through the village, collecting odors and sounds. It carried with it the scent of charred thatch and the puppy's lonely yapping. There were many dead things not buried—dogs, chickens, two large pigs—and Jones angrily brought the blanket to his nose. Then figures began to move, half-crouched, in the light of the newly risen moon. Jones started.

"Who's that?" he hissed.

"Hook. Is that Jones?" The sergeant let himself down and sat next to Jones. He found little room; their thighs were pressed tightly together. "Not much cover here, Andy. You'd better do some more digging."

"I can't. I hurt my hand. Where you been?"

"Around. Don't say you missed me."

"I like t'keep an eye on you, that's all." Jones shivered; his teeth made a clicking noise. "It amuses me."

"The dog," said Hook. He listened to its yapping for a moment. "Wish we could do something."

"Why don't you shoot it?" But Hook ignored the challenge, and, after a moment, Jones cleared his throat tentatively. "Sergeant . . . Ah . . . did you . . . I mean, is anything out there?"

"Yes. I think so."

"What? What's out there?" Hook felt a prompt stiffening in Jones' thigh.

"Relax. No sense worrying. We'll know better tomorrow. Nothing will happen until then."

"But tomorrow—" Hook put his hand gently on the corpsman's bicep.

"Listen. You lived through today, Andy. A lot of people didn't. What more can any man ask?" With a deliberateness that infuriated Jones, Hook then began taking an exhaustive inventory of his own pockets. He counted several small objects, peering closely at his palm. Jones sputtered.

"Well. Go on. Say it."

"Not so loud. Say what?"

"About them people back there. The dead ones. Say it— Say I told you so. Go on."

"Come now." Hook cupped his kneecaps and massaged them with a slow, even rhythm. "You're a big boy, Andy. You have two eyes and a brain. No one needs to rub your nose in it: you can judge the Riffs and their methods for yourself." He paused. "Besides—I'm tired of using dead people as arguments. Some of those Indians were my friends. I lived up here for a year with José Ix when we were first trying to organize the Indians. No offense meant, Andy—but I'd hate to think those poor people died just so I could prove a point to you." His hand moved from his left kneecap and touched Jones' thigh. "Don't worry. I give you my word—they're all right now. Their innocence is triumphant. I wish I could be as sure of my own."

"No. No. No!" A voice materialized in the silvery darkness. The syllables were blurred, as though shouted through a heavy mask, but the anxiety was evident and swiftly aggravated. "No. No. No! Don't take it away! I'm falling in. No!" The voice rose to an ultimate shrillness, and was shattered to a hoarse whisper. It began to mount again. Some trick of the atmosphere made its origins protean. Jones' pupils widened. The voice issued from the left, from beneath them, from the devastated village. "Ohhhh. It's dark. I can't breathe. Help! Help!"

"What is it?" Jones hissed saliva over his chin.

"Hall. He's having dreams. I've got to go."

"Shut up! Shut up!" A new voice, grating and furious. Garbini's voice. And then the dull sound of slapping. "Shut up, you nut! Shut up!"

Hook dislodged Garbini's fingers from Hall's throat, lifted him bodily and, as though with a great shrug, tossed Garbini a full three yards beyond the foxhole. Hall was thrashing about in the dirt: His dread fantasies and the reality of Garbini's throttling hands were now inseparably mingled. Hook found Hall's glasses. Then he straddled the convulsing form, withstood the private's first violent reactions and, by gently massaging the sides of his neck, drew Hall back to consciousness. Hall spat dirt and began to fumble for his glasses. Hook slipped them on. There was silence. Then Hall sobbed once.

"Take a couple of breaths, Tom." Hall complied, but sobbed again at the nadir of each exhalation. Without shame he cradled his head in the bend of Hook's arm.

"When will it stop?" he said.

Hook could not answer. He drew the slender body toward him. Hall was sweating freely; moisture surfaced whenever Hook touched his clothing. Hall began to shiver. Hook was disturbed by his thinness. All the bones were there: the blunt hips, the individual vertebrae, the corrugation of his rib cage. Hall's throat began to work spasmodically; his protuberant Adam's apple bobbed up and down. Hall searched for it, as though the bobbing were painful for him. Hook grasped his hand and stilled it.

"Want a drink?" Hall nodded. Hook unscrewed the cap of Hall's canteen. The private sipped methodically, as if straining out dangerous bits between his tongue and the roof of his mouth.

"My neck hurts. I must have been trying to choke myself." Hall shook his head. "Good God. It's come to that already."

"No," said Hook quickly. "I did it. When I was trying to wake you up."

"Sure. Thanks, Clarence. But it's no good." He sat up. "What a mess. Funny thing is—I was a soldier once, wasn't I?"

"You saved my skin—that time in C-City." Hall sighed.

"It was the greatest day of my life. I was Plastic Man. I was Captain Marvel. But now the hands are gone. I have to watch them." He laughed. "Then I don't know if it's my hands shaking—or my eyes. Or the whole fucking world."

"Listen," said Hook urgently. "It happens to the best of us.

129

You've been down here a long time. The things we saw today, they were—"

"No." Hall smiled. "It isn't that. I'm sorry. I wish it was. The poor, bloody, butchered Indians—I couldn't care less for them and that's the ugly truth, Clarence. I feel sorry for one person—me. That's all I have strength for. I'm rubbed as raw now as a piece of hamburger."

"Isabel?"

"Yes." Hall hissed, letting the air from his lungs gradually. Then he drew out a cigarette and lit it. The match danced and wavered before he could touch it to the cigarette's end. "I don't want to go home. I'd sign up again, but I'm no good for that either now."

"Tell me. You never have."

"How could I?" He puffed savagely. "You've never been married. You've never even touched a woman. And they fall down on their knees and crawl, begging, when you come in the door. How could you understand? How could you know the way I feel—a stupid sap like me?"

"Try."

"Try? You remember that whorehouse in Mexico City?" Hook swallowed noisily. "You were such a good sport. That's what got me. Standing there stark naked, fiddling with your cross, one woman with her fingers in your beard, another, naked, on your shoulders, another trying to pull your left leg off—and the madam standing on a table, screaming in Spanish."

"Kind of pissed on the parade, didn't I?"

"Well, you sure talked me out of a screw."

"And you think you have problems." Hook pulled nervously at his beard. He cleared his throat. "Ah—but about Isabel. Did you get a letter, is that it?"

"No. We don't write."

"Do you think she's . . . I mean—"

"Look, Clarence, I'm going t'do you a big favor. I'm going to spare you my problems. Don't ask me. Please."

"Why not? You've told Garbini, haven't you?"

"Yes. Because he understands. He's got that kind of mind."

Hall crushed out his cigarette. "And because I knew he'd make me suffer for it."

"I don't see that."

"Sergeant." Hall leaned forward. Hook could smell his breath: it had a fetid, unpleasant odor, but Hook did not avert his face. "I've done you some favors. You do me one. Okay?"

"If I can."

"Did you find Riff tonight?"

"I think so. I think they've got the spot picked. Can't be sure, though."

"What's the odds?"

"Oh—" Hook shrugged. "Three to one. About usual."

"Horace tells me you're sending him out—with José and Gutierrez. In a few hours. I want to go with them."

"No." Hall cursed. He grasped Hook by the arm.

"I have to."

"No."

"Clarence, please."

"They're small men. The trail is pretty well overgrown. Besides, I'll need you down here."

"Bullshit. You made it. You're twice my size."

"No."

"You've got to—you owe it to me."

"That's another reason. The answer is no, Tom."

"Why? Why? In God's name, why?"

"Because you're not ready for it. You just think you are."

"Not ready for what?"

"Not ready to die."

"You're wrong. So wrong. My mouth is watering for it. That's how ready I am."

"I know." Hook stood up. "That's what I mean." Hall slumped backward and drew off his glasses.

"God damn. You're a pretty rich diet, Clarence. I sometimes forget you're Jesus Christ on earth. I guess I don't even have the right to die."

"None of us has that right. Except perhaps the innocent. Do you know any of those?"

131

"No."

"Then maybe none of us."

When Hook finally found him, Garbini was lying full length on his right side, his head propped in the palm of his hand. He rolled his dice aimlessly, half mesmerized by the tumbling, luminous dots. Garbini knew that Hook was standing near him, but he feigned ignorance and, to make the pretense more plausible, he began to repeat the senseless order of the numbers half-aloud: "six, six, twelve, eight, seven, five, eight, three, seven, seven, seven—"

"Joe."

"Six, four, nine—"

"Joe."

"Yeah. Who is it?"

"Joe. I don't want you to do that again—ever."

"Oh. It's Sergeant Hook. Sit down." Garbini smiled. "Want to roll some crap?"

"Did you hear me?"

"Sure. Sure I did." Garbini sat up; he began to speak with a threatening nasality. "Sure I did. But he's a crazy man—you know that, don't you? Them dreams of his get on my wick. They make me nervous, and when I get nervous, Sergeant— well, you know how it is."

"Don't do it again." Garbini spat explosively.

"You know what's wrong with him? Do you, Sergeant?"

"No. And I don't want to. It's his business."

"But you should." Garbini stood. His chin touched the fringes of Hook's beard. "After all—he could fuck up some day. He could get us all killed. It's your duty. Hall's got this idea, see— he's afraid he'll fall into his wife's big, warm hole. Fall in and never come up again. He thinks it has teeth." Garbini laughed nastily.

"That's enough."

"No. It ain't enough. Not by a long shot." He grabbed the front of Hook's uniform; the gesture was nearly insubordinate. Hook quickly undid the grip of Garbini's fingers. "When we

132

first got here, he showed me her picture. In a bikini, yet. I didn't ask him to. He did it to make me burn. God, what a body that woman has; if she was my wife, I'd screw her 'til her eyes fell out. But that skinny creep, he can't cut the mustard." Garbini ground his teeth together.

"I forgot," said Hook sympathetically. "You've got your own problems, haven't you, Joe?"

"Yeah—yeah, I do. That's right, pretty boy."

"Shut up, Joe."

"Aw, gee—that's it. See what he's done? He's got us mad. You and me. He's a menace, Sergeant, that's what he is. I shouldn't be mad at you. This is crazy." Garbini laughed. "Crazy. Crazy. You're my friend. You're gonna take care of me—right, Sergeant?"

"Right, Joe."

"You're gonna see I get home O.K. You're gonna see nobody hurts my face. Promise?"

"Promise."

"Yeah. Yeah. You're a good man, Sergeant Hook. Look— I'm sorry I blew up. I really am. Shake on it, huh?" Hook met and grasped the hard, scale-covered hand.

"Okay, Joe," he said. "Get some sleep."

Falk slept with two fingers in the corner of his mouth. Hook watched him for several moments. Now and then the lips would curl, and Falk would nibble gently at his fingertips. His large frame was bowed in a fetal pose, kneecaps and elbows touching. Hook knelt and drew a blanket over Falk's shoulders. The private smiled, his eyelids fluttered; he sighed as though with pleasure. Hook remembered then what he had said to Hall about innocence. Hook prayed. He assumed now, from what he had seen in the shaman's hut, that he would die in the next day's conflict, and his eagerness, the utter absence of fear, had begun to trouble him.

". . . It comes. Let me meet it with patience only, not with lusting. I have sinned and my repentance, without grace, is not sufficient. Let me fear, for no man dares meet death with

133

such assurance—it is a sin in pride. Free me from a martyr's greed. Save me in spite of my yearning. Annihilate the self in me. Let me pass knowing neither regret nor relief. Let me merely pass. Teach me to die while I yet live—"

Hook started. The breeze had circled the camp. Now it drifted down in soft volleys from the northwest, and it carried with it a single, incongruous noise. A quiet snap-snap, sounding there no louder than the cracking of a wooden match between thumb and finger. Hook rose and picked up Falk's M16. Seventy yards beyond the camp's perimeter, where a descending ramp of knee-high grasses ended, he saw a small clump of sapodillas outlined in the moonlight. A squared silhouette, resembling the bulky frame of a ferry boat plowing through the grassy highlands. Hook hesitated. Then, as was his peculiar custom, he held his breath, flexed his knees, and brought his shoulders almost to his ear lobes. He waited patiently. Three minutes. Seven minutes. The breeze combed the sapodillas once again, agitating the branches, and then, seconds later, it touched Hook's outer ears. One man, he thought. Two at most.

Hook let himself down on his belly. Then he commenced the tedious, painful crawl: knee, elbow, knee, elbow, knee, elbow. The wind, which had betrayed his antagonist, now camouflaged his own approach. It made wakes in the high grass, disguising his straighter, more purposeful wake. Stones bruised the sensitive domes of knee and elbow. Often he would pause, await a fresh gust, and then crawl forward a few feet. It took him nearly a quarter hour to cross the seventy yards to the fringes of the grove.

At the base of the first tree he waited. An owl began to hoot: Hook bit his lower lip. There was a throatiness at the end of the long, low, whistling moan. A human throatiness. Hook stared into the shadowy grove. Sweat, the physical result of his intense concentration, burned at the corners of his eyes. He rose to one knee and braced Falk's M16 against the tree's rough bark. He swallowed. Then he, too, imitated the sad, long hooting. Something moved in front of him and to his right. He hooted again. A figure rose from the undergrowth; it began to walk toward him. Hook aimed at the oncoming knees. The figure stooped as it approached, peering left–right, and some quality of its stride—the hunched shoulders, perhaps; perhaps the agile apelike swing of the arms—caused Hook to hesitate. He lowered his rifle.

"Halt!" bellowed Hook. The figure halted; indeed, it became immobilized with shock. The helmet popped off and bounced, clunking; hands pounded at chest with heavy spasms; a squeaky, feminine "Eeeeee-uh" escaped through the teeth. Then the figure dropped head first into the undergrowth.

"Don't shoot me! Don't shoot meeeeee!" Hook stepped away from the tree.

"Get up."

"Sergeant Hook? Is that you?" Huddled, hands over cranium, knees in its stomach pit, the small form began to whimper. "It's me, Raoul. Raoul. It's me. Put your gun down. It's me, Raoul."

"Get up." Hook stood over him. He heard Raoul's hysterical giggling. The Camaguayan sergeant stood uncertainly, saw that Hook's M16 was still leveled at his chest, wobbled, and sat abruptly on the ground.

"Get up."

"Yes. Yes." Raoul stood again. "You scared me, Sergeant Hook. You scared me."

"What were you doing, Raoul?"

"I come to piss, Sergeant. That is all."

"We dug a trench for that, Raoul." Hook began to rummage carefully through the smaller man's pockets. He found a penknife, a bottle of pills, two pairs of socks, a fat wad of pornographic pictures, some scraps of paper, a pencil stub, and an empty C-ration can. He tossed the can aside.

"You see. Nothing. I come to piss myself. That is all. Hey! Hey! Don't do that!" Urgently, Hook drove his fingers deep into the folds of Raoul's groin. With indignation the little man pushed his hand away.

135

"Pretty dry there," said Hook. "You didn't piss, Raoul."

"I was going to, but then you scared me. Why do you do that? Why do you scare me?"

"Scare? I almost killed you," said Hook. "You don't belong out here."

"No?" Raoul had recovered his composure, and now he became angry. "But I am a sergeant, too. You have no right to do this. No right. I will report this to Colonel Smith."

"I see."

"We must trust each other. We are allies." Raoul bent and retrieved his helmet. "Why are you so big a man? Why must everyone obey you? I am a sergeant, too, but no one listens to me. It is not fair. I am as good as you are. You Americans, you think you are all gods."

"Sure, Raoul."

"Well—I am a good guy. I will forget this, Sergeant Hook." He smiled. "So. We understand now. Let us go back." Raoul took a step toward the camp, but, as he moved, the muzzle of Hook's rifle shot upward to catch him in the soft parts of the throat. Raoul gasped. "Wha-wha," he stammered.

"Not so fast." Hook drove Raoul backward, his rifle jammed horizontally across the compact, muscular chest. "Don't strain your bladder, Raoul. Not because of me. Go ahead."

"What—what do you mean?"

"You came to piss—so piss."

"Here? In front of you? No. I could not."

"Shy? But back in C-City, they tell me that Sergeant Raoul will do anything. And in front of cameras."

"I cannot." Hook lowered the M16. Then he brought the butt down swiftly, striking, scraping the length of Raoul's shin. The Camaguayan yelped. He tried to nurse his smarting shin, but Hook would not let him bend.

"Piss, damn it."

"No. My leg-oh! Don't hit me. I will tell Colonel Smith. No!" Hook raised the M16. Raoul's fingers hurried to his fly.

For a moment the zipper's nub eluded his fumbling. The wind blew against his pants leg and the injured shin burned, paralyzing the critical nerves of his limb. Raoul nearly fell, but at last, cursing, whimpering, he managed to undo the fly. Raoul plucked out his member and held it tentatively between fingers of both hands. "I cannot. I cannot," he muttered. Then he laughed. Hook watched, unmoved. Raoul closed his eyes tightly and began to concentrate on the secret mechanisms of his bladder. There was a spurting. A tiny jet erupted, faded almost as it appeared, and dribbled, breeze-blown, over Raoul's boot. The Camaguayan whimpered and covered his face with his hands.

"I am nervous," he said.

"Let's go, Raoul." Hook jabbed him in the kidney. "I've made a mistake. I haven't paid you enough attention. We'll sleep together, and tomorrow we'll walk together. We'll get to know each other very well." Raoul stumbled forward, his private parts still bared.

"I will tell Colonel Smith. When we get back, then I will tell him."

"Raoul," said Hook mildly, "I'm not sure you will get back."

WRITTEN ONE WEEK BEFORE: LETTER FROM PRIVATE LANCELOT FALK TO HIS FATHER

Dear Daddy:

I got your letter just this morning. It made me very sad. Clay sure was a great guy and we all loved him, and if I could have died instead of him—I would have, sure enough. That's the gospel truth, Daddy. I mean it, every word.

But you shouldn't keep on thinking about it the way you do. I mean, you can't forget Clay—nobody could and I wouldn't want you to try. Still it isn't right being so sad all the time, not smiling, not sleeping, not eating, making Mom so worried. Mom's not strong like you and she might take one of her fits again, you know what the doctor said. Daddy, I hope you don't get mad at me—I mean, my writing like this. I never did talk back to you, the way some guys do, and I'm not talking back now. What I mean is, Clay was lots of fun. He was always happy, playing the guitar or drag racing or dancing with the girls. It seems to me it's wrong you mourning so much. Clay wouldn't want you to. I know that. I just know it.

And anyway, Daddy, I been thinking things over. I guess being down here in Camaguay kind of helped it along. What I mean is, we all have to die. That sounds funny—everybody knows that. But now I figure there's a difference between knowing and, well, knowing. I wish I was really smart so I could explain it right to you. What I'm trying to say is, we're not all going to die at nineteen the way Clay did, but we're none of us going to live a million years neither. You and me and Mom and Mr. Hawley and the President. All of us, we've got to die. And it seems to me, if it's going to happen to everyone, I mean—it can't be so bad then, can it? I've seen kids die down here, kids of ten and eleven, babies even, and some of them died real terrible. I don't mean to compare no foreign boy to Clay, that wouldn't be right, but, Daddy, they died. They died.

I guess I can't explain it. But I want to, Daddy. So much. It seems real important somehow. Times are, I get a real sad feeling, and I know I'm going to die, too. Soon. Maybe right here, right now. And you know, it's not too bad. I'm not scared of it or angry about it. I figure I'll just miss things like you and Mom and home. But, whatever happens, I don't want you to mourn me. I don't want that. That worries me more than anything else. I had a good time, and a real easy life. I see things down here and I know how lucky I was. You and Mom were real swell to me, and it just doesn't seem right to be sad. There's got to be a reason for it, Daddy. I don't know what it is, but there has to be. And its right. Its right. I know that now for sure.

     Love,
       Your son, Lance.
P.S. You tell Mom to send me some more of those nice wool socks.

VII

IT WAS AN INCONSEQUENTIAL VALLEY, shaped like a taut, slung hammock, one of the rare depressions in their long, upward progress. The patrol mounted a small ridge and marched slowly down into it.

"We are here, Lieutenant. Keep walking, don't slow down." Hook cupped his hand around Sanchez' shoulder, quite enveloping it, and drew the slight, tense body in toward his hip. "Remember. We don't know. We must let them surprise us." Sanchez made no reply, nor did he struggle against the enforced intimacy of their bodies. He stared ahead, at the valley, at its thickly wooded fringes, and the plastic sphere that was his strong desire to kill rose up to obstruct the narrow passages of his throat.

The valley resembled some now disused golf fairway. On the left the forest ascended gently to a height of perhaps three hundred feet, and the fairway, with its shin-high, yellowing grass, doglegged to the right, away from this high ground. On the other, lower edge the cover was ragged in places; it overlooked the open field from a height of no more than a dozen feet. And, at the center, there was a sand trap: an elliptical bowl, the pool of a dry stream bed, and the pivot of Hook's planned defense. Small birds flopped about in it, tossing up spurts of reddish sand, leaping down, wings spread, from the foot-high rims of the bowl. It was another lovely morning. Hook sensed acutely and with gladness his own body's need to live.

"Let us not be eager. We are going for a walk. It is a nice, sunshiny day. There is no enemy." Sanchez nodded reluctantly. "Do you remember what I told you?" Sanchez nodded again. Behind them a Camaguayan shouted laughter at the sun. Hook had told only the IC's; the Camaguayans' innocence was part of their cover. The file was drawn out, bunched at irregular intervals. Hook depended on the Riff officers' complacency and their greed for bodies. Ahead, at point with Falk, Sergeant Raoul slouched forward uneasily. He glanced back at Hook for the fifth time since they had entered the valley. And now the men at point were only a hundred yards from the Riff kill zone.

"Again," said Sanchez abruptly. "Tell me again."

"All right." Hook inhaled, wondering then if his men would have any chance at all. Sanchez was a good soldier, but he lacked imagination, and even the best of the Camaguayans, Hook knew, were unable to relate tactics to the more brutal and straightforward aspects of battle. "There is the sand pit. You remember that? They will attack just beyond it. At least I hope they will." Hook gnawed thoughtfully at his beard. "You and Raoul and Falk and the two men on the right—you will take the point. You will walk through the sand, walk slowly, as if there is no hurry. They will not fire at you. The Riffs want to hit us in the middle. But the rest of us, we will not follow. I will stop the men when we reach the sand, as if I am lining them up. And while we are grouping, you will still walk. The Riffs will wait. I'm sure of it. They want to kill us all. Then I will yell, 'Go!' When you hear me yell, you and your men will run, head down, run hard. Someone will shoot. They are not so well trained as that. But you will be by the big tree before they do, outside the zone. We will still be in the pit. And their machine guns will be aimed at empty grass. Between us."

"Yes," said Sanchez. "I see this. Last night I did not."

"We are counting on you, Lieutenant. Your men will have the most important part. The Riffs will fire from both sides and then I will shoot the purple flare, and Baxter and Gutierrez and José Ix will come down from the hill, throwing their grenades and screaming like hell. The Riffs on the left, they will think they are pinned between two forces."

"If they are on the hill. If. I do not trust the Indian." Hook grunted noncommittally. Two hawks soared above, flat wing-tips paralleled.

"Well. We must hope. But that is your moment. The Riffs on the left will be stunned and we will pin them down from the pit. Then—then you must charge the machine gun on the right. I think there will be few men there. The cover is poor. Ten men maybe with the machine gun. The rest will be on the hill. Falk has the grenade gun. It will help you. But you must move quickly."

"It is difficult," said Sanchez.

"Yes. But it is the only way. When you have engaged the machine gun on the right—then I will move with my men against the hill. We will charge from the pit. Our timing must be perfect. If it is not, then they will shoot us down in the back."

"My men are not good at this," said Sanchez skeptically.

"I trust your men." Hook removed his hand from Sanchez' shoulder. The sand pit was now only fifty yards ahead. "If I am killed, then you are the man in charge."

"I am the man in charge now."

"Yes," said Hook. "And you are brave. I know that. Take my rifle." Sanchez shook his head. "Yes. You must. The little guns are no good here. I will drop back now. Remember. Show nothing. We are on a picnic. Good shooting, Lieutenant. And keep your eyes always on Sergeant Raoul. Always."

Hook slowed his pace and then halted. Garbini passed with the M30 cradled against his hip. Garbini bared his teeth in a grin of stark malevolence; he began walking toward his designated position at the far edge of the sand trap. Hook removed his helmet. He tilted his head lazily toward the sun, displaying the bulk of his dark beard. This show, he hoped, would gain his men an added few moments; the Riffs would not fire until the chief prize, Hook himself, was securely within their kill zone. He began to shout cheerfully. He gesticulated in a broad, theatrical manner, swinging his helmet high above his head. Hall and his group of five Camaguayans passed. An agitated tic had appeared under Hall's left eye, and yet Hook thought he detected a look of joyous excitement. Flocks of swallows buzzed the fairway in close and complex formation. Against his will, Hook glanced at the shadowed eaves of the forest, but they were muted, discrete.

Sanchez and his men were proceeding through the sand. Jones passed. The red cross on his helmet had been carefully and skillfully obliterated. Jones was humming, but the sound emerged as a poorly organized series of moans. Garbini, moving perhaps too swiftly, too purposefully, had reached the far end of the bowl. He slouched in a pose of easy aggressiveness, and when a Camaguayan tried to pass, Garbini blocked his way with the M30's ugly barrel. One by one the Camaguayans began to collect in the small depression. They milled about, perfect in their innocence. And now Sanchez and his men were fifteen yards beyond them.

They're getting anxious now, Hook thought. They want to shoot, the ones who've got rifles for the first time. Provided they haven't planned this for some other place. Provided they haven't captured Horace and José and Gutierrez. Those things provided—I am now the cynosure of all their gunsights. Hook grinned. He bent down and plucked a few grass blades, imagining a dozen rifle barrels being depressed as his torso inclined forward. "Help these," he murmured. "As for me—not as I will but as Thou wilt." Hook straightened and put the leaves of grass in his mouth. Sanchez's party had increased its lead to thirty yards. Hook put his helmet on. "Show's over," he said.

Hook began to gather stragglers. The pit, only twenty yards across, was crowded now; the Riff officers could wait no longer —despite the unsatisfactory angle they would open fire; probably, Hook thought, they had already sent riflemen to the left. Now, the last man in the file, fat Armando, strolled up, picking his nose delicately, a surgeon at work. He smiled at Hook, and caressed his belly with the deep affection of a pregnant woman. Hook returned the smile. Then he grasped Armando by both shoulders and booted him sprawling into the pit.

"Go!" he shouted.

Sanchez' men began to run. For three seconds the forests were silent, unprovoked by their motion. Hook, Hall, and Jones began throwing dazed Camaguayans to the ground. These protested awkwardly, struggled upward, kicking sand. Then, from the left flank, a single shot snapped at them, and its report echoed through the valley.

"Fire! Fire! Fire!" shouted Hook. He alone remained erect, tempting the Riff machine gunners. And then it came. Amid a deafening percussive roar, a pair of deadly machine gun streams leaped toward the sand trap, shredding the grass, one from the left flank, one from the right. Hook dove. Garbini replied with his M30 and, for a moment, the torrent from the machine gun on the left rose, sputtered, and died. Garbini swung around, and, half standing, fired at the right flank.

There was little cover in the sand trap. Hook knew they would have to counterattack at once. The Riff ambush was imperfect: the sand trap was not enfiladed; rather, it stood at the apex of an angry cone of fire. Both enemy concentrations were farther ahead, but already there was small arms fire from the left flank directly opposite. The Camaguayans were reacting poorly. Hook doubted if half would follow him. Jones fired his pistol ineffectually, while Hall crawled through the pit, leaping, pummeling, exhorting the Camaguayans to return fire.

"Ready?" shouted Hook. Garbini replaced the barrel of his M30 and nodded, saliva streaming over his chin. Hook knelt, tried to find Sanchez' position, and was driven to his chest by a close burst from the right. He flipped over on his back, raised the flare gun, and fired at the belly of the blue, cloud-strewn sky.

The whoosh-pop of the flare gun was subsumed by a strident, hammering clatter. Hook rolled on his side, stared at the hill. The edges of the sand trap were being tattered by the

143

Riff fire. Explosions of red grit blinded them, stung the skin of their faces. Now about half of the Camaguayans were returning a sporadic fire. One man was weeping, his face swathed in a yellow handkerchief. While firing his M16, Hall began to hit him savagely about the head, but the Camaguayan merely rose up, into the beating, as if seeking unconsciousness there. At the north end of the pit Garbini had been forced down by the concentrated fire of the two Riff machine gunners. Hook crawled toward him, spitting sand. A stone, driven by a bullet at a glancing angle, clunked heavily against his helmet.

"Where the hell's Baxter?" shouted Garbini.

"Get ready," said Hook. "Get ready. We'll have to move out alone."

"Oh shit! Shit! Shit!" groaned Garbini in an acid monotone, but, as he cursed, he readied the clumsy machine gun.

"Look!" yelled Hall.

Explosions, muted by the deafening torrent of sound, began to appear on the hill slope. They advanced downward in three areas: one thrust directly opposite, two curving in, pincering the Riff machine gun. The fire from the left began to falter. "Ready! Ready! Ready!" shouted Hook. And then Sanchez began to move forward. Falk engaged the Riff M30 with his grenade gun. The Riff gunner hesitated and then pivoted around to pin down Sanchez' tiny, charging squad. For a brief moment the sand trap was freed from the vicious, shattering machine gun fire.

"Go! Go! Go!" shouted Hook.

He rose up grasping two Camaguayans by their belts as he did so, and then he began to charge across the open field, carrying the two reluctant soldiers as he might two duffle bags. Small arms fire pinged and whizzed, but the farther they ran toward the hill, the farther they were beyond the ultimate range of the still silent machine gun. It was uphill; the friction of the grass impeded their legs; sweat formed on their foreheads—the sweat of exertion and the sweat of dread commingled. Fifty yards they ran into the anonymous, erratic

144

fire. Hook's Camaguayans raced forward on their own now, shrilling angry curses. Garbini was to the right and behind, hampered by the heavy gun. And Private Hall led the charge: he ran with huge strides, arms high, chest bared, the M16 unfired in his hand. But Sanchez, behind them, had failed to destroy the other machine gun. It turned now and clattered at their retreating backs. Angry divots were dug by bullets on either side of Hook. Then the Camaguayan on Hook's left was pierced through the upper spinal cord. His body lost co-ordination. It crumpled, and the lower half vaulted grotesquely over the fallen torso.

As he ran, Hook smelled the hot, rich odor of the trampled grasses. Smelled and wondered at the beauty of their scent. He had time to think, for the working of his mind was accelerated, and the first growths of the hill came only slowly toward him. Butterflies, unaffected by this human skirmish, continued to flutter over thistle tops, scampering like memories of a better time near the running soldiers' faces. It seemed to Hook that their charge would never end, that his feet were locked in a gold-green treadmill. He began to pant and knew the other men would be slowing down. Another fifteen yards, another ten, shortening the range of the Riff riflemen. He spotted one now: a face, an arm, a muzzle. The muzzle was discharged. The face disappeared in panic. "Good God," he thought. "They're retreating. They're retreating." Hook let out a long, instinctive whoop of triumph.

Hall reached the woods first. He stood at the edge, fist upraised, refusing to take cover. A breeze blew; branches above him shook as if in scorn of his challenge. The forest was nearly silent now. Hook on Hall's right plunged through the tall grass at the forest's edge, driving forward into the thick undergrowth. He heard Garbini's M30, but it seemed to have no opposition, seemed to be firing in annoyance. Across the valley, Sanchez and the other element of the Riff ambush were still engaged, but he could no longer hear the enemy machine gun. Glancing back, Hook saw eight men lying prone—dead or malingering—in the sand trap. He subtracted quickly: no more than ten men could have made the charge with him. Too few, and now they were badly separated. Hook knelt and listened.

He decided to move up the incline a few yards and then turn to his right. If he proceeded swiftly, he could perhaps flank what was left of the Riff machine gun position. Hook rose to a half crouch. The lower branches of the thick tree cover made walking difficult, and the dry, twig-strewn ground reported his progress at each step. Firing from across the valley had ceased now. The Riffs, true to their tactics, were pulling back. Hook continued to move forward and then dashed, half slithered blindly twenty yards to his right.

Jones was there—a tiny Riff draped across his shoulders like some playful, piggybacked child. The Riff's left arm was hooked around Jones' throat. Hook watched, horrified, as the knife was raised and plunged over Jones' shoulder, into the corpsman's chest. Jones shrieked and tumbled forward, throwing the small body from his back. Then he rolled over, helpless, clutching at his chest. Dazed, the Riff dove forward, groped for the fallen knife and then brought it, in both hands, high over Jones' convulsing back. But Hook had crossed the clearing by then. He caught the little man by his hair and lifted him a full two feet off the ground. Then, with nice precision, he grasped the man under the jaws and snapped the small, dark head backward. The neck broke with an audible crack. Hook tossed the dying Riff aside.

"Help! Ohhhh-aaah! Help me! Ohh!" Jones shrieked and whimpered in turn with the crippled bellows of his breath. His maroon-brown skin became oddly grayed. Blood leaked from between clenching fingers; Jones saw his blood, squealed in terror, and began to kick the earth with his heels like some peevish child. Sergeant Hook dragged him into the cover of a tall patch of ferns. With difficulty he wrenched the rigid fingers away. Then he tore open Jones' shirt front, while the corpsman screamed—hearing in the ripped cloth the ruin of his own vital tissues. "I'm bleeding. Oh, God. It hurts. I'm bleeding. Get me out of here. Hook—help me, Hook."

146

"I'm trying, Andy. Relax. Relax."

Jones' agony was genuine. Hook feared the onset of shock. The corpsman's eyes had shrunk, and they flickered wildly now, seeming unable to focus. Cautiously Hook examined the bubbling wound. The Riff's knife had missed: there was only a superficial slit, no more than an inch in length. The blade had glanced off the hard corrugations of a grenade; it had struck a rib just below the left nipple. The bone was painfully bruised, perhaps fractured, but that was all. Quickly Hook opened Jones' kit and took out packing and antiseptic.

"Andy. Hold this." Jones' fingers fumbled awkwardly, clutched at the gauze.

"Hook. I don't want to die. Get me out of here. You've got to. Get me out of here. Get—" Hook cut off the rising voice; he forced his palm over Jones' open mouth.

"Listen to me. You're all right. He missed—you've had deeper cuts shaving, believe me. He hit the rib. It hurts, but that's all. Now shut up—Riffs're all over the place." Jones gagged against the pressure, and a flood of saliva rushed between Hook's knuckles.

"Don't lie to me."

"I'm not lying. Now listen, I've got to get out of here." Jones shook his head vigorously. "I've got to—there's a battle on somewhere. Just lie low and shut up. Don't draw attention to yourself. You've got yourself a Purple Heart, that's all."

Hook stood. He watched as Jones crawled, gasping, farther into the jungle of ferns. The Riff was dead, having touched feebly at his broken neck with the last reflexive motions of his hand. Another boy—no more than eighteen. The Riff wore gray track shorts and sneakers; his thin shirt said *"Tigres"* on it in fading letters. Hook knelt, put his fingers to the forehead, and prayed. Jones' .45 lay nearby. Hook checked it, found the magazine empty. He laughed once: Hook had realized then, for the first time, that he carried no weapon at all, that he had made the charge with only a knife and two grenades. He was astonished by this. "You see. You see," he said. "I'm ready now."

He slipped the .45 under his belt and began, once again, to move toward the Riff machine gun.

He found Garbini lying with Gutierrez behind the huge, fallen trunk of a mahogany tree. Garbini was smoking a cigarette while Gutierrez wrapped a filthy Ace bandage around his ankle. Ants crawled in full regiments up and down the length of the log, some with pieces of foliage debris borne like pennants on what appeared to be their shoulders. Hook knelt and surveyed the position. There was a clearing almost thirty yards square beyond the trunk. Nothing moved. In the limpid silence Hook heard only the faint, crackling whirr of the busy ants.

"Damn ants," growled Garbini cheerfully. "Worse than the damn Riffs."

"Did you get any?"

"Riffs or ants?"

"Riffs."

"Oh, sure. There's my kill." Garbini pointed across the log, at a patch of gorse only ten yards beyond it. A large green bird lay, its body shredded. Gorgeous gold-green-scarlet tail feathers, a yard in length, were scattered over the ground.

"A quetzal," said Hook. "Is that all?"

"All," said Garbini. "All? That's an officer, ain't it? A colonel at least." A shrill voice was heard.

"Green Bay Packers!"

"Detroit Lions!" yelled Garbini. "Washington Redskins!"

"Baltimore Colts!" answered the voice.

"Wrong division!" shouted Garbini. He squeezed off a short burst on the M30. "I'll get you, you dirty Riff."

"Cut it out, Joe. Cut it out. I'm tired."

"Come ahead, Horace," said Hook.

Baxter stumbled into the clearing. His eyes were puffed and bloodshot. He tottered as he came forward. José Ix, behind him, seemed unaffected by their long night's watch. He nodded at Hook. Gutierrez waved his four-fingered hand: Gutierrez had made his attack on the Riff right flank and hadn't seen the other two for five hours.

"Any signs, Horace?" Baxter shook his head.

"They got away. Ran like hell. There was blood where the machine gun was. And heel marks like they dragged off a body. Least that what José says. Right, José?" But the Indian hadn't heard Baxter. He was staring, aghast, at the patch of gorse.

"Who did that?" he said in a querulous voice. "Who— Who did that?"

"José—" said Hook.

"What's he mean? The parrot? I killed it, with my little M30. So what?" Garbini grinned; then he frowned. José Ix crossed himself twice: once for each of his religions.

"It's bad. Bad."

"José," said Hook gently. "You and Baxter go across—see if Sanchez needs help. José? Did you hear me?"

"It's bad. It's bad." The nostrils of his large, bent nose flared in an instinctive dread. He seemed eager to leave the place. José Ix looked once at Garbini, then he spat: not at Garbini, but rather as though he were creating a barrier between himself and the act. He turned then and trotted to the left, toward the open valley.

"What the hell was that?" said Garbini.

"The quetzal is sacred to the Mayan Indians," said Hook. "It is forbidden to kill one."

"That fat parrot? Oh, great!" Garbini raised both palms in a gesture of exasperation. "You mean I can't keep the feathers?"

"I wouldn't. They're pretty serious about it here."

"Jeesus. What a life I lead." Garbini wanted to protest further, but Hook turned to Gutierrez.

"You did good work, Corporal. How do you feel?"

"Hokay. Pree-good, you know. We knock them to hell, yes?" Hook grinned.

"Looks like it. Sure does." He removed his helmet.

"Shit," said Garbini. "And now it's prayer time."

Falk was dying. His thighs were splayed and they twitched convulsively. Only a primitive awareness survived in his mind.

149

The lower segment of his body did not now pertain to him: it was an enemy, jarring his fragile torso. The pain originated in his groin, was driven slowly upward through the kidneys with the force and penetration of hard metal skewers. In his chest the lungs struggled fitfully to make breath, but already he was strangling in the weight of his shattered body. He pressed his face to the earth and shrieked through his nose, blowing out thin red bubbles of blood.

"He is a hero," gasped Sanchez, panting as he tried to maintain Hook's pace. "A hero. The grenade was this close to my body."

Raoul stood as they approached. He had been squatting close to Falk's body, loathe to comfort him, palms pressed across his ears. Hook knelt. Falk's hands clasped and unclasped. They throttled thin blades of grass, uprooting them one after the other in a meaningless rhythm. The shrieking that echoed in his ears was heard by Hook as muffled whimpers. When the sergeant touched Falk's shoulder a mass of reflexes knotted, drawing his head, neck, and chest into a dreadful spasm.

"Lance. Can you hear me? How is it?"

"Uuuuuh." Falk remembered Sergeant Hook. He tried to speak, but his jaws would not open. With difficulty he raised his head up. He was terrified by what he saw: the valley's dissolution; the greens and browns and yellows amorphous, pulsing with the fervid rush of blood behind his eyes. And, when he opened his mouth to speak, shredded bits of his lower lip fell out, suspended in bloody saliva. He understood the ruin of his body. And he began to sob.

Hook injected morphine into Falk's upper arm. The shape of his body was outlined on the grass by an aura of spattered blood, except for one circle, a pristine green-yellow, where his helmet had lain. Hook sprawled flat and brought his mouth close to Falk's ear.

"Lance. Can we turn you over? Could you stand that?"

"No." Falk gurgled, speaking as from liquid depths. He found Hook's hand and scratched it with his nails. "I—"

"What is it?"

"Uuugh—"

"Lance. You've done a great thing. I'm proud of you." Falk's throat began to emit a thin whistle. He scratched again at Hook's hand. The sergeant leaned close, until his ear touched Falk's cheek.

"I didn't want . . . to." Falk inhaled carefully. "It was . . . in the books I read . . ." He inhaled again. "It hurts . . . so bad . . . I'm crying . . ." He inhaled again. "A reflex . . . That's all . . . The books about medals . . . I didn't want to. It was like my daydreams. It wasn't real."

"It was a great thing Lance, no matter what. No matter why."

"But . . ." He scratched desperately at the back of Hook's left hand. "I didn't want to do it." He inhaled, then spoke almost shrilly. "I didn't want to do it."

"Take it easy. Please."

"Am . . . I dying?" Hook clenched his fists.

"I think so." Falk groaned. His lips moved, forming a single word. He expelled it with a thick, purpling clot of blood.

"Good," was what he said.

Falk's head dropped. Blood had begun to seep heavily from beneath his chest and abdomen. His legs ended their ugly spasms. One slight tremor passed through his upper body—a last untying of the tensed, live nerves. Falk died.

Hook stood up. The front of his uniform, from throat to knee, was smeared with Falk's blood. A group of Camaguayans had gathered to watch, but Hook did not acknowledge their presence. He removed his helmet, and the sun glistened on his thick, black hair. Hook stared upward, into the torrid light. He challenged it. The sun, in his vision, became a flat, purple disk. For a long moment he stood there, rigidly erect, staring. Then a wide wisp of cloud obscured the sun. Light dulled in the valley. The ground around Falk's body lost its strong definition. And Hook, nearly blinded, turned away from the sky.

Lieutenant Storch sat, barefoot, on a flat rock. Now and then he would belch through clenched jaws, a ponderous, hoarse rumbling. There were yellow corns on the backs of his toes. Storch opened a canteen and poured water over his feet. He moaned with pleasure.

"Falk is dead, Lieutenant," said Hook quietly. Storch nodded. He indicated the canteen: L.F. was printed in blue ink on the fabric covering. Hook frowned, but did not comment. "Feet bad, sir?" he asked. The toes wriggled. "You shouldn't go out on trips like this." Storch produced a glottal laugh. Then he turned his back on Hook, as he stroked downward, his fingers between his toes.

Hook walked away. Thoughtfully he sucked at the back of his hand; it stung now where Falk had scratched him. He wondered why he was still alive, and realized then just how assured he had been of his own imminent death. The valley had quickly reasserted its placid loveliness. Only the torn grass around the sand pit reminded Hook of violence. The little birds had resumed their bathing. Sanchez came toward him from the far side of the valley. He was walking western again, long, bowlegged strides, the confidence in his prowess restored.

"What is the count, Lieutenant?"

"Only two. One of my men. One of your men."

"Wounded?"

"Just the big black man, Jones, and that is nothing." Sanchez spat in his disdain. "The Riffs have had a beating. They are in the hills now, running still."

"Perhaps." Hook stared doubtfully toward the valley's northern access. "You did good work, Lieutenant. Your men were very brave."

"Some. Some." Sanchez spat. "But there were eight who did not charge with you. And I will make them pay for it."

"Please. Few men are soldiers, Lieutenant. Punishing them will do no good." Hook rubbed at his forehead with the back of his hand. "What is the Riff body count?"

"One."

"One? How can that be? I killed one myself."

"Yes. That is the one. There was blood in some places, but the bodies were dragged away."

"One," said Hook. "One. We'll be here for a hundred years."

"Yes? That is good then. This is a nation of cowards and lazy, stupid men. Even General Amayo is lazy and stupid. I am sick of it." Abruptly Sanchez made a fist. There was nothing to strike; instead, he prodded the sinewy, hardened ball with his fingers. "We need to be brutal. The war is good for us. It will destroy the lazy, stupid ones. It will kill the old beliefs. And we will be strong. You Americans help us. You are smart; you are not afraid. And you are killers."

"Yes? Are we?" Hook sat on a rock. Even sitting, his head was higher than Sanchez' head. "I am too tired now, Lieutenant. And I am very sad. One of my best men is dead." Sanchez spat again, provocatively, close to Hook's boot.

"That. That. I don't understand. How can it be? You tear a man's head from his neck with your bare hands. A man? I saw it—a boy only. Tear it off like a flower from its stem. And then you are sad because one single soldier has died. Or one rabbit. How? You are crazy, that's what I think."

"No," said Hook wearily. "You are right, Lieutenant—you do not understand. We make war out of love. And God allows it out of love. Only an animal kills without love."

"Do you call me an animal?"

"No," said Hook simply. "Not yet. Not yet."

Sanchez would have persevered, for he was becoming very angry. The skirmish had frustrated him. Sanchez had killed no one, had seen only one distant, retreating back. Now Hook stood up. Jones and Garbini had emerged from the woods and were approaching slowly, laughing. Garbini supported the corpsman: his arm encircled Jones' back and his hand was wedged in Jones' far armpit. Hook could see the Negro's eyes.

153

Even as he laughed, Jones was examining the grass, the sky, Garbini's ragged profile—and seeing these things, Hook knew, with an exultant, joyful perception.

"How is it, Jones?"

"Fine, Sergeant. Only hurts when I laugh."

"Then you better stop laughing," said Hook quietly. "You were lucky back there."

"Sure he was," said Garbini. "Lucky he didn't have to treat himself. He put the damn gauze pack on upside down. Would you believe it?" Jones giggled.

"I was nervous, man."

"Falk is dead."

"No," said Garbini. "Not old Lance. God damn. I can't believe it. Lance dead? Son of a bitch. Ah—how'd he get it?"

"He fell on a grenade."

"Son of a bitch. A hero." Garbini pulled his arm away from Jones' back. The corpsman tottered once, but recovered his balance easily. "Look, Sergeant—" Garbini took out his wallet. "I won these two fives off Lance just yesterday. You send them back to his ma." Hook accepted the money. Garbini hesitated, the slit of his wallet still gaping. "Old Lance. I didn't get to know him too well. His folks were real poor, that's right, isn't it?"

"No," said Hook. "His father is well to do. Does it matter?"

"Well to do, huh?" Garbini stared at the two bills. "Is that right? Ah . . . Sergeant—" He smiled at Hook. Hook stared at him without expression.

"What is it, Joe?"

"Nothing. Nothing." Garbini folded his wallet. "Poor Lance. Just a kid. You can never tell, that's for sure." Garbini walked away. Hook stuffed the two bills in his pocket.

"Can you keep up, Jones?"

"I–I guess so." Jones fingered his chest tenderly.

"Good. We'll be moving out in an hour. When we've buried the dead." Hook turned away.

"Sergeant—"

"Yes."

154

"Ah—back there. About the Purple Heart. Were you kidding?"

"No. You were wounded in action. You bled. That's that."

"God damn. A Purple Heart." Jones considered this for a moment. "Listen, Sergeant," he said with a shy smile. "We don't get along too good. I mean, I can't always swallow your line of crap. But I gotta give credit where it's due. You saved my life back there."

"Yes," said Hook. "I guess I did. I guess that makes the difference."

"Difference?"

"Yes. Between the seventeen-year-old boy I killed here, and the one in the farmhouse. That difference."

"Look, Sergeant—"

"Never mind," said Hook sadly. "I'm glad you're alive."

WRITTEN FIVE DAYS BEFORE: NOTE FROM LIEUTENANT HARRY STORCH TO HIS FRIEND

You're a fucking balls-up, Fatty. Hook's letter got through to Colonel Smith's ADC. It cost me fifty bucks to get it back, and that Jew prick Goldberg sneering at me while he counted my money. You can kiss your case of Scotch good-bye friend. I guess I can't trust nobody in this damn army. But don't worry, Fatty boy—Hook will be with me till the day they bury him. No matter what I have to pay. No matter what I have to do.

Harry.

The Riffs did not attack again that day. Gradually, as they marched, the somber, wooded spur of the ridge loomed nearer. It was chilly; a thin mist formed at the base of the ridge and descended, undulating, to meet them. The

Camaguayans were silent. The shock of the battle reproduced itself again and again in their minds. They remembered the deaths, the dreadful clamor, their own individual acts. The eight who had not charged began to seek each other out: they touched hands like members of a secret order; they gave and received a tacit consolation. Their comrades, those who had charged because of shame, or because of an insane exhilaration, or because they had been dragged forward by the Americans—these especially were intolerant of the eight malingerers. Once a silent, determined fistfight had broken out. Sanchez allowed it to continue until one man, the man who had hidden in his yellow handkerchief, was beaten to his knees.

Throughout the battle Hall had tried to get himself killed. The attempt had very nearly exhausted him. Now, as he walked, he came to an abrupt conclusion: death alone was not sufficient. It would not satisfy Isabel. With an increasing excitement he began to consider several kinds of maiming—years of helplessness in some dreary veteran's hospital. Blindness did not seem extraordinary enough; nor did the mere loss of one or two limbs. He settled finally on the spine: total paralysis, a dream perhaps of infancy. But he was not sure how this end might be achieved. A fall, a bullet; there were diseases, too, that he had heard of. Hall wondered if he could find someone to help him. He made no decision, but, while he walked, these thoughts of some sensational, conclusive act were wonderfully consoling.

Garbini whistled, improvising. He was a very talented musician. The sounds, especially his low notes, possessed a disturbing vocal quality: in turn they exhorted, interrogated, admonished. For the last fifteen minutes Garbini had been taunting José Ix, posing him unanswerable tone questions. The Indian had begun to irk Garbini. Whenever they passed each other, José Ix would invariably cross himself twice, and a look of troubled awe would perturb his eyes and forehead. Garbini didn't like the implications. As a distraction, he fingered the thick, squared bulge in his pants pocket. His whistling ascended to higher registers. It abandoned its taunting and began cleverly to mock the twitter of the evening birds. Garbini was not unhappy. During the battle's confusion he had stolen Raoul's pack of pornographic photos. He had not yet had a chance to examine them, but he anticipated a pleasant night.

Raoul, just behind Garbini, was busy nursing Jones. He walked with his arm around the corpsman's buttocks, whispering his comfort, patient in spite of Jones' constant, whined complaints. In part, Raoul was using Jones' body as a shield. Both Hook and Sanchez were suspicious now. Hook did not concern Raoul, but Sanchez, he knew, was a dangerous psychotic. When at last they had overrun the Riff machine gun nest—abandoned then but for ejected shells and two neat piles of human feces—Sanchez, furious in his frustration, had permitted the muzzle of his M16 to play longingly over Raoul's body. But Falk's agony had saved him, and Raoul had decided he would desert before Sanchez found a better opportunity. "Come," he said to Jones. "Be brave. Don't show them that it hurts."

But Jones wanted very much to show them. He admired his new role: wounded soldier. It intrigued him. He had complex plans for his triumphant return home, and he doubted only whether his scar would seem sufficiently impressive. But his attitude toward the event was ambivalent. A sip of water, a familiar sexual fantasy, and the paraphernalia of his ordinary life would subsume the experience. Then, disconcertingly, it would reassert itself—often so suddenly that it caused a physical reaction, a painful, violent shrugging free of his shoulders. The powerful, thin forearm that crushed his throat; the Riff's hot, explosive hissing gasp; then the knife's terrific hardness, the pain, the assumption of death. He would sweat abruptly, become dizzied remembering it. Jones tried to force the event entirely from his consciousness, but the shocked, frayed instincts of his body betrayed him again and again on the march.

In the slanting, low rays of the setting sun, Baxter's shadow extended, gigantic, from the soles of his boots. He could en-

vision no end to it. Elongated through infinity, his waist slithered across a grove of boulders more than thirty yards away.
Baxter saw the other marching shadows, enlarged beyond all
distinction. He lifted his foot and shook it, detaching one of
the shadow's long props. He raised his left hand and smote the
trunk of a distant pine tree. Then he laughed. Another shadow
overtook his, coalesced with it, became a single blackness glid-
ing on four shapeless pseudopodia.

"Getting chilly," said the other shadow.

"Uh," said Baxter. "It's the man. Get out of my shadow. I'm
big now, big as they come, and I'm enjoying it." He smote another pine tree.

"I haven't had a chance to thank you, Horace." Hook
stepped back, politely disengaged his shadow from Baxter's.
"One heck of an assignment that was. You've come a long
way. Right now you're as good as any in this man's army."

"Aw, shit," said Baxter. He murmured an incoherent phrase.
He began to finger the plush circle of his lips. "I'm sorry about
Falk, though."

"Yes. That spoils our little victory. Lance was growing up a
bit, too." Hook sighed. "I didn't think you knew him very well."

"I didn't." Baxter hesitated. "It was his accent. Ever since
that Wallace guy first run for President—I mean, them
southern-type accents make me feel sick all over. I guess Falk
wasn't like that, though."

"Poor Lance. He didn't think much about it. He just wanted
his father to like him a little."

"Yeah?" Baxter slowed; their shadows merged again. "How's
that? I mean—I never had a father at all, so that kinda thing
makes me curious."

"Oh. There was a brother. Daddy's favorite child. The
brother was killed in Vietnam, near the war's end. They
blamed Lance for it, I think."

"See—now I'd never've guessed a thing like that. I thought
Lance was pretty damn sure of himself. Real secure. Hell, I

think all white men're secure. After all, they're white, ain't they?" Hook laughed. "Now that's funny. That's the first time I heard you laugh. You're a heavy smiler, but you don't laugh much at all."

"I'm a pretty dull sort."

"It's all that religion, I figure."

"Could be." Hook pondered this. He jammed his hands into his pockets. "No. That's wrong—it shouldn't work that way. Tell me, Horace, do I come across like that? Fanatical? Kind of crazy?"

"Well . . ." Baxter became cautious. "Let's say, uh . . . there ain't too many of you around just now."

"Still," said Hook, "I saw you once. Back at Hill 506, when we were pinned down by that burning am-track—I saw you cross yourself. I remember that."

"Yeah? Well . . ." Baxter shrugged. "It's like pickin' your nose, a real tough habit to break. My aunt brought me up a Catholic. But, you know—I'm not too clear about things. I mean, I'd rather not talk about it."

"I understand." Hook hummed for a moment. He watched the flight of an oriole until it disappeared in the deep pine woods. "Still. It's a nice thing to have handy."

"You believe in the whole works, that right?"

"I do. The whole shtick."

"Okay. I respect that." They walked in silence for a long moment.

"How's the arm? Looked like you were throwing pretty hard back there."

"Not too bad. Not too bad. But that's different. Maybe—I don't know—maybe I will get me an operation. This arm don't look natural, know what I mean?" Hook cleared his throat.

"It's all part of a plan, Horace. Remember that." Baxter looked up at him.

"Yeah? You mean God don't care for me to pitch? He'd rather I's a garage mechanic or a busboy? That what you mean?"

159

"Who knows? Maybe he wants you to develop a knuckle ball. One thing—you'll know your body better than most nineteen-year-olds with a little smoke and nothing else. It'll mature you."

"Maybe. Still I can't think he cares about baseball. It don't seem proper."

"Well. I'll say one thing. He hasn't been much of a Yankee fan lately." Hook sighed. "Look at that. One heck of a hill we have to climb tomorrow."

"Then climb back over it again."

"And down all these miles."

"And through that lousy swamp."

"Doesn't seem too sensible, does it, Horace?"

"No sir. There's a reason though, ain't there?"

"So they tell me," said Hook. "So they tell me."

"God isn't a colonel, is he?"

"No, Horace. Hadn't you heard? God is a sergeant."

And Hook laughed again.

WRITTEN TEN DAYS BEFORE: LETTER FROM PRIVATE HORACE BAXTER TO HIS AUNT

Dear Aunt Min:

I got the cross you sent me. It's very nice and I know it must have cost a lot—I saw where it says sterling on it. Im glad Father Bully blessed it in church and asked everyone to pray for me.

Aunt Min, dont worry, Im not afraid of death. I don't want to get all busted up like some of the boys here have but being dead is another matter. We all got to die. Theres no two ways about that—it don't even help to be white.

I've done some thinking about it. And I gess if I was shot right now Id be—well Id be anoyed. Thats what Id be. You

see Im 19 years old now and I just got sort of settled down and Id have to pack up and move on again. But thats all Id be and maybe after a while Id like the idea. Things aint all that good here in this life. Someplace else I could be richer or smarter or even taller maybe.

Then you ask me if I still believe in Jesus Christ. Well not the way I used to. I mean not like when I won them gold stars in Sunday School. Thats for sure. I gess I got to say—some ways I believe more and some ways I believe less. But does it matter really? Aunt Min either God's going to take care of all us guys—us little guys with no brains and no big hopes—or he better dump the whole bunch of us. We don't count anyway. Sometimes I wish he wouldnt bother—if he bothers. Its like going for a job from some big white personal manager. You get so scared taking up the mans time you start bad-mouthing yourself just so you can get out and go back where you belong.

But Ill think about it Aunt Min and when I get back home again well sit down by the kitchen table and well talk it over. I gess theres got to be some reason for all this. A pretty big reason too—otherwise I dont want to be down here trying to kill people like I am.

Well thats my filosofy. Except for one thing. The most important thing of all. Being Christian got to have something if such a wonderful person as you, Aunt Min, can believe in it.

Love and kisses,
Your son Horace.

Hook stepped out of the forest. He descended cautiously along a steep causeway of broken boulders, toward the encampment. Isolated Riffs had returned: he had heard their quiet calls to each other—the sounds of owls and small night animals. These few scouts did not disturb him. He expected only harassment until they had crossed the ridge. It was cold.

The moon had risen and loomed now overlarge in the blurring aura of its own diffused light. Near it flared the pinprick of Venus. Hook's knees ached; his extremities were numb. He had prayed, without moving, for more than an hour; now he experienced a fresh gladness in the things of the night. He hesitated, then stared upward at the moon and its intense, tiny companion. For several moments he remained still, as though fixing the heavens in his mind.

The camp was quiet. The eight malingerers, now very much subdued, had been placed on extended sentry duty by Sanchez. The lieutenant had gallantly sacrificed his own sleep in order to supervise their persecution. Garbini lay sprawled, examining something carefully in the meager light. Now and then he would exclaim quietly to himself: "Son of a bitch. Look at that. Would you believe it? Son of a bitch." Hook crossed the encampment to the place where he had last seen Jones. Raoul sat near the corpsman, his lips busy, very close to Jones' left ear. Hook cleared his throat. From the way in which Raoul started, Hook sensed that the two men had been discussing him.

"How is it, Jones?"

"Uh—" Jones shrugged and then winced. "Not so good. I can't sleep."

"Has the dressing been changed?"

"Yes sir, Sergeant Hook." Raoul stood up. "I have done that. I am good at these things." Raoul smiled. "Well—I will go away now. If you are needing anything, Ondy, please call me." He backed away, bowing deferentially to Hook as he did so. When he had left, Hook sprawled next to Jones, who sat cocooned in two blankets, his own and Raoul's.

"We've got a pretty stiff climb tomorrow. Think you can keep up?" Jones was silent. He gnawed at his lower lip. "Well?"

"I don't get much choice, do I?"

"No." Hook was disappointed by his tone. "I could leave you here with a few men, until we get back from the lake.

But I doubt if the Riffs would let you alone. You'd be a lot safer with us. How's the pain?"

"Bad. Hurts when I breathe."

"I'll detail two men to help you."

"Raoul wants to do it. Let him help me. That's all I need."

"Raoul's a sergeant. I can't order him to take care of an American private. He's got other duties." Jones laughed harshly.

"Yeah. That's what Raoul said you'd say. But Raoul said it don't matter where he is—you think he's too stupid to do anything anyway. He might as well be in the rear with me." Hook opened his mouth; he shut it. He wondered if Raoul wanted to be assigned to Jones, to be beyond Hook's own immediate surveillance, for some special reason. Jones coughed and then groaned plaintively.

"Did Raoul say anything else?"

"Yeah." Jones stared at the sky. Quietly he said, "Raoul told me how you killed that Riff." Hook looked instinctively at his hands, and the gesture did not elude Jones. "That's right," he whispered. "That's right."

"I had to. I didn't have any weapon with me." Jones laughed. Then he began to cough.

"Sure," he said finally. "You forgot your gun."

"Well, I'd better go. I seem to bring out the worst in you." Hook stood up.

"Had enough? Is that it? Can't face the truth?" Hook hesitated. Then, with deliberation, he sat down again.

"What's the truth, Jones?"

"Truth is you're a first-class hypocrite. All this big Christian talk. Answer me. Go on. Are Christians supposed to kill?"

"Supposed to?" Hook jammed his hands under his armpits. He stared at the soil between his legs. "No," he said. "Of course not."

"Well," said Jones triumphantly. He took out a cigarette and lit it. "Well? Is that all you've got to say?" Hook did not reply. "Christian. Christian. I'm sick of Christians. My mother was a Christian." Jones inhaled and blew smoke, belligerently, toward Hook's face.

"So you've told me."

"I've had it up to here."

"What have you had? Do you know? Do you know anything at all about it?"

"Enough. Plenty."

"I don't think you know anything. You wouldn't be so confused, so angry, if you did."

"Tell me then."

"All right. I'll try." Hook leaned close to Jones' huddled, blanketed shoulders. "One—it's not about these things." He indicated his hand, Jones' hand, the earth itself. "It's not about bodies or things. It's not about pleasure—not even about pain. Christ's kingdom is not of this world. It was never meant to be. Remember that. The great point of the Christ adventure was His death, not His life. His Resurrection, His triumph over our mortality. It's not the healings and the good works that matter. If it was, then He was unspeakably cruel—Christ was —if He left one maimed man, one blind child unhealed. He said, 'The poor you have always with you.' He said there would be wars. He sent His disciples, the men He loved, knowingly each to a terrible martyrdom. Because this world, these lives, are relevant only in a greater context."

"You know," said Jones, "it sounds to me—it sounds like you don't think a human life is sacred."

"Of course it's sacred. It's a gift from God. But it's not supremely sacred. In terms of salvation, in terms of eternity—it matters very little at all."

"Sure. But see, then you contradict yourself." Jones became agitated. "If it don't matter—then why all this crap about helping people? Killing to help them? Everybody's gonna die. They're all gonna be poor. So what the hell?"

"I'll tell you why," said Hook. He placed the tips of his fingers together, one hand against the other. "Because the act of giving is for the giver. Not the recipient. That's the whole point. You remember back in East One, how that woman spat on me. She hated me for my charity. It's often that way. But it doesn't really matter. I can't help her—I can't make her rich or healthy or immortal. But a true gift of love, any sacrifice, helps the giver. It's healthy. That's the meaning of charity— not the mere passing of money or services. The gospel recommends good works for our sake. For our sake. For love's sake. Not for the sake of a materialist utopia in which men are richer or happier. For the giver's sake."

"Man, you're giving me a headache." Jones spat between his feet. "It sounds like a lot of horseshit. It don't even make sense."

"All right," said Hook. "Simply then. Christianity has to do with the saving of souls, not lives. It has to do with an eternity beyond this world. The whole of Christ's teaching means only this—you give up your life to have another life. I killed those boys. I will have to account for it. But their lives—their lives have just begun."

"Hook. That kind of talk. You can justify any kind of crime with it."

"I know," said Hook simply. "And people have. There are great dangers: I think sometimes only saints should be soldiers. But it's the truth, nonetheless. The only truth there is."

"Okay." Jones scraped his butt out. "I'm getting sick of this. It bores me. I'm still waiting—the day you die, that's when I want to be around. We'll see about life then." Hook stood up. He knocked small clods of mud from the bottoms of his boots.

"One thing, Jones. You're getting pretty friendly now with Raoul. I'd watch it. Keep an eye on him."

"Oh?" Jones laughed. "Is that so? You can't stand nobody who don't kiss your ass. What's the matter with Raoul? Think he's gonna kill me in my bed?"

"I'm not sure. But I don't think he's with us."

"I'm not with you either, Hook."

"No," said Hook quietly. He fingered his beard. "But that

doesn't worry me. What you do is predictable. Selfishness always is. Good night, Andy. Sleep well."

I don't get it. Voice, everything he does, face, beard. Shaking all over when he left. Had to smoke. Couldn't light up though—hands kept clenching. Why do I hate him like this? Saved my life. Stupid, but honest man, good soldier. Think I want to hurt him—no, I want to kill him. I want to kill him. Why? The Riff knife? Infected? Am I crazy, sick? It's getting much worse now. Go blind, can't see at all when I talk to him. Got to get out of here. Can't be me. It was never like this before. I'm afraid. I'm afraid.

VIII

TWO DAYS LATER, in the morning, they crossed the ridge and descended to the shores of Lake Negro. The ascent was exacting; the diminutive, heavily burdened Camaguayans had had a strenuous climb. Furthermore, Jones' condition had impeded their progress considerably: through Raoul he had demanded rest at more and more frequent intervals during the day. As a result their night camp had been made in a cave high on the far face of the ridge—no more, in reality, than an elaborated niche and not deep enough to shelter even half the men. During the night it had rained heavily. The wind was chill; the ground was rocky and steeply inclined beyond the cave; lightning flashes stunned them. No one slept. Sanchez, angry and frustrated, had punched Private Armando above the eye. The unfortunate Armando, blinded by darkness and the harsh, wet wind, had urinated on Sanchez' boot—mistaking it for the boot of a friend. He was unconscious for more than ten minutes: the only man who had rested at all that night.

The foliage was transformed abruptly several times as they descended. From rocky scrub to pine forest, to a scented tangle of mahogany, sapodilla, and bracken. And, in the lake valley itself, to their dismay, the jungle appeared again as though by some immense illusion. It became hot and humid: an increase in temperature of nearly fifty degrees from the night before. Mosquitos swarmed, scattered like pollen out of the inhibiting undergrowth. The sun vanished. Once again, their progress was roofed over by sweating branches and vines. Unseen birds, monkeys, insects commented rudely on their slow intrusion. The ground was marshy, having been drained, just a few weeks before, of the lake's spring excesses. Though they had been advised by Hook beforehand, the men were uniformly disgusted. They progressed to the southeast, to the village where Rodriguez awaited them, at a rate of barely a mile an hour.

The lake—bloodied by the sun's setting, burnished by the dawn light—had possessed an ephemeral charm when seen from the ridgetop. Now, invisible, present only in the moisture it gave to the humid air, its remembered beauty became a symbol to the men of loathsomeness and deceit. Lake Negro was shaped roughly like a Valentine heart, with a rounded hole in its eastern auricle. The hole was an island sacred to the Mayas and covered by the overgrown ruins of a modest ceremonial city which dated from the seventh century. Three years before, Hook and José Ix and Rodriguez had spent two months in a hut beside the lake's marshy, malarial shores. Hook was familiar with the unhealthy terrain, and he knew it would have a poor effect on an already deteriorating morale. He hoped to meet Rodriguez late that afternoon. The next morning, if there were no complications, they would begin the arduous trek back to San Pedro.

There were complications; the village was deserted. When they reached it at sunset they found no evidence either of Rodriguez' company or of the dozen or so Indian families that had once lived there. The few huts had been emptied of all but the least valuable, least transportable items. There was, however, no sign of violence or even of a hasty, unpremeditated leaving. Aware of the significance of this to their mission, the men sullenly took over the large, three-sided thatched huts. They had arrived two days late for the rendezvous, but José Ix and Hook both agreed that the village had been abandoned for at least two weeks. Three days were all they could afford to wait. As they settled down uneasily for the night, a thunderous, torrential rain began to fall.

Hook and the two lieutenants had appropriated the headman's hut. It offered them only a minimal protection from the storm. When the wind veered, and a freakish gust blew

168

from the west, they were drenched by the pelting rain. The mosquitos, moreover, had chosen the same shelter. They harassed Sanchez, who retaliated with curses and sharp slaps; Storch, naked to the waist, accepted the annoyance with a series of sighed grunts. No one slept; no one spoke. Both officers had tacitly agreed to hold Hook responsible for Rodriguez' absence. Storch found a broken *metate*. He worked the grinding stone backward and forward in the slot, crushing bits of dirt and straw—as intrigued as an infant with a simple toy. Sanchez stabbed his own toy blindly into the earthen floor.

Hook ignored the sounds: the rushing of the downpour, the rhythmic thwacking of Sanchez' knife, the scraping of the broken *metate*. He was puzzled. He wondered why he was yet alive, and why Falk had been selected in his stead. Falk, he realized then, had brought his childhood, intact, to the moment of his death—his leaving as unquestioned as had been his coming. Whereas he, Hook, had been too eagerly resigned. Pain, he said aloud. I will need to have pain. It has been too easy. There has been no sacrifice.

He struck something with the side of his foot. Groping in the dark, Hook found a small stone incense burner. There were still a few damp lumps of copal inside. Hook lit a match, shielding it with difficulty against the eddying wind. The odor of smoldering copal invaded his sense and, for a moment, the smell gave birth to a vision of terrific vividness—a vision of hot sun and alien voices and the textures of rich, heavy cloth. The damp copal sputtered; it went out. Eagerly, Hook searched the air. He lifted the burner to his nose. But the aroma had lost its influence. Disturbed, he rose and walked out into the rain.

In a flash of lightning, the huts resembled huge, hunched toads. Doggedly, Hook splashed from one to the other, water swirling around his ankles. He found few men asleep. As he had feared, the Camaguayans were bitter and perplexed. He joked with them, suggested cures for complaints that Jones had blithely ignored, wrote letters by the light of a candle's stub. He settled an argument over personal belongings and listened patiently to an elaborate description of woman's infidelity. He counseled the two soldier-lovers, accepting, without scruple, the ever-changing roles they played: male now; female a moment later; alternating easily, cleverly. The Camaguayans liked to touch Hook. They would gather near his body, as though deriving both warmth and confidence from it. Often he found items of property missing: a match pad, a chewing-gum wrapper, some coins. Relics, he knew. He did not begrudge them this petty thievery.

Jones and Raoul were alone in the last hut. They lay side by side, their presence diminished, at first glance, to a pair of orange, glowing cigarette ends. Raoul was naked, lying under a single blanket. Solicitously he nursed the weakened, irritable Jones, held a cup of some unknown substance to his lips. Jones was silent during Hook's visit. Raoul chattered pleasantly, but the sergeant's presence seemed an embarrassment to him. Jones moaned often, stroking his bandaged chest almost fondly. Hook left them, depressed for some reason he could not understand. Outside he stared up at the teeming sky.

"Soon. Please," he said, his opened mouth filling at once with the rain. "Soon. I'm tired."

Long before dawn Raoul had disappeared—and the radio with him. They had difficulty waking Jones, who could remember almost nothing of the previous night. Soon after Hook had left them, Jones admitted, he had felt an irresistible need to sleep—for the first time since he had left the *Sting*. Hook wondered if he had been drugged: Jones mocked this suggestion, but, secretly, he had entertained the same idea. The Camaguayan watch was totally ignorant. As was their habit, they had hurried back to their huts soon after the rain began to fall. Hook and José Ix followed Raoul's spoor, but they lost it almost at once in a wide swampy area just north of the village. Raoul's trail through the jungle, Hook thought ruefully, showed few signs of hesitation despite darkness and the unfamiliar terrain.

The implications were very serious. Raoul had effectively isolated them from whatever aid the GHQ at San Pedro might supply. Furthermore, they could now learn nothing of Rodriguez' plans. No one in San Pedro would even know whether or not they had reached the rendezvous. Sanchez was furious: he excoriated Hook publicly in a strident, eager voice. When he had finished, Storch, standing near him, spat just once. He had already commandeered all Hook's chocolate. Hook accepted these insults. He had misjudged Raoul—not the man's intentions but, rather, the quality of his determination. The Camaguayans were shocked by Hook's deflation. The state of his omniscience was debated among them, and, in a very short while, Hook noticed they no longer seemed to obey his commands with their accustomed willingness. Something, he knew, would have to be done very quickly.

Small patrols were sent out regularly during that first day. After the torrential rains, footing in the marshy areas had become extremely treacherous, and even the experienced IC's could not penetrate very deeply into the steaming jungle. No contact was made with Rodriguez or with the dispersed inhabitants of the village, nor was Sergeant Raoul's spoor rediscovered. Hook encouraged his men to work, but the Camaguayans were balky and unenthusiastic. A plague of the jungle runs had developed suddenly, and three straddle trenches had to be dug—one, with convenient parallel logs, for the private use of Storch, who soon made it his permanent headquarters. Some foliage was cleared. Clothes were hung up to dry on the strands of a tattered village fishnet. A hissing, smoky fire was lit as a signal for Rodriguez. Hook knew it might benefit the Riffs as well, but he hoped the moatlike swamp would discourage a massed attack. These things were accomplished slowly and to the soft, susurrous murmur of voices discussing Sergeant Hook's damaged status.

At noon Hook climbed a towering, solitary pine which stood just behind the headman's hut. The tree's bark was scored, and the regular stumps of the branches provided convenient footholds—doubtless, he suspected, it had long been the village crow's nest. The sun's heat was torrid once again. For a quarter of an hour Hook stared across placid Lake Negro, hidden only three hundred yards to the southeast. There was no sign of human activity on its shores. The rounded island appeared to float on the inverted cone of its own reflection. To the north and west he saw the unbroken green roof of the jungle, misting gently now under the sun. Hook was uncertain what to do. They couldn't remain much longer. They couldn't leave Rodriguez' supplies behind, and to carry them back to San Pedro would be a cruel hardship for his nearly exhausted men. Swaying at the tree's slender apex, Hook prayed for guidance.

Garbini watched his descent. He gnawed hungrily at the purple flesh of his own mouth. Mosquitos orbited his head like erratic electrons about a bloated nucleus, but they were ignored. When Hook jumped the last six feet Garbini laughed exultantly, spattering saliva. Hook frowned. He intuited something perverse in the rich flush of nervous excitement that suffused Garbini's face. Garbini laughed again; he rubbed his hands together, as though in a mime of washing.

"Pickin' fruit, Sergeant?" Hook examined him quickly. There was thick mud on Garbini's boots, and a high water mark on his pants leg that reached to a point just above his knees. Hook scraped pine resin from the palms of his hands.

"Where have you been?"

"Oh—around." Garbini giggled suddenly, as though surprised by some secret thought. "I like it here. Always wanted some nice lakefront property."

"I see. Find what you were after, Joe?"

"Why—" Garbini touched his chest carefully with an opened palm: a gesture of surpassing innocence. "What's there to find, Sergeant?"

"That's what I'd like to know." Vengefully, Garbini repaid Hook for his suspicions.

"Sure fucked you up, didn't he? Raoul, I mean. Caught you with your jock strap down. Me, I never did trust that little bugger. Anybody five feet tall with a pecker like his—got to be trouble. How long we stayin' here?"

"Another day at least."

"Long trip for nothin', huh Sergeant? Colonel Smith's not gonna like it. Man, this war's like pickin' fly specks out of sugar with boxing gloves on."

"Joe. Don't go off like that again. I might need you."

"Sure, Sergeant."

"Do you have something to tell me?" Hook sniffed once, as though the air might enlighten him.

"Me. Not me. If I did, you'd be the first to know. I mean," he said seriously, "you're like a father to me."

"Yes. I know."

"Well. I suppose you're pretty busy. Guess I'll go see Jonesy." Hook watched Garbini cross the village. From his cheerfulness, from the way he walked and the way he challenged those who passed him, Hook knew that Garbini had sinned once again.

Hall was busy. He leaned the barrel of his M16 on the flat rock and jammed the stock against a small depression in the earth—so that it pointed upward at a forty-five-degree angle. Then he backed carefully toward the muzzle, staring over one shoulder, like a woman examining her hem in a full-length mirror. The aim seemed right, though his knowledge of anatomy, he realized, was extremely primitive. Hall fingered his spine just above the hips and nodded. He picked up the long, curved stick with the tiny fork at its end. He inhaled and reached behind his back with it. His hand shook, but after a moment's fumbling he pinned the trigger. Hall corrected his aim once more. He sighed, then jerked his arm backward. The M16 toppled and fell, clattering, from the rock.

Hall tossed his stick high in the air. Dejected, he sat on the rock and rubbed his skinny forearms together. That made, altogether, five abortive attempts in one hour. He had anticipated the sudden devastating agony so often now that he was emotionally exhausted. His stomach, tormented by eddying juices, went into spasm. He groaned. His glasses became fogged, and for several moments he sat, miserable, staring into opaqueness. It was certainly a very difficult business. He hoped Isabel would appreciate what he was doing for her.

Hall had second thoughts. After all, there were intestines and things in there. His bladder, for instance, where was his bladder? He palpated his abdomen inexpertly. He might die anyway, and, even if he succeeded, would it be fair to burden Sergeant Hook? Shouldn't he wait until they got back to San Pedro? He took off his glasses and waved them briskly in the air. Hall thought of the professor—comforting Isabel, explaining what had happened with, perhaps, a judicious use of medical charts, grave but reassuring. He would wait. Anything worth doing was worth doing right. Then Hall remembered something. A Tarzan movie that he had once seen as an adolescent. Little pygmies with blow guns. The poisoned darts, he recalled abruptly, had paralyzed their victims. Hall was on his feet at once, hurrying toward the village to find José Ix.

Garbini did not see Jones at first. The corpsman lay sprawled in the darkened, far corner of the hut—compelled to crawl there by his illness and the animal instincts it had awakened. He was huddled under his blanket despite the sweltering heat, and his head was propped, lolling, on the empty pedestal of some family's household god. Garbini's presence did not register on his attention. He nipped at the first cigarette of his last pack, eating the bitter strands of tobacco as he sucked. His feet wriggled, pocking the blanket, in a quick rhythm exacted by the chaotic turmoil of his thoughts. Garbini bent low under a thatched eave, and stepped into the hut's fetid darkness.

"Jonesy—"

174

The corpsman started. His cigarette popped from between forked fingers. It fell, depositing a hot ember in his lap. Jones shook the blanket out wildly. Then he searched, his hands in a minor frenzy, for the bent, half-smoked butt.

"Damn it, Joe. Don't do that again."

"Sorry. Sorry." Garbini took off his helmet and squatted. "Phew—smells like a monkey's poop in here. Why don't you come on out?"

"No," said Jones sullenly. "I don't like the light."

"How d'you feel?"

"Bad. Bad. I got a hundred fever. I been shivering." He touched his chest. "It hurts like hell if I move wrong. Even if I breathe too heavy. And I got a lump there. I can feel it."

"Hmmm," murmured Garbini significantly, as though rendering a professional's opinion.

"Hmmmm? What's that mean? Huh? You ever seen a lump like this before?"

"Yeah. Once."

"Here on the chest?"

"Yeah." Garbini nodded soberly.

"What . . . what happened?"

"The guy died."

"Jesus." Jones covered his mouth with one hand; his chest, tenderly with the other. "How long was it?"

"Oh. About two weeks."

"Jesus." Jones' voice broke, then disintegrated entirely. For a moment he could not use it at all. "Did it hurt much?"

"Guess not. The poor guy stepped on a land mine—two days after he left the hospital. Blew him to red confetti." Fury and relief stunned, stymied Jones. He cursed as Garbini cackled, slapping at the fiber-covered hut floor.

"You prick. What d'you care? It's not your chest."

"Come on, Jonesy. Be good. Only a joke—that's all. No harm in a joke. You're gonna be O.K." As proof of this statement, Garbini emptied his nose: he held one nostril shut and blew vigorously through the other. A long strand of mucus sagged lazily to the hut floor. Garbini pinched it off between thumb and forefinger, then repeated this operation with the other nostril. Jones stared, galvanized by his own revulsion.

"Joe," he said finally, "I'm worried. Suppose I get an infection. Suppose I get real sick. Suppose I can't walk out of here. How's Hook gonna get me down to San Pedro? That's a long way."

"Don't worry, Jonesy." Garbini wiped his nose with the back of his sleeve. The reddened, bulbous nose seemed to bend—left, right with the sleeve's motion—as though it were on a hinge. "With your luck, a Greyhound bus'd probably come by. You were lucky when that guy hit a rib. As a matter of fact, you're lucky Raoul didn't slit your throat for a good-bye present."

"Not Raoul. He wouldn't. We were friends."

"Ha! That shit. He'd'a sold the hairs on his mother's mound —and pulled them out himself. One by one."

"Yeah, who told you that—Hook? Raoul didn't like fighting, that's all. He thought the war stank. And I agree with him. From what he told me, Raoul was an artist. His father was a big fashion photographer in—"

"Fashion!" Garbini shrieked. "Fashion my fanny. Here. Take a look at these fashions."

With an elaborate flourish, Garbini drew out the sheaf of photographs. He tossed them to Jones. The corpsman glanced at the first, looked more closely, pushed his nose to the paper, and then crawled hastily toward the light. Garbini laughed. He lit a cigarette and leaned back on one shoulder to enjoy Jones' reaction.

"That's him," said Jones in an awed whisper. "That's Raoul. Where'd you get these?"

"Oh—he gave them to me—as a memento, I guess."

"Hey! Hey!" Jones waved the pack in erratic circles above his head. "There's a man in here. Another. Oh, God—no wonder he's always grabbing my behind." Garbini chuckled, choked on half-exhaled smoke, and lay prostrate, coughing.

"Keep going," he gasped. "There's two sheep, a cow, and one very surprised goose in there."

"But he—I mean, he never made a pass at me."

"Maybe he was prejudiced."

"Damn. The filthy little queer." Jones began to cough. He pressed his hand to his chest, bracing it against the convulsions, but even the pressure of his hand became intolerable. He moaned.

"Hurts bad, huh?" Garbini seemed to smile—a meaningless, characteristic rictus—but Jones saw significance in it. He moved forward, driven by the terrific fury that now welled continually within him.

"You—you bastard. You like it. You like to see me suffer." He spat as he said the words. Garbini frowned, puzzled by his anger.

"Hey. Kinda irritable, ain't we? What's the matter, Jones— you afraid to die?"

"Yeah. I am." Jones' voice became boyish, shrill. "You want to make something out of it, you ugly, stupid dago?" Garbini's mouth opened slowly: it remained open for a long moment. Then he shut it with a hollow, decisive click.

"Ugly, stupid dago? Ugly, stupid dago?" He repeated the words, incredulous. "Say that again, nigger, and I'll bust you—right there, right where it hurts. Don't talk big, friend, not unless you can back it up. I'll break your black ass in two." Garbini stood up.

"Wait!" Jones yelled, suddenly afraid to be alone in the shadowed hut. Garbini hesitated.

"Jones. I liked you once. I thought, man, this is a cool cat. I mean the way you got on old Hook's wick. But I was wrong. You ain't worth the water to flush you down to hell. You're a drag, Jonesy. A first-class drag and I'm sick of it. That piss little cut ain't gonna kill you. No sir. And it's a God damn shame. That's just what it is. So long, you chicken-shit, yellow cock-sucker. I just hope you rot in this hole. I just hope you rot."

177

Jones threw something at Garbini's back—the first thing his fingers found on the hut floor. A handful of dried, brittle henequen fibers. The strands floated, gently, back to earth. And Jones cursed.

WRITTEN THAT AFTERNOON: LETTER FROM SERGEANT CLARENCE HOOK TO HIS FRIEND

Dear David:

I wanted you to know it, my last exhilaration. This morning, early, I parted with my hands. I apperceived them—even those ten fingernails that seemed so odd, like eyes, like saddened windows, like visors. I cupped myself in my own palms, and I sensed the usefulness, the free co-ordination, the hymns that rest in my fingers. The inventory is almost taken, David. There isn't much left of me now.

And, every moment, I am more fully surely assured of our acting here. This pain, this suffering—what is it? Nothing. At worst a thing that adds meretricious realness to the body's life. But pleasure will do that, just as surely. I have seen, as though from the blurred edges of my eyes, the great ladder of the universe. I'm sorry, David. We are not the be all and the end all, as you would have it. We are debtors even for our pride.

There is a man here, Jones by name. A Negro. A smart, handsome boy. And I think my waiting now depends on him. He hates me. Not for my whiteness, or for my authority, nor even for my knowing him. He hates—I have seen it through his eyes and it is immense, beyond his man's capacity. As though we bore between us the far extremes of some huge reality. Fell opposites and yet, I feel, interpenetrating. There is a reason for his being here.

I know. You will have studied these words for the signs of my madness. And you will find them. Do not take comfort, David. I have come to destroy. To eat away the fine, familiar

order of your humanism. I am antisocial. A sport. A tear in the fabric. I am indeed mad—mad with passion. I want you with me, for you, of all the others, have always seemed beautiful. A fierce blindness, the same that I have felt in this boy, Jones. You have a little time left, David. Only a little. I give you fair warning.

This is the last letter I will write. I wonder sometimes if I should have written more. But there are writings enough to undeceive those who would be undeceived. This is a solitary thing—a secret coming and going. There must have been many such, private, unannounced, in our long nighttime. Goodbye, David. It is not the end.

     Love,
       Clarence.

Their faces began to swell again: unbitten flesh was scarce, and the mosquitos stung the tumid lumps of their other stingings. A hollow semblance of alertness was maintained. Men ordered to sentry duty slept in open defiance of courts-martial. Some said that Rodriguez was dead; others, more imaginative, said that he had deserted to the Riffs and was preparing, at that very moment, to attack the village. There were those eager to follow Raoul, had they known the path he had taken. All now doubted Hook's authority, but the doubting remained silent, furtive. Hook had witnessed this phenomenon before: like a bully among bullies, his influence waxed and waned with the events. The Camaguayans, as did the Puritans, considered success the outward and visible sign of a divine election.

A ritual was instituted that afternoon. One Camaguayan, returning from a fruitless, difficult patrol along the lake shore, dropped a fist-sized stone near the open side of Hook's hut. This mute act of defiance was adopted enthusiastically by the other men. One by one, as they finished sentry duty or returned from some particularly unpleasant detail, the Camaguayans would drop a new stone beside the first. Within just a few hours, a foot-high pile had been accumulated—an emblem of their increasing disenchantment. In time even a poor night's sleep, an unsavory meal, a bad hand at cards, became the occasion for yet another stone—as though Hook were being held responsible, as indeed he was, for each evil without distinction.

Lieutenant Storch was dumb and unhelpful. From dawn until dusk he squatted on the two parallel logs, satisfied to watch the pile of stones increase—sitting there, in fact, so that the onus would fall more patently on Hook. He had acquired a new orderly, fat Armando, who brought him food and water and, on occasion, spread dirt over the trench's bottom. Armando liked his job: it gave him a certain status. As a good servant should, he imitated his employer in all things, dropping his lower lip, belching, maintaining a pregnant, sullen silence. Storch smoked what seemed to be an inexhaustible supply of cigarettes, lighting each with the end of the last, nearly extinguished butt. He ignored the mosquitos, who retired from his pale, bare buttocks sated and apparently somewhat crazy, for they circled aimlessly, making jagged, banking dives. The Camaguayans avoided his trench; the squat, inert figure attained, in their imaginations, the singular uniqueness of some malevolent idol. Late that afternoon one of the logs lost purchase in the loose dirt of the trench side, and the idol toppled silently into its own detritus. Two dozen eyes watched, horrified, unwilling to give assistance. But Storch merely replaced the log, loosened his soiled shoes, and sat again, his pants draped like a deflating cloth balloon around his knees.

The rock pile toppled, subsided of its own crescent weight. Hook knew that he was expected to act decisively, that his idle presence in the village both irked and disconcerted his men. In plain view, therefore, he began to prepare himself. He removed his shirt and blackened his face, arms, and broad chest. He slipped a knife into his belt. Then he wrapped Storch's .45 in a goose-necked polyethylene bag. The Camaguayans watched, suddenly excited. He told Sanchez, who sat, sulking, his back against the crow's nest pine, that he was going out on reconnaissance alone. The lieutenant would gladly have denied Hook, but the thought of having the command to himself titillated Sanchez, and, instead, he merely shrugged. Hook crossed the village quickly. The Camaguayans watched him surreptitiously, their attention disguised by games and small acts of housekeeping. And from the darkness of the last hut, Corpsman Jones followed Hook carefully with the muzzle of his own cocked .45.

A hundred yards along the trail, Hook encountered Private Hall on his hands and knees, his bent form almost submerged in the undergrowth. Hall was profoundly intent. He murmured, "She loves me, she loves me not," as he culled plants from the confused mass around him. Already Hall had plucked a dozen small, six-leafed growths with orange berries the size and shape of grapefruit pips. Hook frowned. He was familiar with these berries and their use, but they were, he thought, yet two weeks from their dangerous maturity. Hall acknowledged Hook's greeting slyly, shoving the plucked heap behind him.

"I lost something—ah, my ring."

"Need some help?"

"No. Oh, no. I just found it. Here. See? It's on my finger."

Hall stood up, brushed his hand nervously against the side of his nose, and deposited a brown streak just under his eye, a pendulous, murky tear. Hook nodded. Then he bent down and picked up one of the plants. As he talked, he began deliberately to eat the berries. Hall gasped, made fluttering, winglike gestures, and then sat heavily. When Hook left, Hall was flicking orange berries high in the air with the bony thumbs of each hand.

Hook followed the tortuous, sodden track for a quarter mile. It ended at the lake shore, in a cove, the anchorage once of several native canoes. But for his undershorts, he removed all his clothes and wedged them in a tight bundle in the fork of a tree branch. He tied the polyethelene bag to his right ankle. Then, knife clamped in his teeth, he stepped out into the thigh-deep water. For a moment he paused, absorbing the shock of its coldness. At last, silently, he pushed off from the shore.

It was a half-mile swim to the island. Hook paced himself, swimming on his back, floating. Except for two tiny black V's —condors drifting—the sky was an unblemished blue-white. Idly he lifted one pale, hairy leg above his chest until the toes appeared to probe the blue-white itself. Floating there without the perspective of either shore, he seemed suspended, related to nothing, alone. He thought of Breughel's *Icarus* and the poem it had inspired. With willingness, Hook contemplated the insignificance of his own body, balanced precariously on a shifting line between two measureless enormities. He would exhale and sink, inhale and rise, kept buoyant, kept uncommitted, by the thin, yielding bags of his lungs.

He remembered her body and the shock of that first recognition in the shaman's hut. He questioned the realness of the event; questioned then his own questioning; questioned reality itself. Hook sighed, drove the last cubic inches of air from his chest. His body contracted itself, knees bent, arms in at the sides. He sank, sitting, dragged down by the weight on his right ankle. Water passed over his face—thinly enough at first so that he saw the sky's brilliance clearly, shimmering. Then deeper, until the day's light was only a less substantial shadow. As though at a distance from him, his starved lungs began to writhe. He struggled with his consciousness, struggled then upward, shocked by the deepness of his descent. He broke surface gasping and sputtering. "Not that way," he said between clenched teeth. "Not that way."

Hook swam strongly then, as though in expiation. Within twenty minutes he had penetrated the island's marshy circumference. The water was brackish there, a dark body secretly skeletoned by thick, slimy roots. The lake had risen during the rains and was now subsiding slowly. Trees on the shoreline had been overrun, their trunks submerged still in a yard of water. Green scum joined putrescent leaves and bulbous water lilies. Frogs fell from their perches and flopped awkwardly into the water, where, as though by transformation, they became each a purposeful, deft dart. Hook stumbled over roots and unseen floating things, found the island's genuine shore, and climbed ponderously into the unsupporting air. An anaconda, startled, whipped its immense, filled-hose of a body away from his intrusion.

Hook examined his .45. The land ascended steeply from the shore's apron, through tall grass that sizzled with a fervid insect life. Fifty yards above he saw the wide man-leveled field. The grass was quartered here, sprouting only from the crevices of the city's ancient pavement. Hook hesitated. To the left was a blunted, square pyramid, its southern sides crumbled and worn, but bare; its northern side overwhelmed, almost to the summit, by the impertinent forest. There was a path: he discovered it almost at once. A ten-foot-tall stele, dragon-bird fangs naked and broken, inclined toward him on a crazy foundation. Hook fingered the cryptic numbers: the holy counting backward and forward that had been a whole nation's business. Now in the jaws there was an empty swallow's nest.

The sports arena, its scoring ring yet intact, opened to his left, buckled in its center by some subsidence of the earth. As he neared the pyramid Hook found copal incense burners, each marking some present reverence. His heart beat strongly; it filled the silence that had begun to frighten him. Knife in hand, he climbed the long, stepped side of the pyramid. The temple room at the top was a tiny square with hugely thick walls, festooned now with somnolent bats. As dark, as cold, as incommodious as it had been in its architect's conception. Hook touched the wall; sacred bas-relief and modern graffiti mingled beneath his fingertips. He gasped. The scent of copal was rich and choking. It entered his lungs and would not be expelled. His breath became short. Arms high above his head, he tottered, dizzy, through the narrow portal. Hook stared down at the ancient city.

The waving grass was gone. Hook shrieked, and the sun itself rushed headlong to the heavens' center, wobbling there. A thudding, a gonging: music. The knife's handle grew thicker, awkward now between his joined and upraised palms. He

183

awaited their assent: a thousand feet firm-planted, where before the waving grass had stood. In another tongue he thought, 'Who is old? The nut or the tree?'

And struck suddenly downward.

Hook was their god again. In his absence Gutierrez had found the head of Sergeant Raoul. It had been impaled on a stick—like some red, round flower half-turned to a bloated fruit. His wrath, the Camaguayans knew, had reached out to strike down the infidel. As a propitiation their symbolic heap of stones was strewn solemnly over the tiny grave's bottom. And, for their sakes, as he spoke the Christian service, Hook raised the eyeless, tongueless head in both hands, high above his shoulders.

IX

*Ive killed him. Ten times. A dozen times. He's thrashing
out there in the dirt right now. Out there shrieking for my
mercy like a woman. What will you do about it? Do something—get me off, for gods sake. I'm not in my right mind.
I swear it. Is it the voices or is it the black, numbing wings
that press on my eyes? At night. And now its always night
in here.*

"I fall. Bang-bang," said Armando. "Very stupid. Yes?" The
fat Camaguayan private winced. His flesh was mottled from the
scalpline to the soles of his feet with angry blue-black-yellow
blotches. There were bruises on his shins and on his metatarsal
arches, on his rib cage, his temples, at intervals along the length
of his spine. The skin around his left eye had begun to pucker;
its white was striated with red, jagged veins. Hook had spent
the first dawn hour bandaging him, stitching a severe laceration
in the webbed tissue between his middle and ring fingers.
Armando leaned his weight on Hook, as the sergeant pared
a broken, bloodied toenail. The Camaguayan's hand on his
shoulder was warm and insinuating.

"Raoul is dead."

"Yes," said Hook. "I know."

185

"He was bad. A very bad man." Hook did not comment. "Very bad. Don't you say that, Mr. Sergeant Hook?"

"He did wrong. He hurt his friends."

"Yes. And now he is got no arms and legs. He is got no nothings." Armando giggled. Then he whispered, "Did you do this, Mr. Sergeant Hook? Did you cut Raoul's head off with a big, big knife? Whooosh-plop."

"No, Armando—I've told you that already. Other foot, please."

"No. No. Of course not." Armando smiled. "But the dirty Red Communists, they were his friend. He give them our nice American radio. They don't cut his head off and pull his tongue out and crush down his eyes like little grapes. Who did this then?"

"I don't know."

"No. No. Of course not." Armando smiled again. "But please, Mr. Sergeant Hook, you are still my friend. You don't be mad for all those little stones. No whooosh-plop for poor Armando. Eh?"

"I'm not mad."

"I am glad—" Abruptly Armando began to tug his injured foot away from Hook's grasp. The sergeant looked up. Sanchez was crossing the village, whipping his right thigh with a lithe, long stick. Armando stammered, "I go now. Please, Mr. Sergeant Hook."

"Relax, Armando." Hook drew the foot back. "You'll be all right now."

Yesterday's temptation had proved too great for Sanchez. Soon after Hook had left, the lieutenant commenced a strutting, thigh-slapping inspection of the village. He required only the most minor provocation: and, when he came upon Armando just behind a hut—strutting, slapping his thigh, imitating Sanchez for the amusement of two others—he sighed with happiness before he shrieked with anger. Armando was considerably stronger, but he endured the beating stoically. Little Pedro, he remembered, had been found dead the year before, a bullet in the base of his skull. Pedro had sung certain topical songs of his own invention. And so Armando had submitted, doing all a favor, permitting Sanchez to release the tension of seven frustrating days.

At nine o'clock Baxter and two Camaguayans returned from an uneventful reconnaissance south, along the lake's shore. Gutierrez returned a half hour later. He had gone east, toward the base of the ridge. Hook and José Ix decided that they would travel north, toward the end of the great box canyon in which Lake Negro rested. This was the logical direction. Rodriguez would have had to come from the north; the villagers, moreover, would probably have migrated away from the unhealthy southern basin of the lake. They would follow the coast, then angle east, toward the ridge, and return through the deep marshes just north of the village.

Lieutenant Storch was not very interested: by the terms of their agreement, the present dilemma was entirely Hook's responsibility. He had found a slick, oblong stone that fitted very nicely into his mouth. He sucked it now, allowing it to protrude between his lips like a dark lizard's head. Hook addressed the half-naked officer deferentially, eyes averted, as if such a conference between superior and inferior were a routine event. He explained the object of his patrol; reported on the state of their supplies; asked if the lieutenant had any orders. The lieutenant did. Storch pointed to a trenching tool that lay near the logs. Hook nodded and carefully strewed several spadesful of dirt over the bottom of Storch's trench. The lieutenant sucked on his stone: he was in command. He had proven it again.

Hook and José Ix left at ten-thirty. They passed Private Hall just outside the village. He sat, alone and shirtless, on a tree stump. Hall hummed intently as he palpated the secret organs of his abdomen: going over them again and again, as though he had deciphered some alien hieroglyphic and was practicing now, becoming fluent.

"He is not all in the head," said the Indian when they had passed out of Hall's hearing. "He should not be here."

"No," agreed Hook. "But soon he'll be going home. Just a few more days."

"He is dangerous. He wants to die. That is like a disease. He will make us all sick."

"Hall was a fine soldier once. He saved my life." José Ix inclined his head slightly: an expression of doubt. "Don't be hard on him, my friend. Few men are soldiers. We fight ourselves first before we can fight the others. Sometimes when this first fighting is done, then there is nothing left for an enemy to kill. The men that war doesn't hurt—those are the dangerous ones."

"Sanchez," said José Ix.

"Perhaps. But the war has hurt him most of all. He will never be a man again. He will die—as soon as the peace comes. There will be no place in peace for such a very small killer."

"Yes. And Lieutenant Storch?" José Ix examined Hook's face, but the sergeant did not respond. "Storch. What of him?"

"He is the lieutenant. I am the sergeant. This is the Army. What more can I say?"

"He wants you to be killed."

"No. Not yet." Hook smiled. "But soon enough. You are right. I'll be in his way soon."

"Yes," said José Ix. "I am sick of men."

"José. Yesterday, in the afternoon, I went—" Hook touched the side of his temple.

"Where did you go?"

"Well . . . Never mind. I'll tell you later. It's not important now."

For three hours Hook and José Ix did not speak. The trek was considerably more difficult than they had anticipated: they were compelled to turn east before half their intended progress along the lake shore was achieved. The hundred small bayous that oozed into Lake Negro, that were Lake Negro, had become swollen and coalesced. The path they both knew now abutted on insurpassable blind ends. Twice José Ix fell heavily, surprising Hook, who had not noticed the slight, slow deterioration of the Indian's reflexes. It was not merely exhaustion: José Ix was suffering rather the consequences of his uniqueness. He ate alone, slept alone, he saw and heard things in a separate sense; he perceived the war and his native land in what was, he realized, a manner alien to that of both the ICs and the Riffs. He was as wary approaching Sanchez and the other Camaguayans as he was in the presence of the enemy. And now, despite himself, he was wary of Hook. He had begun to loathe especially the sergeant's easy familiarity with his language. Twice he fell; twice he regained his feet, half slithering from Hook's proffered assistance.

Their reconnaissance was not a success. Through shimmering clouds of insects they watched the lake's surface, flattened in the breezeless high afternoon as though by some plasterer's tool. The far shore, seen through Hook's binoculars, was of an undistinguished wild sameness. They took turns climbing trees; took turns descending silently. The bits of trail, poor compounds of animal and Indian tracks, suggested no evidence of a recent human traffic. Inland, east toward the ridge, the land sloped gradually upward. The soil was more certain underfoot, and the foliage began to thin somewhat. At two o'clock they discovered the half-buried remains of a small cooking fire, built in the Indian fashion. It was more than three weeks old.

They rested there before crossing the low half mile of swamp that intervened between their present position and the village. Still they did not speak, and now Hook understood that the long silence had been imposed by his companion. José Ix sat apart, his back turned toward Hook. Slowly the sergeant ate his last piece of chocolate, as he watched the alert, angular progress of a lizard through the damp jungle of leaves around them. José Ix began to gnaw at his knuckles. The lizard sensed their presence; it darted into a cave of leaves, its tail, yellow-gray, still obvious and vulnerable. Hook licked his fingers.

"What's wrong, José?" He spoke in the Mayan dialect; the Indian answered quickly and in English.

"I am tired. I think I will go home soon."

"Well." Hook smoothed his beard; the Indian's bitter tone had startled him. "You can do that. You're a free man. But we need your help." José Ix turned to him.

"Yes. Like the fat man Storch needs you. And then you will kill me."

"You? Who do you mean?"

"The Riffs. General Amayo. You—the Americans. All three of you—you fight now for the right to kill me, to take my land away." José Ix smiled sadly then. "Is it not so?" Hook stared between his feet. Carefully he folded and refolded the chocolate wrapper.

"Yes," he said. "Don't trust any of us." Hook stood up. "Let's go, José."

Forty minutes later they emerged from the underbrush at the edge of a wide, sluggish stream. To the left and across the stream was one of the swamp's rare elevations: a moss-covered knoll, its base defended by a windrow of massed logs and vegetable rubbish that had been deposited by the current in its spate. To the right, however, the stream verged away from them, and, on its near flank, there was a level stretch of sand no more than twenty yards across. This seemed the easiest point at which to ford. Hook turned to the right, but José Ix caught his elbow.

"No. Quicksand," he said.

José Ix crossed the shin-high stream, and then began to struggle awkwardly through the windrow. This was not easy: his short legs sank into the thin, treacherous vegetable matter, and, at one moment he was buried almost to the waist. Hook crossed the stream quickly, and lifted the Indian by his collar and belt onto a bare, wide log that ran like a spine along the full length of the mass. José Ix was angered by this, embittered at the treason of his own body. He clambered hastily up the knoll's side, and vanished over the crest, leaving his companion to negotiate the windrow alone. Hook had just reached the solid, mossy soil of the knoll when he heard José Ix cry out sharply. He scrambled, sliding, falling to the top.

The Indian stood in a crouch, as perfectly rigid as some well-trained pointer dog.

"What is it?"

José Ix stepped forward cautiously. For a moment, Hook could not see it; his eyes scanned and rescanned the flat summit of the knoll. The leaves. A pile, he saw, heaped in an unnatural regularity: the oblong blister of a grave. And at the base, seeming itself like a leaf, brown and articulated, Hook saw a human hand. The fingers were cupped downward, outstretched and curled as though in the act of clawing. A woman's hand.

"Careful," he said. "It may be trapped."

"No." José Ix shook his head. "It would not be hidden then."

Gently José Ix removed the haphazard covering of dried leaves. The face of an Indian woman past middle age appeared. She had been raped and strangled; her tongue was bitten off and a burlap shift, her only article of clothing, had been wrenched above her belly. Hook realized, in spite of himself, that this had never been a handsome woman. A down of dark hair covered her cheeks and upper lip. Long before this moment, her nose had been broken, crushed into her face until the round nostrils protruded farther than her nose's tip. José Ix frowned.

"Do you know her?"

"No." Carefully José Ix pulled the shift down.

"The Riffs?" asked Hook, but he knew, as he said the words, that no Riff had done this. José Ix shook his head.

"No. They would have made a show. They would have cut her head off—not tried like this to hide her body. See. The ears are torn. He ripped her earrings off."

"Can we bury her?"

"By the stream. By the quicksand."

They bent to raise the body: Hook at the shoulders, José Ix at the feet. The woman had been dead more than a day, for the rigor mortis that had gripped her limbs had begun already to relinquish its hold. Though small, the stiffened, unresponsive form was an awkward burden. Hook raised the torso to the height of his waist—and then he saw it. He was stunned, terrified that José Ix would see it also. But José Ix already had. The Indian gasped. Hidden under her shoulders was a single yellow die.

"Garbini—" he hissed.

José Ix released the thin, brown legs. They did not fall, but drooped stiffly downward. The Indian staggered away, then turned his back to Hook. And between them, on a pile of sapodilla leaves, rested the die, already phosphorescent in the late afternoon light: it was faced to one, the single spot staring up like a pupil in some square, jaundiced eye. José Ix had made fists of both hands; he held them to his ears, as though each clutched within it some special sound. Hook let the body down. Its bent small finger caught in the lacing of his boot. Patiently, politely, he disengaged it.

"The ugly one. The one who kills our sacred bird. Mr. Private Joe Garbini."

"José—" The Indian acted swiftly then. He darted to his knees, snatched up his M16, and held it aimed at Hook's chest.

"Take your belt off, please. Lie down on the ground."

"Why?"

"I am going back now to kill him, that is why. Then, when I have killed him, then I will go back to the hills. And anyone who comes—Riff, American, Camaguayan—I will kill them. Until I am dead."

"Please, my friend, don't—"

"Speak in your own language!" The Indian shrieked. Then his features became suddenly inert; the muzzle of his M16 inclined slightly downward. "You are an American. Speak in English. I will understand you."

"All right. But you can't do this, José. Why should you risk your life for Garbini's sake? He's a sick man. He must be taken to trial—"

"To trial. Yes. I know your American trials. What will he get for this? A year in prison? I know how your American courts will protect a criminal. You forget, you have told me this yourself. You want to save his life. You are all alike."

"Are we?" said Hook suavely. He smiled. "Then kill me instead."

"You?"

"Yes. You can say a Riff did it. They might believe you."

"No. You did not kill her."

"But I did," said Hook with sudden urgency. "I brought Garbini here. I am his officer. I should have stopped him." He paused. "If you don't kill me, José—if you don't—then I will stop you. Come: it's my life for her life. I must die anyway. Of all people, I would rather you killed me, José."

José Ix opened fire then. He emptied a whole clip into the soft ground between them. Leaves and bits of moss swirled, were spattered in the air. Then they stood silently, staring at the quivering muzzle, hearing its rattle in the high echo chambers of the forest. José Ix closed his eyes. He opened them.

"What can I do?" he spoke quietly, pleading. "I am a chief. These are all my people. And I am helpless for them."

"No," said Hook. "Not helpless. Together we will do something."

"What?"

"First—bury this woman and pray for her immortal soul."

"And then?"

"Then I will do what must be done. And you will trust me."

WRITTEN NINE DAYS BEFORE: LETTER FROM PRIVATE JOE GARBINI TO HIS UNCLE

Dear Uncle Joe:

Just a little note to say how much I hate you. I got your lousy letter, Unk. So you hope I die, do you? Me? Die? Me? I got news for you—you slobbering, feeble old crud—I'm not gonna die. Not for you. Not for nobody. I aint never dying. Never. But you—you got three months left to live. Thats all. Then its bye-bye you ballsless, stupid old cocksucker. It makes me sick. Jesus, I just dont know what things are coming to. There was a time when a man wouldn't dare treat his own nephew the way you do. Uncle Joe, you're a cold, selfish old fart, you always were and you always will be, and youre gonna get just what you deserve. I'm only sorry for Aunt Rosa. Thats all—Im that kind of guy. I dont forget my relatives. And I dont forget it when someone gives me the shaft. May you roast in Hell you two-faced fat scumbag.

Go on, laugh. You think its funny I bet. You think Im a stupid gutless punk. Well, you got another think coming. One thing I can say for the army—they trained me to kill. Im coming after you, you arm chair crook. And nothing, not all your money, not even that bunch of hired thugs, nothings gonna save your rotten hide. Goodbye, Uncle Joe. I'll be seeing you real soon. Thats a promise.

   Love,
      Your nephew, Joe.

"Tough trip, Sarge?" Garbini grinned.

"Yes. It was tough."

Hook swallowed. His hands had become an embarrassment. He pressed them firmly to his thighs. During the tedious last quarter mile of their march, he had thought wholly of Garbini. Now his thoughts of the man and the man himself were, he knew, irreconcilable. Hook had forgotten Garbini's ugliness: the long, yellow teeth; the ruined skin; the dark, grime-filled furrows of his brow. He found this ugliness oddly compelling, for it lent Garbini a potent specificity. He had forgotten, too, the extraordinary quality of his liveness—the laugh, the innocent delight, the mordant, lewd wit. And when he acknowledged these things, Hook acknowledged as well his undiminished fondness for the man.

Garbini was puzzled. Hook, confounded by his thoughts, had allowed the silence, the staring to extend unnaturally. Garbini cocked his head; he sat forward. Hook did seem strangely disheveled. There was mud to his hips and mud even

194

above his elbows . . . as though he had been digging. And the
fingers: Hook was fastidious about his nails—to Garbini a
source of secret amusement. Something had gone wrong. Garbini considered himself an expert on Hook. By anticipating
the sergeant's moods he had been able often to escape dangerous and unpleasant details. He frowned. But the reason for
Hook's distraught appearance did not suggest itself. The murder was now more than a day old; Garbini had quite forgotten
it.

"Sarge. Why don't we get out of here? Huh? I mean we're
not doin' nothin' t'speak of."

"Soon." Hook peered at the sky. Then he touched his beard.
It was the gesture of an old man.

"What's up?" asked Garbini, curious. "Something bothering
you?"

"Ah—yes." Hook cleared his throat. "There's something I
want to check out. José Ix and I didn't have time. Want to
come with me?"

"What? Now? It'll be dark any minute."

"We'll only be gone an hour or so. I don't want to go alone."
Garbini threw his arms in the air.

"Okay. Okay. I'll get my gear. I don't know what you'd do
without me, Sarge." Garbini winked. He got up, whistling
beautifully. And his willingness caused a great anguish then in
Hook.

Garbini chatted constantly as they floundered through the
darkening marshes. Even on the most difficult terrain, he remained only six inches from Hook's back, cannily placing the
sergeant's body between himself and the most likely source of
ambush. To justify his irregular nearness, he would entertain
Hook with discursive, obscene stories. Hook, remembering the
man's crime, was sickened by his eager, harsh whisper, by the
warm puffing of breath on the nape of his neck. Sickened, but
fascinated as well, for Garbini had one inexhaustible subject:
he talked about women: ugly women; degenerate women; disfigured women.

". . . What do you think of that? Huh? Huh?" Hook did not respond. "But that wasn't the worst. Get this—down in Miami I meet this beautiful, stacked blonde. Miss Navel Orange 1967. Maybe Miss Orange Navel. I'm not real sure." He guffawed. "I figure: Hey, Joe-boy, there's something wrong. Why's this bitch giving you a tumble? And I was right—" Garbini, enthralled by his narrative, stepped into a hole and fell forward into the knee-high, stagnant water. Hook dragged him upright by the collar.

"Less talk and more alertness."

"Sure. Sure. Hey, not so fast. Slow down." Garbini scuttled through the water, gaining his former intimate position, his face close to and between Hook's shoulder blades. "Well, about this broad. Man, we spent a weekend in this real posh hotel, swimming pool, room service, the works. Great—I mean, she was heeled, too. Screw and eat, screw and eat. I even ate a little screw." He laughed. "I still couldn't figure it—for a moment, ha! . . . for a moment I thought she's in love with me. Then, get this, Sarge—on Sunday night she starts laughing at me. Laughing and pointing her finger. What's the bit? I say. You're pregnant, she says. Then she hands me a pair of blue bootees. Man." He shook his head. "A pair of blue bootees. Hand-knitted yet."

"To the left here," said Hook.

"Sarge, would you believe it, she had the clap—besides being as fruity as a gay bar on Saturday night. Seems she got pregnant when she's twelve and had to have a real nasty abortion. Hated men. A member of SCAM—Society for Castrating All Males." He whistled. "So she gets herself infected and gives it to every guy she meets. Getting 'em pregnant, she called it. Oh, man—" he cursed. "I busted her one—right in the navel orange. Took me three months t'get rid of it. Sarge, I tell you: if nuts were moths—then, man, I'd be the world's biggest light bulb."

Garbini fell down again. He righted himself with difficulty, his chest pockets dripping water like punctured vessels. For a moment they sat on the tormented, high roots of a cypress tree. As though by previous arrangement, hundreds of tiny frogs began to peep. In the branches above they heard an occasional heavy flapping: wings being settled for the night. Garbini dabbed at his wet uniform with a wet handkerchief. Unknown to him now, they had crossed the stream that flowed past the base of the knoll—upstream perhaps two hundred yards from the knoll itself. Within twenty minutes, as Hook had planned, they would circle and approach the windrow as José Ix and he had approached it earlier that afternoon. Hook heard his pulse in the sides of his throat; while they sat, its pumping accelerated, deepened.

"Tired, Sarge?" Hook had yawned. It was not exhaustion: it was, rather, the surfacing of his nervous excitement.

"Yes," he said warily.

"You know. It's time you took it easy. Everybody dumps on you. Man, you get the dirty end of every dirty stick in Camaguay. And, far as I can see, that's the gross national product here—dirty sticks." He hissed. Strange dimples, extinct craters pocked the skin of his cheeks. "Hey. What say you and me—with Horace maybe—what say we cut out and leave the rest of these pricks t'make their own dinner for a change?"

"I've thought of it." Garbini cupped a hand over the sergeant's kneecap. Hook fed suddenly on his own beard, grazing fiercely, painfully on a tuft beneath his lower lip.

"Say—what're we lookin' for anyway?" Garbini peered toward the shadowy, moist trunks, then toward the level expanse of the oozing stream.

"Riffs. What else? A trail that's used a lot. I want to look at it."

"Yeah. You're a real Tarzan of the apes. I mean, I admire it. I could just about get around out here."

"Tell me, Joe—" Hook stared at his hands, then began busily to work fat pockets of dried mud out from under his fingernails.

"Yeah?"

"Did you ever meet a nice girl? One that didn't give you a disease or break wind in your face?" Garbini smiled.

"I've met them." He ground his teeth together: the sound was sad, determined. "You see my face? Even my own mother —sometimes she used to see me and start talking to herself real crazy." He paused. "And believe me, she ain't no prime rib herself. She looks like a potato that's been left in someone's dark closet. My father's dark closet, I guess. It isn't easy, Sarge. Try to understand. Not like it was for you."

"For me . . ."

"Is it true? I mean, what Tom Hall says—that you ain't never touched pussy?" Hook inclined his head: against his will. "Damn. Damn it. Then why don't you look like me? Why didn't God make me good-looking and why didn't he give you a hamburger face like mine? Why?" Hook turned with an eagerness that startled Garbini.

"Do you believe in God?"

"Aw, Sarge . . . You know me. That's just a figure of speech."

"But—" Hook interlocked his fingers. "You were baptized. You were brought up as a Catholic, weren't you?"

"Am I Italian?" Garbini chuckled. "Sure. But you can con a guy just so long. With me—I caught on when I was ten, maybe. Look, Sarge—I mean that's your bag. It's not mine. I respect you for it, but—" He made an abortive gesture. "Let's go, huh? I get scared in the dark."

Hook saw the knoll first. He waited as Garbini caught up—waited for the first hesitant, condemning signs of recognition. Garbini was ten yards behind him. Hook heard his panting and the sharp sounds of his passage through the undergrowth. Then he saw the face. It came through the leaves like an emblem of the war itself: helmeted, yellow, skeletal. Still without suspicion. And, in the bulging eyes, a dreadful trust. Hook touched his pocket. He felt the familiar, flat cube; as he did so, Hook shot a shapeless prayer up through the branches of the forest.

"Hey, Sarge. Stop a minute. Where's the fire?" He halted. "Jeesus. Am I bushed. How much further is—" The words lodged in Garbini's throat. He saw the stream. He saw the

198

windrow and the knoll behind it. Hook closed his eyes. With an instinctive, lithe move Garbini ducked back into the forest.

"There's high ground over there," said Hook quietly. "We can rest a minute."

"No," said Garbini. "To hell with resting. Let's get this over with. I'm sick of climbing. To the right there. It's flat as a pancake."

"Looks too muddy," said Hook. "Let's climb the hill. It's not so high."

"No," said Garbini wildly. He pushed past Hook. "To the right. Come on."

Hook did not follow him. Garbini trotted swiftly toward the quicksand. Then, as though impelled by some pursuit, he began to run. He leaped onto a fallen log and plunged forward, his right leg outstretched. The leg vanished. As though by an illusion his body was engulfed, foreshortened to the torso. His helmet popped off and skidded over the flat, yielding surface. Hook watched as a terrible understanding convulsed the torso's shoulders and neck. He watched its foolish, panicked thrashings. Slowly, driven down by his own terror, Garbini sank to his chest. "Hook! Hook!" he screamed. But Hook was not there.

Garbini's cries echoed in the jungle's vaulting. They became hoarse. After the first five minutes they lost their verbal form. The sergeant's name became an open vowel sound—a droning uhhhhhh-uhhhhhh. And, in the undergrowth, concealed from the quicksand, Hook spread the prayer book before him. "Lord God, my Father, if ever You have helped me, help me now. Let me bring this child to peace. Help him, for he is dying now. In the name of Your Son, Jesus Christ, who conquered death. Help us. We are both afraid."

Hook stood, the book cradled in his arm, and began walking toward Garbini. Drops of rain pattered down, some already finding their way through the leaves. Garbini continued to howl, his head thrown back. He had sunk now to the shoulders. His hands, disembodied, appeared like strange amphibians at either side of him, their fingers slapping the surface of

199

the quicksand. He saw Hook out of his eye's corner, and his head fell forward on its neck, enervated by the violence of his relief. Hook came to the fallen log and knelt there.

"Hook . . ." The word crackled in his throat. For a moment he could produce no other sound. Hook waited patiently while Garbini swallowed again and again, forcing his own saliva down in lubrication. "Hook. Where did you go? I could have died. Get me out of here quick—but be careful, for God's sake. Be careful."

"Don't struggle," Hook said. "Don't move at all." Garbini nodded with his eyes. The suspension of the sand grains, each sliding against another with the slickness of oiled ball bearings, held his body in an uncertain, shifting grip. Garbini remembered a contest he had once lost. A sledgehammer head coated with grease was lifted between thumb and middle finger. He sensed again, now at his own sides, that futile struggle against weight and slipperiness. He wanted desperately to flail upward, to crack the sucking vacuum. Sweat welled in his eye sockets. He whimpered.

"Hook. Get a branch. Get something quick. I can't stay up much longer." Hook felt a thrill of horror. The disembodied head, dotted now with feeding mosquitos, appeared as some infernal theme of retribution. Fascinated, he stared at it, at the placid, treacherous surface, at the helmet and at the M16 resting nearby. Then the head shrieked. "Hook! Hook!" Hook put a finger to his lips.

"Be quiet, Joe."

Hook's tone shocked Garbini. He blinked the sweat from his vision. Hook remained kneeling, but now, Garbini saw, he had opened a book. Garbini jerked his right arm out of the sand. His body slipped down again. One full half-inch this time.

"Hook! Are you crazy? Please. Do something. Get me out of here. I'm scared."

"Yes," said Hook gently. "I know you are."

Hook slipped one hand into his vest pocket and drew a tiny object out. Garbini's fingertips began to agitate the sand. He stared greedily at the hand as it reached out toward him. It opened. The yellow die landed soundlessly a foot from Garbini's face.

"Oh, no." Hook stared at him. There was silence. Then Garbini smiled. "Hook. Hell. It's no time for games. Help me." The sergeant shook his head. "What do you mean? What do you mean? Hook. For God's sake. You promised you'd take care of me. You promised."

"I will," said Hook. "I'll take good care of you, Joe."

He began to turn the pages slowly, holding the prayer book up at a sharp angle to catch the dying light. And Garbini saw the thin, gold cross on its cover. And Garbini howled.

"Help! Help! Help! Someone help me! Help me! Please God someone help me! Please!" When he was silent Hook spoke again.

"Joe. Listen to me. You must confess first. Confess what you did here. You must do that."

"Confess to what? To what, for God's sake?"

"We found that under her body. You ran away when you saw the hill. You killed her, Joe."

"It's a frame-up. Those Indians hate me, Hook. Ever since I killed that stupid parrot. In the name of all that's holy, believe me, believe me—I didn't do it." His trapped hands, used so often in his speaking, struggled to assert themselves. But the sand reacted. Garbini became rigid; saliva ran down his chin.

"You did it, Joe. Admit it. Until you do, until then, it's hopeless."

"No. No. I won't. I didn't do it."

"I see now," said Hook. "I see what's wrong." He closed the prayer book. "You've made a mistake, Joe. But I can understand that. I haven't made myself clear." He stood up. "You think I've done this to make you confess. I haven't. You think I'll pull you out. But I won't, Joe. This is the end, whether you confess or not. You're going to die very soon. These trees, this sand—they're the last things you'll ever see. Believe me. It's hard to accept death, but you have no choice." Garbini moaned.

"Hook. Have a heart. We're buddies, you and me. I promise—"

"No," said Hook. "This isn't good. You won't understand—not while I'm here, not while you can talk to me. I'll have to go. I see that. If you confess, you'll do it to God—for your own soul's sake." Hook backed. "When you want help call me."

"No! Don't leave me here. Please." Hook walked slowly toward the jungle. "All right! All right. I did it. I killed her." Hook stopped. "But it was an accident. I didn't mean to do it. I didn't mean—"

"You meant it, Joe."

"I—" Garbini began to cry. Hook walked back to the log. There he knelt and reopened the prayer book. The sobbing increased, interrupted by sharp gasps of fear as the sand gave way beneath Garbini's feet. Hook removed his helmet.

"Joe? Are you sorry?"

"Yes. Yes. I'm sorry."

"Not because of this. Not only because you're dying."

"I—no . . ."

"Because you killed an innocent person—out of lust. For this. For those thousands of loveless killings in your life. The cruelness and the hatred. The greed. For all these things, be sorry."

"Hook? What is it? What do you want me to do?"

"Trust me, that's all." He leaned forward. "You've trusted me before, trust me now. Forget about this life. You're dead, Joe. It's all over. You'll never get out of this sand—"

"Stop. Stop saying it. Stop. I don't want to die."

"But you are dying."

"No! No!" Garbini flailed, raised his right arm up. The sand began to seethe. An air pocket burst through the surface, and his body sank once more. Garbini shrieked. His teeth chattered convulsively.

"You don't have much time."

"I'm afraid. I'm afraid."

"Of what? Afraid no one will see your ugliness again? Afraid you won't have to fight in this stinking war? You'll be dead.

You'll be free—for the first time. What's there to be afraid of? Answer me, damn it."

"But—" Garbini gagged. "After. What's after this?" He looked down, toward the sand, as though an answer might be there.

"You were a Catholic. They must have told you, Joe. About Christ. About His death and His resurrection. This—" he pointed at the sand. "It's no more death than Christ's cross was death. If you believe—then you can, you will, rise again. You've murdered, but that's nothing in the sight of God's grace. Forget about this. Forget about me and what I've done to you. Forget about life."

"Hook. Please. Give me another chance."

"You fool," said Hook. "This is your chance. This is your only chance."

"What do you mean . . . ?" Garbini began to gasp. The weight of the sand was oppressive; he fought to expand his lungs.

"Did you think you were immortal? Did you? What am I taking from you? Not life. A few tormented moments, no more than that. We all die. But you have time now to understand it. Let this fill your mind. A man's life is nothing. But in God, with God, life is eternal. I promise you."

"How—how do you know?"

"I have seen it."

Garbini stared at him. The crouched form bulking on the log's edge. A terrific kinetic power massed in the thighs and hands: a grotesque power at the verge of some prodigious leap. Hook's intensity, like radiating body heat, was blown against his cheeks. Garbini thought, "He's crazy. He's crazy." And there was a new fear then. It was irrational; it ignored the fact of his death. It extended beyond it. Garbini feared Hook's enormous madness. And he was speechless.

A mosquito came. It floated down, landed high on Hook's cheek, just under his left eye. A big mosquito—for even from where he lay, suspended in the bowels of the quicksand, Garbini could see it clearly. He saw it clench for its feeding. He saw it hesitate. And when it died, dropped into the black whorls of Hook's beard, Garbini saw it then as well. And saw.

"The bugs!" he shouted. "The god-damned bugs. And that night by the airfield. Hook. You do know. You've got to know. You've got to know—" His eyes widened. "And you won't pull me out. And I am—Jesus Christ . . . I'm going to die."

"To die. To live."

"To live . . ." Hook sighed.

"In the name of the Father, and of the Son, and of the Holy Ghost." Hook raised his right hand: he blessed Garbini with the sign of Christ's cross. "May your sins be forgiven you. May the light of God shine upon you; may He grant you His peace. And may you come to His eternal life, through Jesus Christ our Lord."

Urgently now Garbini prayed. The rain descended more heavily, pocking tiny craters in the quicksand. Hook watched Garbini's lips; he prayed as they prayed. He wanted to touch the face, but he knew that this isolation of their bodies, this figuration of death, could not be broken. Instead he crushed his hands together. And, unnoted, the mosquito's shell, this smallest of miracles, dropped silently from his beard.

"I am the resurrection and the life. He that believeth in me, though he were dead, yet he shall live. And whosoever liveth and believeth in me shall never die. Lord, we brought nothing into this world, and it is certain we can carry nothing out. The Lord gave and the Lord hath taken away. Blessed be the name of the Lord." Garbini began to repeat the words, watching Hook as he did, drawing assurance from his assurance.

"Man that is born of woman hath but a short time to live and it is full of misery. He cometh up and is cut down like a flower. He fleeth as it were a shadow and never continueth in one stay. Lord remember not the sins and offenses of my youth, but according to Thy mercy think Thou upon me." Garbini cried again, without sobbing now—rich tears that swelled at his eyes and burst easily on his cheeks, mixing with the rain and the sweat. "They shall hunger no more, neither shall they thirst any more. For the lamb which is in the midst of the throne shall lead them unto living fountains of water. And God shall wipe away all tears from their eyes." Hook paused. "Joe," he said, "I need your help. Pray for me now—close your eyes and pray. This is a terrible thing I do, and I'm afraid of it." Garbini closed his eyes. Hook said, "I have loved you. I love you now. We suffer together. One body, one soul, one hope. Forgive me, Joe."

Garbini's lips moved once again. Swiftly then Hook stood. He lifted his M16 high above his head, and brought the butt down firmly at the side of Garbini's neck. And pushed him under the sand.

X

RODRIGUEZ DID NOT APPEAR on the third day. No patrols were sent out: the men were rested for their long journey back to San Pedro. Corporal Gutierrez shot a wild hog that morning, and the animal was roasted in the village center. There was a great deal of silliness: wrestling matches, songs, a primitive baseball game with sticks and a bundle of rags. The two homosexuals played strip poker in their hut: one, after a streak of bad luck, had only his blue, frilled panties on. The remaining IC's, soldiering alone now, felt isolated, like glum fathers at some child's birthday party.

Hook sat in front of the headman's hut, his wrists on his knees, watching for shapes in the smoke of the roasting hog. A Camaguayan raced past him, the hog's thigh bone held like an Olympic torch above his shoulder. They had accepted the news of Garbini's death without question: only Baxter had seemed disturbed. "Now that's too bad," he said. "Now that's too bad." And Baxter had licked the circle of his lips like an animal, frightened. The Camaguayan hurried past again. He saw Hook and stopped. With thumb and forefinger he forcefully spread his mouth, revealing a curious smile. Hook smiled in response. The Camaguayan laughed, fungoed a stone toward the lake with his hog's bone, and ran away.

They had found him there at dawn, sitting as now he sat throughout the day. His presence spoiled their pleasure. It was rumored that, in his long night's absence, Hook had found whisky and was now intoxicated. And, indeed, there was a suggestion of this in his dishevelment. Hook's helmet was gone, and his shirt was opened to the waist. During the night he had worried his beard, had parted it in the middle; it extended downward in two sharp prongs, the legs of a narrow, inverted V. His feet were bare, a thing the Camaguayans could not easily forgive him. The hirsute ankle bones, the puffy, white toes seemed huge and repulsive to them. And yet, in passing, they could not suppress their furtive, amazed glances. Hook was not conscious of this. He watched their holiday for hours—as though, by familiarity, he could distance all things.

Lieutenant Storch sat near the hog, while, officiously, Armando served him. Hook saw his bald, white head and the scorched, earless black head of the carcass as though they had been skewered together. And beyond, at the far south end of the village, a dark face appeared at the hut's mouth. Appeared again. It glanced left–right, then toward the sky, like some burrowing rodent surprised. Jones pulled his head in. He had found Garbini's carton of cigarettes. He chain-smoked them now as, over and over again, he cleaned his .45.

Hook saw José Ix and frowned. The Indian, too, was smoking: certainly for the first time, Hook thought. He held the cigarette pinched between his lips, pinched simultaneously between thumb and forefinger. His slightly crossed eyes seemed to regard the issuing strands of smoke with some suspicion. He was walking toward Hook, walking not through the village street, but, from unconscious habits of caution, hugging the thatched walls of the huts. He stopped; he appeared in discomfort. Then he groped for his throat and coughed, spewing smoke through his nose. He sneezed twice. José Ix threw the cigarette down and stamped on it. Hook smiled. Two Camaguayans passed near him, one doubling the other over in a playful hammerlock. The Indian became rigid; his foot quickly concealed the crushed butt. Then he hurried across the open ground, toward the headman's hut.

"Hello, José."

"My friend. My friend." The Indian crouched near him; he clasped his hands in the crook of his groin. "My friend. I have just heard. Why did you do it?"

208

"He was a murderer. He was also my friend. It seemed the best thing. I couldn't put him in prison—not for so long a time."

"But now? What will happen?" José Ix scraped up a handful of loose dirt. He brought it near his face. His brown, hooked nose seemed to probe at it, birdlike.

"I will tell them, José. Not yet. When we get back to San Pedro."

"No. No." José Ix spoke quietly. He shook his head. "Not you. It's not right. You are the best of them."

"I'm not so sure, José." Hook sighed. He flexed his wrists and ankles. "And even the best—even they are not above the law."

"It is my fault. You did it because of me."

"No," said Hook. "I'm sorry, José. I don't kill my friends for vengeance. Not even for you. Don't blame yourself." He touched the Indian's knee. "And José—"

"Yes."

"I don't want to see you smoking again."

"Aaaah." José Ix grasped his throat. "I found it on the ground. Aaaah. Never again. Americans are all crazy."

"Good." Hook smiled.

"I must tell you, my friend. There were tracks today in the swamp. New tracks. Three men, I think. They were here last night."

"Well," said Hook. "The plot thickens. If they attack now— bang, we are all dead. You'll see, we will miss our friend Garbini. A murderer can have his uses. Go get yourself some pig. We will all need our strength, if only for running away." José Ix shook his head. "Go on. We'll talk later. I must think now." The Indian stood reluctantly. "Don't worry, José. There is a reason for these things. I know it. A good reason, but very hard to understand."

José Ix walked away from Hook. Suddenly, then, like a man stepping up on a down escalator, the earth met his out- stretched foot and shot violently under it. José Ix toppled and fell on his side. There was a sonorous rumbling, more felt than heard in the depths of the ground, felt sympathetically in the stomachs and diaphragms of the men upon it. A six-inch-wide crack opened up, as neatly as a coat's unzipping. It cut silently past José Ix's sprawled legs, through the door of a hut, out under its far wall, and into the jungle. The earth roared once again. The crack closed quickly; its edges chafed, crumbled each other.

There was shrill confusion. The hog's carcass fell from its spit, scattering hot embers into Storch's lap. Trees crashed in the jungle. The Camaguayans, panicked, rushed shouting to the village center. One hut began to wobble: a corner of a roof collapsed, and the two queers scampered out, holding their unplayed poker hands. The man in the blue, frilled panties fell over Sanchez and, in his frenzy, began embracing the lieutenant's head. A peccary galloped through their midst, more frightened now of the earth than of men. Sanchez saw the blue, frilled panties and began to whip his embracer around the shattered cook fire. One Camaguayan crossed himself so fervently that he tore two buttons from his shirt front. Flocks of birds rushed from one treetop to another, cawing, cackling, twittering. Storch began to kick the hog. The earth quivered again and there was a hiatus now in their panic. They waited: Sanchez, his whip upraised; Storch, his foot half-cocked; the reverencer, in midblessing. A stilled tableau of chaos.

Hook leaped to his feet. A shriek of agony. Another. Barefoot, he hurried around to the hut's rear. A thin, rotted tree had fallen there and, beneath it, Tom Hall lay pinned and screaming. The trunk was stretched diagonally across his lower back. Hall was fully spread-eagled: his glasses, knocked from his head, rested on the ground—staring back at him like disembodied eyes.

"My back. My back. It's broken. Oh, God—I can't feel anything. Oh, God."

"Easy, Tom. Easy." Hook raised the trunk from Hall's back and heaved it aside.

"I can't move my toes. Hook. Hook. I'm a paraplegic."

"Hold on, Tom. Don't panic. Are you sure?" Hook touched the splayed legs. "That's an awful small tree."

"I'm a vegetable now," he groaned. "That's all." Hall's eyes were tightly closed: lines of stress darted out from their corners. His body was rigid—a flat plane from his calves to the back of his skull. Hook touched his spine.

"Here?"

"Y-yes."

"Try moving your toes again."

"I can't. I can't."

"Well, now. Let's see." Hook pulled Hall's shirt up gingerly. The lumps of vertebrae stood out, their conjunctions with his rib cage clearly visible. There was a red bruise above Hall's left kidney. Hook touched it. "Does that hurt?"

"Yes. Ohhhh. Yes." Hook frowned.

"Now, Tom. I'm going to make a test. Are you ready?"

"Okay. But be careful. What're you going to do?"

"I'm going to tickle you."

"What? Ha! Oh ha ha! Oh oh—eeee. Stop. Stop!" Hall struggled to escape Hook's jabbing fingers. He curled himself into a fetal position, then stared at Hook who sat, grinning, on his haunches.

"Oh. Oh, my," gasped Hall. "I thought it was broken. I really did."

"A miracle."

"That damn Garbini." Hall found his fly open. He peered in, then closed it quickly. "Everything goes right for him."

"Tom. Garbini's dead."

"I know. You don't have to rub it in." Hook sighed. He cupped his beard in his palms.

"Tom. Let me ask you a favor. For a while, until we get back to San Pedro—no more attempts on your life, please."

"Paraplegia," said Hall.

"Well. Whatever. We've got a long walk ahead of us. What I don't need is a basket case."

"Oh." Hall shrugged. "If you say so. But I don't know how long I can wait. Time is getting short."

211

"Yes. But try." The earth rumbled again. A long, interrogative murmur. "All right," said Hook wearily. "All right. I heard you the first time."

WRITTEN THAT AFTERNOON: NOTE, SCRATCHED ON THE FLOOR OF HIS HUT, FROM CORPSMAN ANDREW JONES TO HIMSELF

I wont do it. I wont do it. I wont do it I wont

~~~~~ XI

HOOK DIED the next day. They had abandoned the village just after dawn, following a track that led toward the northeast, through the swamp, to the base of the ridge. Hook was at point. José Ix was ten yards behind him. The rest of the patrol had already begun to lag. There was a mist just over the ground, and the thatched pyramids of the huts appeared to be smoldering as they passed them. All Rodriguez' precious supplies had been destroyed the night before: a distressful act that verified, for each man, the futility of his personal efforts. They were glad to leave the village.

Hook's left leg came off at the kneecap. The mine's concussive force crushed his right shin and ankle and heaved his lower body six feet in the air. His bloody left leg, unbooted, struck José Ix in the face. Hook fell, landing on the back of his skull, in the undergrowth to one side of the track. His vision became abnormally vivid. He saw the patterns of the leaves above him as though telescopically. And he reached up once, in curiosity, as though to finger them. Then he waited for the pain.

It came with terrific verve and articulation. Not, as he had first expected, from the wounded parts—instead, it came from his kidney and stomach from a frantic pulsing in the chest and throat. He raised himself on one elbow. His pants legs, he saw, were shredded and bloody. His right leg had been crushed toward him, reversing the knee joint: it wore his right foot at a crazy angle, an upright T. Hook tried to utter his surprise, but his mouth was choked with churning bits of flesh. Dizzy, he

213

toppled backward. Without blood, he knew, he would die very quickly.

Hook heard sounds behind him, but the shock wave had confused his hearing, and the sounds were oddly garbled. Camaguayans lay prostrate for thirty yards on the trail. One man, eyes pinched shut, fired his M16 at the treetops. José Ix began to shout for Jones: the blood of Hook's amputated leg had painted a garish red band across his shirt front. Baxter ran up, stopped, and struck a tree trunk with his clenched knuckles. The body of a small, green bird fell, dead or stunned, from the trees above. When Jones arrived he was cursing.

For several moments, Hook imagined he lay amidst the curved, black stubble on Jones' chin. He saw wide pores and one curious, terraced pockmark. Then Jones shook his head. He stared unhappily at the sergeant's ruined lower parts. His pupils tightened with fear. Hook saw this. He wanted to speak, to encourage Jones, but his breathing was too erratic then to support coherent sound. Jones swallowed. In Hook's new, magnifying vision the Adam's apple swept downward—a large and crestless dark swell.

"Do something, you useless prick."

Baxter kicked Jones in the lower spine. The corpsman whirled around, but Baxter's M16 was leveled at his eyes. Jones nodded. Quickly then, holding his breath, gagging, Jones began to tie off the oozing stump. His hands reddened at once; the clotting blood glued his fingers together. He became nauseated. In the naked mechanism of the knee joint, Jones recognized Hook's death. "Now," he said under his breath, "now you're more my size, big man." There were wounds in the groin and in the lower abdomen as well. Jones forced the right leg down from its crazy angle. It crackled, responded to his touch like some crudely stuffed toy. Hook whimpered. Jones heard him eagerly and with a curious glee.

There was something Hook wanted to do. He listened as full, mature shrieks now were expelled rapidly at his lips. The pain had become predictable: a rhythmic, undulating line that had great peaks but no intermissions. And yet it was the nothingness that terrorized him—gaps in the familiar pattern of his sensations. He knew the left leg was gone. But there was no feeling whatever in the other leg, in his man parts, in his hips. His mouth burst open again. Pray. That was what he had wanted to do. But his mind was a turmoil of sensation and antisensation. And his new vision had become phantasmagoric. It settled upon Baxter's doughnut mouth. Hook floated there, lolled as though against the fat, inflated sides of some bobbing life raft. And then he passed out.

Jones did a fair job. The tourniquet was effective. He gave Hook an injection of morphine and one of blood expander. The right leg was put in a crude splint, though, Jones knew, it required amputation. Baxter and Gutierrez carried Hook back to the village on an improvised stretcher. He was placed, still unconscious, in the headman's hut. Baxter, who could not endure the odd, evanescent grins that distorted Jones' mouth, left the hut at once. José Ix stayed for an hour, watching as the corpsman cleaned Hook's wounds. Just outside the hut Private Hall clutched excitedly at the Indian's shoulder.

"He's a paraplegic, isn't he?"

José Ix frowned. "Yes? What is that?"

"Oh. Never mind," said Hall slyly. "You wouldn't understand."

José Ix shrugged off Hall's hand. He walked slowly toward the village center. Power abhors a vacuum: already Sanchez had lined up his Camaguayans for an inspection. His voice had deepened in timbre since Hook's wounding. The supple whip touched the thighs of each man in turn, as he strutted along the line. Lieutenant Storch had abdicated his interest in their joint command. Instinctively, dolefully, he had returned to his place at the latrine trench, though this had been filled in the night before. He toed the soft dirt thoughtfully. And José Ix stared toward the jungle with a new interest. Yes. He would leave the army soon.

Hook's eyes opened. At first he could recall nothing: the darkness of the hut bewildered him. He thought that the dawn had not yet come, that this setting out had been a dream pre-figuration. He raised his head slightly. The morphine drunkenness rushed to his eyes, dizzied him. Hook wanted to vomit. And then the pain returned. He imagined it as a dark snake with feathered wings, for it would slither up from his belly in heavy waves, dancing out along his ribs with aching flickers, constricting his lungs. He gasped and fought to turn on his side.

For a moment Hook was certain that he had moved. The instinctive commands had been relayed through his nervous system: the feet twisting, the pelvis being swiveled. But his chest remained inert. Like a pantomimist, he sought to re-create the outlines of his lower body. He moved the toes of both feet. He wriggled them. He tapped the balls of his feet together. Then he lifted the left leg high in the air—and watched for the rising above his chest. There was nothing. Suddenly Hook remembered. He groaned harshly. Pain and the knowledge of his loss overwhelmed him.

"Stop moving."

"Jones," whispered Hook. He reshaped the name a dozen times before he could say it. A leathery shell of dried and bloodied phlegm coated the roof of his mouth. He broke it off with his tongue. Jones squatted beside him.

"What is it?"

"Pain's very bad." Jones nodded. "Morphine."

"I gave you morphine."

"How much?"

"Quarter grain."

"No—" Hook grimaced. "More. Half grain for my weight."

"You don't weigh so much as you think. Not no more." Hook frowned, not comprehending.

"Pain," he said. The snake, as though summoned, began to writhe again. Hook breathed, inflating a barrier against it.

"Hurts bad, huh?" Hook nodded. Jones drew a morphine syrette from his kit. He prepared Hook's left hip for the injection. Then he paused, cocked his head. He seemed to be lis-

216

tening. "Hook?" Hook opened his eyes. "You sure you want this?"

"Yes."

"I mean, since I met you—all you ever talked about was death and pain. How great it was to suffer. You remember?" Jones shrugged. "Hell, man. I didn't think you'd want to miss it, that's all. Any of it."

"What . . ."

Hook frowned. Jones was smiling. The teeth were white and, it seemed now, very sharp. There was something about the eyes: Hook suddenly remembered Garbini's dice. He made a tentative, awkward gesture with his left hand. Jones thought he wanted the syrette; he withdrew it from Hook's reach.

"Not so fast, Sergeant. Let's talk this over. Remember. You were going to teach me something. Yeah: about how a Christian dies." He paused. "You know you're dying, don't you?" You don't think a shit-ass medic like me can save you. You know it's all over." Hook blinked. He had meant to nod but he couldn't remember how. "Well. I want to learn from you. About how human life don't mean a thing." Impudently, Jones leaned close, until his mouth nearly touched Hook's beard. The wounded man gasped. He tried to squirm away.

"Jones," he said. "Who are you?" The corpsman giggled.

"Sorry. Hook. It's just your old friend Jones here. Who'd you expect—Jesus Christ? He's white, remember?"

"No," said Hook. "Not Jesus Christ." The snake began to burrow. Hook moaned. He wanted very badly to urinate, or thought he did, but the required instincts were no longer there. His hand wandered toward his stomach. Jones intercepted it.

"Okay. You better have some." Jones touched the syrette to Hook's flesh.

"No," said Hook. "Wait. I'll wait. Not now."

"Hell. What's the sense in suffering?"

"No. Later." Jones shrugged. With a large gesture, a gesture Hook could see, he replaced the syrette. Hook whimpered.

Jones felt laughter in his chest. It surprised and disconcerted him. He didn't understand it.

"Water," said Hook.

"Thirsty?"

"Yes."

"Damn. I don't know. I think you took some fragments in the gut. The book says no water." Hook closed his eyes. "Is there anything else you want?"

"Go—ask Storch to come." Jones left.

Alone, Hook's mind became quickly distracted. He raised his two hands up in front of his face. He studied the balls of his fingers, pressing each one lightly with the edges of his thumbs. The pain rushed, slithering, over him. Hook arched the part of his spine that was still alive. For a long moment he was blinded by a red, light-spotted veil. The odors of his lower body drifted toward him: smells of rottenness and excrement. The snake coiled itself. Hook withstood its springing. "Please, no. Not again."

But it came again. And again. The organs in his thorax seemed to be breaking up. He heard a hollow, sucking groan—a desperate contraction of his stomach. Then he was panting: he could not expel breath soon enough to satisfy his hunger for breath. "God. God." He gasped. "Forgive me. I can't pray." Then, without shame, Hook shrieked.

"Storch don't want to come. He's digging a new john. He didn't say nothing, but I think he's pretty pissed at you." Hook waved his hand: a fluttery, undisciplined spasm. "Hurts, huh? Not so much fun as you thought?"

"It's—very bad." Hook's head rolled from left to right. "Morphine?"

"Not yet," Jones smiled. "Jesus Christ, Hook—I'd be pretty mad if I was you. That god of yours—he's gotta be some kind of sadist."

"No." Hook fingered his lips. "You're wrong. I deserve this. Pride—"

"Nobody but nobody deserves this." The corpsman spat. Hook found Jones' hand and squeezed it tightly. Jones was surprised at his strength. "Well, don't worry." He undid Hook's grip. "There's angels and harps up there. Just waiting for you." Jones laughed.

"Why—why do you laugh?"

"Why? It's funny. That's why. Isn't it?"

Hook did not reply. The ghost of his need to urinate returned. It became an excruciating, hot pain: a hard volume of liquid driving at, tearing apart a choked and tiny passage. He pounded the earth with his fists. Jones watched, interested. Then he leaned forward and, with a languid movement, smoothed Hook's hair back. It felt brittle, as though coated with a hardening moisture. Hook smiled.

"Thanks."

"Uh-uh." Jones shook his head. "No. Just wondered how it felt. Hook. What's going on in there? Your life—is it passing in front of your eyes?" Hook seemed to ponder this.

"No," he said finally. "Everything's crazy. The pain—" He twisted his neck then; he craned to look at Jones. "It's you. I don't understand. You seem to have no feelings."

"I have feelings. One feeling anyway. I hate you, Hook."

"I know." Hook winced. "But why?"

"Who knows? Maybe it's because you're a first-class phony. Maybe because everybody thinks you're so great."

"No—" Jones made an ambivalent sign with his fingers.

"So. What does it matter? This way you'll suffer good. You want to be a martyr, don't you? I'll help you."

"Want? No. No more pain."

"Morphine?" Hook bit his lips closed.

"Garbini," he said. "I killed him."

"Huh?" Jones frowned. "You mean you couldn't pull him out?"

"I pushed him under."

"You—" Jones stood up. He put his hands on his hips. Then he laughed. "Why? Why?"

"He killed a woman. Raped her. I wanted him to make his peace."

"And did he?"

219

"I think . . . I–I don't know."

"Son of a bitch." Jones slapped his jaw. "Son of a bitch. You were right. You do deserve this. I hope you suffer good."

"I am. Thank you."

"No," said Jones abruptly, angrily. "No. That's too easy." He dropped to his knees and began searching through his medical kit. "I want you to live now. I want to see you locked up. I want you cut down to size. You friggin' bastard. Who do you think you are—God almighty?" Jones paused. He rubbed his chin thoughtfully.

"Why—why are you looking at me like that?"

"Oh, brother. You're a sly one, Hook. This is a trick, isn't it—a trick, so I give you morphine. Without you having to ask for it."

"Jones," Hook groaned. "You're driving me crazy. Go away."

"You didn't kill him. You couldn't. You're too soft."

"I did."

"Maybe. Maybe not." Jones tapped his knee. "If I could save your life, I would. But I can't. And anyway—how could I prove you killed him? It'd be your word against mine."

"Jones. Stop. Let me die. That's enough, isn't it?"

"You want to die?"

"Yes!" shouted Hook. "Yes. Oh, God, yes."

"I don't believe you."

"I don't care. I don't give a damn if you believe me." Hook joined the four fingers of each hand together. He plunged these two hard wedges under his rib cage, wrenching upward, but the pressure did not diminish. "Get Baxter," he gasped.

"Baxter?" Jones frowned. "Why Baxter?"

"Get him."

"Okay."

But Jones walked only just beyond the hut's wall and no farther. He stood there, smoking and listening to the rich variety of Hook's groans. In the village center now even Sanchez had settled down, languidly impatient, to wait for Hook's death. Jones had an idea. He grinned. Then he stubbed out his cigarette and rushed inside the hut.

"Hook! Hook!"

"What—what is it?"

"A seaplane. It just landed in the lake. They're gonna fly you out."

Hook rose up on his elbows. He contorted his neck and shoulders until he could see toward the hut's open wall. Then Jones was laughing. Hook stared at the corpsman—and knew it had been a trap. The pain, exacerbated by his movement, began to slash at his torso, an indiscriminate, heavy knife.

"Oh, no . . ."

"You blew it, Hook. That was it, baby. I saw it. In your eyes. Oh, yes—right there. You wanted to live."

"No. You surprised me."

"You wanted to live."

"No."

"Yes."

"Yes . . . I did."

"You fraud." Jones slapped his knee. "You lying, pompous hypocrite. God, you disgust me. It's easy to kill, ain't it? But when it comes to your life—then Hook, baby, it's something else."

"Get Baxter, please. Where is he? Where's Baxter?"

"He didn't want to come."

"No—you're lying."

"It's true. I said to him, 'Horace, the man's dying.' But he didn't want to. It's just you and me, Hook."

"You . . . and me."

Hook closed his eyes. Jones was curiously annoyed by this. He felt alone: as though the overt conflict between them had occluded a more distressing, internal conflict. But Hook had not passed out; after a few moments, the sergeant's lips began to move. Something seemed to brush against Jones' scalp: a crisp tightening of the skin between his ears. He wanted to shake Hook; he wanted to press his hands over the moving lips. Jones was agitated. Systematically he began to pluck hair from his nostrils. The tweaking pain made his eyes water, his nose run. Hook groaned.

221

A spasm, visible to Jones, began to constrict the sergeant's torso. It was born low in his abdomen, shuddering upward, seeming to coil within the chest, issuing at last as a choked shriek. The broken stumps jiggled with its force. At first it occurred with ten-second intervals. Then the frequency increased, until the final thrashings, up and through the throat, ended as another terrific wave was conceived below. Hook's body arched to meet it. In horror Jones remembered a woman he had once seen in labor. The flailing hands; the splayed thighs; and the scream now shrill, more feminine in its register. "Shut up. Shut up. Shut up," Jones snarled. Instinctively, he moved forward to suppress the sound.

His hand was caught. Hook's fingers had wrenched it away from his mouth; now they held it, to the wrist, in a huge, painful grip. Jones gasped. He heard the crackling protest of his knuckles. "Let go—" he hissed. But Hook would not let go. Jones shook his hand, twisted it, tried to pinch Hook's flesh, but the grip only tightened. Jones brought his other hand down with a chopping, futile blow. Then, horrified, he saw that Hook was drawing him slowly closer. Jones fell backward, opposing his weight. And, instead, Hook's body, drawn forward on that powerful arm, began to slither toward him.

"Jones. Jones."

"Let me go."

Hook's eyes were wide, intent and without motion. The skin of his face was bloodless white. Jones whimpered. The sergeant's great, broken body wriggled across the floor like some disjointed serpent. The stumps left tracks on the fiber-covered earth. Jones was paralyzed by his fear. And then Hook's right hand rose up and caught Jones' collar at the neck. Its fingers sunk into the soft places of his throat. Jones squealed, gagged. He knotted his own fingers in Hook's beard, pushing the ghastly face away. But his co-ordination was gone. Hook's torso was slung across his lap. The lips, the brittle filth-caked beard, rubbed against his cheek, in an awkward, stinking kiss. And the right hand closed slowly on his windpipe.

"Don't kill me, Hook—"

"Listen to me . . ." Jones felt the moist lips as he heard Hook's voice. "Listen to me. You were right: it is you and me. But it's no more my fault—no more my fault than yours. You can't help it."

"You're hurting me. Hook, you're—" Jones scraped at the back of Hook's right hand, as inexorably the fingers found a deeper purchase in his throat. Jones' vision doubled. It was as though the whole of Hook's once-massive strength were concentrated there beneath his jaw.

"Stop," groaned Hook. "Jones. Don't accept it. This is not your business. You have no part in it. Listen to me—"

Hook pulled himself up on Jones' chest. For a brief moment the right hand relaxed its hold. Jones threw himself backward then, striking the sergeant's temple with the side of his knee. Hook fell heavily, face downward, into the dirt. He lay stilled.

Jones caressed his throat. Panting, he dove for his medical kit. The contents spilled out, over the floor. Hook had begun to stir. Jones took a syrette and, moving with caution, approached the crumpled form from the far side, away from its terrible hands. He yanked up the shirt. Hook flailed backward.

"No," he said. "No morphine. Save it. The pain is gone."

"Gone—what d'you mean?"

"Nerves are shot. That's all. Jones. I see it now—as it was on the island . . . I'm dying. A thousand times. A thousand times." Hook raised his face from the floor. He seemed puzzled. "That's what He meant. You must be born again. But here. Here."

"Hook. You're driving me nuts. I don't understand you."

"I know. I'm sorry. Jones—take a piss for me, will you? It's the only thing I haven't done." Hook laughed. And died.

XII

THEY BURIED HIM at once, without ceremony, for there was little time. Storch's half-dug latrine was deepened. The leg was placed beside him, lapped under his arm, as though Hook had been in the habit of carrying it with him. The Camaguayans had already forgotten Hook: they could not long remember a god who had come to pieces right before their very eyes. It was two o'clock. They might reach the base of the ridge by nightfall. Lieutenant Sanchez had his men lining up before the last spadesful of dirt had been dropped on Hook's grave.

"Jones?" The corpsman looked up. Baxter stood just beyond the hut's entrance, his hands in his pockets.

"Yeah? What?" Jones continued to pack his equipment.

"Did he say anything? I mean, before he died?"

"Sure. He said, 'It hurts.' He said that a lot."

"Nothing else?" Jones stood up and hooked the medical pack across his shoulders.

"No. Nothing else. You saw him—he was half crazy with pain."

"Yes," said Baxter, "that's why I didn't come t'say goodbye. I didn't want to see him—not like that. He was a pretty good guy." Jones spat.

"Boy. I'll say one thing. He sure had you all snowed. Wake up, Horace—back home he wouldn't even've asked you to dinner."

"That's not true. He was a religious man." Jones laughed. He started to walk ahead.

"Ha! Religious. You should've heard him. At the end there,

when the pain was real bad, he started cursing God, Jesus Christ, the Virgin Mary, Joseph—the whole damn family."

"I don't believe it."

"No? Why didn't you come see for yourself then? Or were you afraid?"

"I—it wasn't that—" Lieutenant Sanchez shouted. The line had begun to move out. José Ix came toward them.

"Horace. You and I, we are in the rear. He told me. Sanchez. To my face. He said he doesn't trust me."

"That's your business, friend," said Jones.

"No." The Indian shook his head. "It is your business, too—you, Mr. Doctor who wears his red cross on the back of his head. We are like lost sheep now, and it is a long trip home."

"Fuck that," said Jones. "I'll get back to San Pedro. I'll get back, if I have to walk over your dead bodies. So long, suckers. Take good care of the rear." Jones began to trot ahead.

"I do not like him. I'm sorry."

"Hell. Don't be sorry," said Baxter. "He's sick, that's all. José, have you seen Tom Hall?"

"The thin one? No. Perhaps he is at point with Sanchez."

"Yeah. That must be it."

Baxter and José Ix hurried to their positions at the end of the moving line. Small, serious men, they had already discovered a secret kinship. Baxter checked his M16. José Ix made a last, careful survey of the village. They stepped into the undergrowth. The foliage at the sides of the trail vibrated with their passing. Then it settled slowly and became still.

L

Rio San Gabriel

Rio Negro

Plateau

SAN PEDRO

THE